Untied
Shoelace

*To Tom
Eat A Cupcake
for Me!*

Pam Kumpe

Pam Kumpe

Pam Kumpe

Untied Shoelace

DEDICATION

To my *Church under the Bridge* family
Church for the homeless and those with a home

To *Pastor Cody Howard*
Who loves others like Christ does

**

To *Manuela Witthuhn*
My friend who was killed by a serial killer

**

To my twin sister *Melody Johnson*
The good twin

To my sister *Beth Malia*
Gone, but remembered

Pam Kumpe

Untied Shoelace

DISCLAIMER

This is a work of fiction. Names, characters, businesses, places, events and incidents are either the products of the author's imagination or used in a fictitious manner. Any resemblance to actual persons, living or dead, or actual events is purely coincidental.

Pam Kumpe

CHAPTER ONE

ONE SCARY NIGHT

I SHIVERED AND STEPPED BEHIND the goblins and the angels on the porch, turning to Tin Can Mahlee. "Stop mumbling. The kids are gonna hear you. I'm trick or treating even without Daddy."

Tin Can Mahlee ignored me and cuddled her Prince Albert Tobacco can. "Why is it always so dark? Side Car Ace is in jail again. Nothing good happens on Halloween." The cold wind whistled around the house as if agreeing with her.

She leaned toward me and I could feel her breath on my neck. "We've got to make camp for the night. I told your daddy I'd keep you close. Them railroad cops might see us. Let's go." Mahlee clutched her tin can and gunny sack close to her chest and rocked side to side in her boots.

I spun around, bumping my head on Mahlee's can. She raised her hand trying to keep the can from tumbling from her grasp and the lid popped off. I reached for the can and she shoved me away, but not before I saw the gun. "Leave my stuff alone." She protected the trinkets and slapped the lid back on.

I moved closer to the kids who were busy yelling Halloween chants and twisted my head sideways. "Daddy promises to take me trick or treating every year. It's not my fault he got to losing nickels in a card game and hit that guy, and when did you get a gun?"

A cowboy looked at me and a giant monster knocked on the front door. The kids shouted trick or treat, rushing the lady at the door. Mahlee stomped in her boots off to the side and she joined in with their voices, only she was yelling at me. "You never mind about my gun. What's mine is mine. What's in my tin can is none of your business."

I frowned at Mahlee and then I scowled at the cowboy whose bugged eyes felt like darts. "What are you looking at?" I stuck my tongue out at the cowboy with the pretend hat. His face was full. Not scrawny like mine. He barely looked nine. Without the hat, he was just another snotty boy.

The pretend cowboy spoke to me. "Are you from Boone? I haven't seen you at school." The cowboy lassoed me with his words while I danced around him.

"I'm passing through."

The cowboy squinted at me, turned to the door, and held up his bag. I held out my paper sack, the one I'd found in the alley behind the jail. The lady with big teeth and happy eyes dropped popcorn balls into our bags.

I rushed to Mahlee who had moved to the side of the porch and gave her my *what for*. "I don't care about your gun. I just asked when you got it. I'm following these kids. Keep your secrets inside that rusty can. I have some of my own. Tonight, I'm getting a sack full of candy and I'm saving Daddy the chocolate. He loves chocolate."

Mahlee stepped in front of me. "If you start wandering these streets we might get lost. The rain's coming in from the west. We need a dry place for the night. Under the bridge will work. We'll meet your daddy in the morning and hop a train out of here."

Untied Shoelace

I put my hands on my hips and gave her the Annie Grace Kree frown. "You're not my mama. If she were alive, she'd take me trick or treating."

"I'm the only mama you got. Since your pa saved me from them bank robbers, I owe Side Car Ace my life. I've been watching out for you since the day he untied me. Nothing's changing this Halloween."

I'll never forget seeing Mahlee with black eyes. That day, Daddy and me had hiked down this trail by the ocean and we came upon three men at a camp site. They had Mahlee tied to a tree. One eye was swollen shut, both were purple. Her lips were bleeding and her clothes torn.

Daddy walloped the men using a pipe he found on the ground and then untied Mahlee. We ran off and hid under a bridge for most of the day and all three of us rode the next empty boxcar out of town.

Mahlee tugged on my arm. "Come with me."

I pulled free. "No. I'll be ten in January." I pranced around Mahlee like a kitten. "Daddy promised me that 1946 was bound to bring good things. He also promised me a birthday cake. Besides, I'll be old enough to ride the rail by myself if I want to. I don't need you looking after me."

A brown wrinkled monster limped by. An angel floated on her toes and the Lone Ranger galloped by in boots. "I'm trick or treating. You'll have to follow me if you want to know where I am."

Earlier today, we rode the rail south and hopped off in Boone. Stopping here came with a promise to take me trick or treating, but Daddy landed himself in jail again. Daddy's keeping his promise. He just doesn't know it.

My yellow shirt had sweat marks under the arms and my ragged overalls made me a perfect Halloween hobo. At the houses, I fit in with the kids who sleep in beds with soft quilts.

They don't eat candy for supper or dig through the trash for old bread, either. These kids have real food like fried chicken and corn on the cob.

Lately, Daddy's love for card games, for the bottle, for ladies who stay up too late leaves me with Mahlee more than him. She disappeared one October, two years ago, but one day she found us again, and started riding with Daddy and me again. Her secrets slip out in loud prayers when she mumbles of the darkness. They slip out on Halloween or when that lid pops off her can.

The train yard cops nearly caught us when the three of us rode into town, the banging sticks on the boxcar walls, and their yelling sent us to a ditch. I hid in the woods and rolled down the hill to get away after watching Daddy and Mahlee slide down the slope. Even at nine, I run faster than Daddy, faster than most hobos and faster than railroad cops.

Halloween fun will wash away the soot from today. I stepped to the next door behind a purple monster, an alien, and a kid with a sheet on his head. A ghost. Not scary, though.

The night dropped darkness in town and more goblins appeared. I jumped at the chance to fill my sack with sweets. We don't have a lot of candy on the rail or food of any kind. I tagged along with the kids and strolled down the streets with monsters and blended in with the angels. Four Indians with plastic tomahawks danced by chanting what sounded like a rain dance song.

Mahlee shuffled in the shadows, close enough for me to see her, but far enough away to leave me alone. To have Halloween with strangers made my life seem not so strange. Later, I'll write a poem and share it with Daddy tomorrow. I scribble my poems on paper sacks and keep them inside my overalls. Someday, I want to be a writer.

The porch lights were on at most houses and I never had to say a word. The kids in front of me did the talking. I opened my sack and followed their lead. "Thank you. Thank you."

The pretend Cowboy told a ghost story to the Indians. "Watch out for Micah tonight. He's the man whose arm got cut off at the sawmill four years ago. He lurks in the alleys on Halloween looking for an arm to replace his and he leaves blood stains on the ground. A trail you don't want to follow."

The pretend Cowboy turned to me. "He might be looking for little beggar girls from out of town, those no one will miss."

Mahlee came to my side and slipped her hand into mine. I stopped following the cowboy. Mahlee knew ghost stories made me shudder and even when she's mad at me she knows just when to show up. She tromped along with me as we moved on, leaving the cowboy to deal with the Indians.

We came to a house at the end of the street. A mansion with steeples. They touched the stars. At the gate we stopped, and the two-foot Lone Ranger called back to me from the corner, three houses away. "Ms. Magnum's a witch. She puts hexes on people. I'm not going to her door." He pulled his reigns back, pretending to ride a horse, and scuffled off to catch up with the alien. He left me standing there with the gate swung open, clutching Mahlee's hand.

The porch light shot a beam at us and Mahlee yanked me along with her. "Let's see what goodies this witch might have behind that door. I'm with you. So you're safe." Mahlee giggled a spooky laugh like she does when she teases me.

The witch opened the door. Her teeth shined as bright as the porch light, and a man with a kerosene lamp lumbered across the front room, joining the witch at the door. "What are y'all doing?"

"Trick or treating." I held my sack out.

His eyes swept us and he gave Mahlee another glance. Probably cause she's taller than most street lights. "You're a little big to be trick or treating."

Mahlee moved back a step. "I'm tall but not too old. I love candy."

The witch invited us inside. "Y'all come on in. I'll fix refreshments."

My feet followed her to the kitchen, her words wooing us. Mahlee marched with me. The aroma of freshly-baked sweets drifted to my nose.

The witch asked us to sit at the big table. "This is nice, we never have any company." She placed steaming hot cups in front of us.

I pushed my cup away. "I don't drink coffee."

Mahlee planted her elbows on the table and wrapped her fingers around the cup. "I do."

The man with the lamp limped by and scooted his feet across the dining room floor. I pulled on Mahlee's sleeve. "Is that the one-armed man?"

Ms. Magnum brought a plate to the table and patted my arm. "My husband got hurt in a sawmill accident. Micah's headed out to check on the cows. He'll be back."

I scooted the chair across the floor, ready to escape, but the smell in the cup changed my mind. I stuck my nose near the rim.

"Child, that's not coffee. Have you never had hot cocoa?" Ms. Magnum asked.

"No ma'am. I guess not." I peeked into the cup sniffing the chocolate.

"You're in for a treat. I've got homemade gingersnaps to go with the cocoa, too."

Mahlee and me emptied our mugs and didn't say no when she offered more.

We left with Ms. Magnum telling us to come see her whenever we're coming through Boone. We were in good spirits, with gingersnaps and hot cocoa in our bellies, and more gingersnaps for later. We stepped from the porch to the cobblestone walkway leading to the road. When the first drop of rain hit my nose, I remembered the Indian dance from those kids. "Mahlee. It's starting to rain."

"Girl, I told you we needed a place to sleep tonight. We need a place with shelter to stay dry." Mahlee scolded.

I turned back to Ms. Magnum. "Do you know where the mission is? Or a place we could stay?"

Mahlee gave me the squinted evil look. "Leave her out of this. We need to go."

Ms. Magnum called from the porch. "You can stay here. I have a soft feather bed in the guest room upstairs. You want to spend the night?"

Hot cocoa. Gingersnaps. And now a bed.

Mahlee threw her arm over her head, waving it, and her gunny sack sailed above her head. She acted as if she'd seen a ghost and her right arm clutched her tin can. "No. I'm not staying here." She pointed to an upstairs window. "There's a shadow on the second floor. It's probably a ghost ready to hex us for sure." Mahlee grabbed my blonde hair, holding me as if she had the mane on a horse. "No bed. No ghosts. No more hot cocoa."

"Bye, Ms. Magnum. Thanks for the gingersnaps." I glanced at the window and saw Micah peeking from behind the curtain. I gave the one-armed man a wave.

Mahlee makes me shake my head a lot. She can be brave one second and scared the next. I just stay out of her way when her arms start swinging.

"Girl, come on. We are leaving this part of town."

We cut through the alley behind the house, close to the jailhouse and other brick buildings, and headed to the woods near a bridge by a creek.

Mahlee mumbled every other step, "He's got one arm and he's not getting mine …"

CHAPTER TWO

TEN DOLLARS WILL BE FINE

IN THE COURTROOM ACROSS FROM the jail, Mahlee and me sat along the rear wall, in the last row of chairs. Last night, we slept under the bridge and I woke up tired. I could go to sleep in this chair, but I've got to listen to the judge. He will let Daddy go this morning. That's a reason to stay awake.

A long line of men who spent the night in a cell came into the room. I counted sixteen prisoners; men caught for hopping trains, loners locked up for stealing, and others brought in for crimes worse than Daddy's fight.

The judge strutted in from a side door. His warty nose and bushy eyebrows were familiar. One arm of his robe hung flat against his side. Goosebumps popped up on my arms. I slugged Mahlee who told me to stop. "But it's One-Armed Micah."

Mahlee frowned and put her hand over my mouth. "Quiet. They'll make us leave. His name is Judge Micah, not One-Armed Micah. Don't call him that. You'll get us sent from the court room."

The Judge pounded his gavel on top of his table. A man stood. The judge handed him his fine and called another name. Each prisoner stood, received his fine, and sat down. Finally, Daddy got called.

Daddy leaned toward the judge. "I've got no money. I lost it in the card game. I can't pay my fine."

The judge pounded his table again. "Then you'll spend another night in jail."

Mahlee shuffled to where the judge sat, motioning for Daddy to step aside. When he didn't, she pushed him out of the way and turned to the judge. She stepped to the side of the judge's table, whispering into his ear. No one knew what Mahlee said to the judge, but whatever she said it caused him to slam his gavel five times. I jumped. Even the bailiff flinched.

The judge raised his hand and pointed at Daddy. "Mr. Gill T. Kree, come forward. Are you ready to leave Boone, Missouri? Are you ready to be on your way?"

Daddy's nostrils flared and his eyes got big, a look that told me he didn't understand what had happened. Neither did I. The beginning of the end became the end and Daddy wasn't spending another night in jail. Judge Micah didn't look scary anymore.

Daddy turned to the judge. "Sir? You mean I can go?"

"Yes. Leave town now."

"Daddy. You're free. The judge let you go."

Daddy nodded at the judge and we marched from the courtroom. Mahlee glanced at the judge and smiled a Tin Can Mahlee hobo smile. She shuffled up beside us, humming. She hummed this tune when Daddy saved her life in Houston, too.

I poked her in the ribs. "What did you say to the judge?"

Mahlee held my hand and kept tromping, not answering me.

As we headed for the tracks, I knew the town of Boone held more than goblins and monsters, and a one-armed man. The town held more than witches and jails, too. Angels in disguise lived in Boone. I had gingersnaps in my pocket and thankfully, Mahlee at my side. The whistle on the steam engine called to us.

St. Louis here we come.

CHAPTER THREE

LOFTY NIGHTS WITHOUT DADDY

HOPPING A TRAIN OUT OF Boone sent us east. The weather changed, dipping cooler with each bump of the rail.

"Daddy, you got any cheese in your bag?" I nestled closer to his side and curled my feet under his warm legs. A gust of wind blew through the open boxcar door. Those gusts get worse during the month of November. A few snowflakes drifted by the open door as the fluffy, white clouds turned gray hiding the sun. None of the snow stuck to the trees, but the clouds announced winter just the same.

Daddy pulled a wad of cheese from his satchel, a hunk discovered yesterday in a trash bin behind the grocery store.

Grandma Elsie would never approve of our swallowing anything half-eaten or chewed, but when you're hungry and your pockets are empty—you eat what you find. "Thanks, Daddy. Do you have to play cards in St. Louis tonight?"

Daddy nodded and pulled his hat down. He leaned on the boxcar wall and drifted off to sleep.

When it comes to gambling Daddy doesn't win much. He usually gets caught cheating. I wish he'd stop playing cards. The game has him. He doesn't have the game.

Daddy peeked from under his hat. "Get a little rest. We got a ways to go." He ran his fingers through my hair, the pony tail slipped free, and my hair rippled on my back.

18

"I'm not tired. I'm hungry. Any bologna?"

Mahlee piped in. "Weather's changing. We'll need to catch a train out of St. Louis at sunrise to miss the snow."

Daddy raised his hat again and peeked with one eye beneath the brim. "I'll make sure we leave early tomorrow."

For the next two hours, we rode through the mountains and my ears popped. The cheese and bologna were gone. Daddy and Mahlee napped and I sat with my feet dangling from the door of the boxcar as the train crept around the mountain bends.

As Daddy and Mahlee slept the tears ran down my face. I was still hungry and my clothes were dirty. The danger on the rail is real and Daddy has some secrets, kind of like Mahlee does. But the thrill of adventure has hitched itself to my soul, and I love the hum of the boxcars rolling down the tracks. We eat when we want, even if food portions are slim, and we sleep when we want. We call the shots.

Daddy came for me at Grandma's house in Texarkana in the spring of 1941. He yelled at Grandma with words of love for me and words of hate for her. "She's my daughter. I can take her with me if I want to." Even at five-years-old, I wanted to go with him, but no one asked me.

Grandma Elsie argued with Daddy. "Leave her be. She's safe and happy here. Riding those freight trains is no life for a child. Besides, I raised her. I've had her since her mother died. She's as much mine as she is yours. Don't take her from me."

As Daddy carried me out the front door, I glanced over his shoulder. I didn't expect to see Grandma cry hard or make loud squeals, but she could do little to get me back. Being kidnapped by my daddy made me feel special.

A jerk of the car nearly bumped me from the boxcar. The train slowed and I knew it was time to wake Daddy and

Mahlee. "Wake up. The train station is around the next curve. It's time to get off. We're in St. Louis."

Daddy stretched one leg and pushed against Mahlee's foot. "Mahlee. Drop and roll time."

"Side Car Ace, we better wait for the train to slow down. Those rocks are sharp."

Daddy's hobo name is Side Car Ace. A card shark in Kansas gave him the name. Mahlee's hobo name is Tin Can Mahlee cause of her trinkets. I don't have a hobo name, yet. I'm plain ole Annie Grace.

When we go into towns, Mahlee keeps next to me, even when I tell her not to. When Daddy disappears at the taverns with the booze and girls, she stays by my side, protecting me from the wild hobos who might bother little girls. I'm glad she stands several inches taller than most men and can take them out with one hand if she needs to.

Mahlee wears all of her clothes, three skirts and two tops, at the same time. She wears them old work boots. They clomp when she steps. I always know where she is. Her shoes clop on a cobblestone street like a horse stepping.

Too many nights, Daddy sleeps in jail. Sometimes, he and his friend, Peg Leg, take off on adventures. He's supposed to meet Peg Leg in St. Louis. They got business to tend to.

"Daddy. Can we go to a mission tonight before you go off to the card game? Maybe they will have a bed for Mahlee and me. I could use a bath. I don't smell good."

Daddy sniffed my sleeve and wrinkled his nose. "We'll see. I've got places to go." He put his arm around my shoulder, holding onto me, and we moved to the doorway. "Time to jump."

Untied Shoelace

The three of us dropped to the gravel and dirt below as the train pulled into the station. The railroad cops came for us with those big sticks as the train inched to a stop.

The clanking sound and yelling told me they were hitting the boxcars with sticks to scare out any other hobos. "Get out of those boxcars. Off the train. We catch you and we're taking you in."

My silent Geronimo had placed me in the bushes, along with seven other hobos. Mahlee landed beside me, her tin can rattling with untold secrets. Brushing myself off, I waited for Daddy.

Cops swung at the running bodies with their sticks. A hard thud made one man cry—a man who sweet talks his little girl. My daddy.

Whack. The stick cracked on something. "I've seen you here too many times."

I peeked from behind the bush. The cop had Daddy by the collar. "Off to jail." They arrested him and a few other hobos.

I kicked the dirt with my navy Keds, the ones with holes. I ran for Daddy, but Mahlee yanked me by my coat, forcing me to hide. She covered my mouth. "You ain't goin' after him," she whispered. "They'll let your daddy go in the morning. Come on. We got to find a spot to sleep till sunup."

Mahlee moved in a different direction and I protested. "Daddy's the other way. Turn around. We have to stay in St. Louis."

Mahlee peered at me with her *don't you run off* look.

I sighed and stepped in brown spongy dirt. It stuck to my shoe. It smelled. I shook my foot, but the gunk didn't come off. "I have horse poop on my shoes now." I rubbed the bottom of my shoes on the taller weeds beside the trail, hoping to get rid of the smell. I ran to Mahlee. "This trail heads out of town, away from Daddy. I want my daddy. I'm going back."

Mahlee disappeared in the fog of the cold sunset.

"Wait up. I'm coming."

"Keep up," Mahlee shouted. "Not waiting for ya." Her voice went deeper into the thicket, an echo running alongside the tracks, telling me to hurry.

Standing in the woods alone on a trail in the dark made me shiver, especially with the eyes of critters surrounding me. I called to Mahlee. "Wait, I need to clean my shoes off." The autumn leaves stuck to the soles of my shoes and the owls called to me. I wasn't in the mood to talk. It was too cold. The wind whipped through rows of Christmas trees. Daddy would simply call them pine trees.

Mahlee yanked on my collar. "Keep up with me. See the barn on the hill behind the main house? The home belongs to Eddie Card. He runs the mission in St. Louis. I've known him since I turned twelve. His barn is also a carriage house. We can sleep inside. If he finds us, he won't shoot us."

Mahlee unlocked the latch. *Screech. Screech.* We slipped through giant double doors and they squeaked even louder when they shut. A milking cow craned her neck chewing on her cud. A harvest moon shining through the windows above the loft lit the entire barn. A bunch of chickens and a horse stared at us from the other end. An old horse-drawn wagon sat beside a big, black, shiny car. Several bales of hay were stacked near a ladder leading to the loft. We climbed up and studied the unfinished floor—our bed for the night.

The windows let silvery moonlight in from the Christmas tree fields. I could see night rolling in across the twinkling lights of St. Louis below. My daddy was there. A lump formed in my throat.

Mahlee tossed her gunny sack on the floor. Her tin can tumbled from her sack. The lid on the Prince Albert tobacco

Untied Shoelace

can popped off and Mahlee's stuff tumbled out. I tried to grab her things, but they fell to the barn floor below, except for the gun. Mahlee snatched the gun from the ledge before it fell.

Diving from the ladder, Mahlee swam in the air as she sailed from the loft. She gathered up her Popsicle stick, the blue ring, a roller skate wheel, and a picture of a baby. *Was that a baby picture of Mahlee?* She shoved her trinkets inside before I could see the rest of the contents, her secret world once again hidden inside of the can. Mahlee climbed the ladder and sat down on the floor.

I spotted an old trunk. A stack of horse blankets lay on top. We could use them to wrap around us tonight. I carried four blankets to Mahlee and tripped on a shoebox beside the trunk. I opened it and inside the box I saw a pair of red PF Flyers with white shoelaces. I've always wanted a pair. Could they be a present for me? My fingers wiggled. "Look what I found. New shoes."

Mahlee shook her head. "Those shoes belong to Eddie Card."

"I'm going to look at them."

"You need to leave them be. Put the box by the trunk and bring me some more blankets."

I tossed a blanket at Mahlee and sat down, crossing my legs with the box on my lap. "Touching them won't hurt." A glance at my stinky shoes made the decision easy. I had to see what size the shoes were and peeked at the end of the box. My heart raced. "They're my size. Maybe I could wear them to sleep in." I kicked off my Keds and pulled on the right shoe, then the left. My toes wiggled and I smiled.

Mahlee watched me and curled up in the blankets. "Are you coming to bed?"

"I will in a minute. These shoes can jump and run. I can outrun railroad cops in these red shoes."

I stood on top of the trunk and jumped down. I got on the trunk and jumped again. Mahlee snapped her fingers. "Time for sleep. Stop the jumping."

We cuddled together inside the blankets. Mahlee held onto her tin can with a death grip. For the next couple of hours, I tossed and turned, and kept looking under the blanket to make sure the shoes were real. If I keep these shoes, they'll be my first new pair in five years. The others came from missions or trash cans. These feel like home.

A *tic-tic-tic* on the roof sounded like ice falling into a glass. It was the first winter storm and it was creeping in as Mahlee snored under her blankets. The barn turned chilly and my eyes popped open again. I pulled out a brown paper sack and a pencil from my gunny sack. The moon gave enough light for me to see and I found a blank spot to scribble a poem. A new one for Daddy. He loves my poems.

> *Down from the loft, Not so soft,*
> *Mahlee's tin can fell.*
> *She got her trinkets, quick and fast.*
> *Secret things from the past.*
> *I found new shoes in a box*
> *Red PF Flyers for me,*
> *I pray God will let it be.*

My warm and happy feet grew sleepy and my eyes blinked heavy. I snuggled under Mahlee's arm and dreamed of Christmas at Grandma Elsie's house. Daddy promised we would make it to her house this year. He means it when he promises. But sometimes his promises get lost in towns we pass through.

CHAPTER FOUR

PF FLYERS RUN

I HAD TO MAKE SURE my feet had the red shoes on. I yanked the blanket off. The shoes were real. It wasn't a dream. Would it be okay to borrow them?

I don't pray to God much cause if Daddy hears me, he tells me God never helps him. Mahlee talks to God. She thinks God does listen and I needed His permission to keep the shoes. I moved to the window and scanned the sky.

"God, it's me. Annie Grace Kree. I'm nine, almost ten. I'm a little mouthy, but I don't cuss much. Did you see these shoes?" I held my foot in the air in the window. "They're PF Flyers. The best running shoes a girl could have. I wanted you to know, I'm borrowing them for now. Thank you. I'll make good on this. I promise I'll return them someday." I put my foot down. "Oh yeah." I folded my hands back. "Amen."

Mahlee wiped her eyes. "You done, girl? We've got to go. Eddie Card is headed to the carriage house. I can hear him whistling."

We scurried out the screechy doors, to the woods, and down the trail. We headed to the jail to deliver my poem to Daddy, to get a hug, and to find breakfast. "I don't remember going this far last night." I called to Mahlee.

"Take the dirt road to the right. The jail is on Clark Street. We're close," Mahlee assured me.

I stopped. Up ahead, smoke rose in a puff of twisted gray plumes. "What's on fire?"

Mahlee caught up with me. "I'm not sure. I see smoke right over them trees."

My PF Flyers raced down the road and Mahlee clunked after me in her boots. I could hear the sirens blaring. We rounded a block of brick buildings. A crowd had gathered. The whole town must have come out to watch the fire.

A fireman yelled orders to everybody. "More water. Watch out. Stand back. The roof's hot. She's coming down."

I squeezed between legs and arms, and inched closer. Flames rose from the jail. "My daddy is in there." I pushed to the front.

A cop grabbed my arm and held me tight. "No, girl. Get back."

The roof of the jailhouse crashed to the ground. The entire building became a big bonfire and the fire popped like fireworks on the Fourth of July.

Tears rolled down my face. "Where's my daddy? I want my daddy." I tried to pull away from the cop, but he held on tight.

Mahlee appeared. "Come with me."

I yanked my arm from the cop's hand. "Why?"

"The prisoners have been taken to the City Rescue Mission. Your daddy is safe."

I glared at Mahlee. "Are you sure?"

"Yes, I'm sure."

I followed Mahlee all the way to the mission and bolted through the doors. A scrawny man rushed by me and knocked me to the floor. "Watch out mister." He didn't even look back.

The smell of bacon and eggs filled my nose. My tummy rumbled. Mahlee moved toward the smell of the food, but I had to find Daddy before I could eat.

A man sitting sideways, two tables away rubbed his eyes. "Daddy, is that you?" He didn't turn around.

The cook came to an opening in the wall. "We've got more bacon and eggs. Come and get it."

I pushed my way through the line of people. "Daddy?" I shoved by two men. "Get out of my way. That's my daddy."

I jumped into his arms. "Daddy, don't ever leave me again." Daddy squeezed me tight and put me in his lap. I wish this feeling would never leave.

"Annie Grace, where in the world have you been? I wasn't sure where you and Mahlee ended up last night."

"We slept in a barn with warm blankets."

Mahlee set a plate of biscuits and bacon in front of us. I crammed a strip of bacon into my mouth. Mahlee pulled up a chair and handed me a biscuit, which I slipped into my pocket.

I wiggled my toes and held my foot up for Daddy. "I found a new pair of PF Flyers at the barn, too. They fit, and I borrowed them."

Daddy smiled and touched my foot. "Tie them shoelaces."

Before I could, the door flew open and bounced against the wall. Two cops rushed into the mission. One shouted, "We need all prisoners to go line up at the curb." The other one slapped a stick in his hand. "A group of you were released because of the fire. We're looking for Peg Leg and Side Car Ace." The cop smirked. "There's a reward." His lips curled into an ugly grin. He turned his head left and right, watching the faces in the room.

The men in the room became a mob. They ran into each other, jumping and screaming. Two men dodged out the side door smashing the glass when the door flew open. A group of men raced ahead of us. The wonderful, delicious bacon went flying through the air and tumbled to the floor.

Mahlee, Daddy, and me dropped to our knees and crawled to the back of the room and through the kitchen. One of the cooks stepped on Daddy's hand, but he kept going. We slipped out the back door and down the alley. We headed south to the tracks.

Peg Leg showed up from a side field as we ran for the train leaving town. If it hadn't been for my new shoes, I would have fallen behind. The four of us caught the first MoPac rolling by. We landed in different boxcars, but we were safe and together. We were on the run, again. The fastest shoes in Missouri were on my feet, and I needed them.

CHAPTER FIVE

UNEXPECTED SPELLING BEE

FOR DAYS MY PF FLYERS have outrun Mahlee at the hobo camp. We're waiting for Daddy and Peg Leg to return from their business in Memphis. I run to the tracks to watch for him when Mahlee's not making me practice my reading. She dishes out the rules. I try to break them.

Mahlee and me are staying with White Beard. He knows us, and we're welcome. The November days are getting shorter, and I'm not sure if we've missed Thanksgiving. It doesn't matter. I'm not too thankful, right now.

"Girl, time for you to read."

I moved closer to the campfire. "Do I have to? It's too cold to read."

Mahlee pulled *The Hero of Strange Hill* from her gunny sack. "Let's find out how the story ends."

I opened the pages. "I read better than most hobos. Better than you, even better than Daddy or Peg Leg."

"Read, girl."

"I'm smart enough. I can make hobo stew from lettuce and old taters. I can catch a train in one Geronimo leap. I can glide on the catwalk on the top of a boxcar, too. Reading isn't going to make me hop a train better."

"Glide? I think you're dreaming." Mahlee's eyes sparkled with interest at seeing the book. This is our fifth time to read the book this year. I spilled out the words from page eighty three.

Andy's heart ached as he thought of his mother and how different life would have been had she lived, and how different life would have been if his father had not gone away. When Andy went to bed, his pillow got soaked with his tears. As yet, though, he could not imagine going home, to the house where it happened.

Mahlee's chin touched her neck and her nose rattled with her famous snore. I tossed the book onto her sack and headed to the tracks.

The tobacco smell drifted in the air. Cigarettes. The kind Daddy smokes. I balanced myself on the top of one rail and jumped the ties. I gathered shiny rocks and filled my pockets with them between jumps.

Down the tracks, a Negro man crouched on the rail. "What's your name?" I kicked at a rock. "Where you headed?"

"I'm Skip. I'm headed south. Looking for work." His skin was browner than most, and wrinkled, too. He wore a gray-striped engineer's cap, black slacks, black boots, and a torn jacket.

Skip ground out his cigarette. "You got a name?"

"Annie Grace Kree." I pointed to the woods. "I'm staying with White Beard and Mahlee. You ever read? Mahlee makes me, but it's boring. I can spell though. I'm the best speller this side of the Mississippi, maybe in the whole world."

He raised one eyebrow and laughed.

"Is Skip your real name?"

"Real enough."

"I don't have a hobo name. I hope to get one before I'm ten. My daddy is Side Car Ace. My mama never got a hobo name. She died. Daddy said she's bones in the ground because she's dead, but I think she's in Heaven."

Skip grabbed another cigarette. "What's got them pockets weighted down?"

I fished the rocks from both my pockets. Daddy's poem floated to the ground. Skip stood and picked up the paper. He handed the poem to me and I shoved the paper into my pocket. I held my other hand out with the rocks, letting him see how shiny they were.

Skip grinned. "Want to play a game with me?"

"I don't know. How do you play it?"

"You say you're such a good speller. I'm gonna give you a word to spell and, if you miss it, you have to toss a rock away."

I didn't have to think long. "You're gonna see. I'll keep my rocks."

We bounced down the tracks together. "Betcha you can't spell engineer."

"That's easy. E-N-G-I-N-E-E-R."

He gave me word after word and I spelled them all. "C-A-B-O-O-S-E." I never lost a rock.

After a while, I glanced down the tracks. "Mahlee's gonna be looking for me. I've been gone too long. I've gotta go back." I paused, letting Skip mosey on.

He removed his striped engineer cap, turned, and came back to me, bent down and placed his cap on my head. It slid down to my eyebrows and I pushed it up. Skip touched my nose with his finger. "Thanks for the spelling bee. You are the best speller this side of the Mississippi."

I grabbed a shiny red rock. "Take this. Put it in your pocket. It'll bring you good luck."

Skip slipped the rock into the inner lining of his jacket, shuffled down the embankment, and headed away. He spun around and waved. "Bye, Annie Grace. Keep on spelling and take care of my cap."

CHAPTER SIX

A SHOELACE IS BORN

MAHLEE PULLED ON MY ARM and twirled me around. "Where'd you get the cap?"

I stepped away from her. "It's mine. I was in a spelling bee, right here on the tracks."

"Sure you had a spelling bee. I don't see a soul on these here tracks."

Mahlee's mocking made me want to toss the rest of my rocks at her, but they were precious to me. I'll keep them inside my pocket so she won't see them.

A car skidded to a stop in the road up a ways. The person on the passenger side stepped from the car. A black hat popped up, came around the car, and a man's vest flew open. The shiny butt of a gun stuck out from his belt.

"Daddy. Daddy." He was wearing the vest he found at a mission in Kansas last year. I raced down the tracks to him, he wrapped me in his arms, and his satchel bounced on his shoulder. The butt of the gun poked my leg. "When did you get a gun? Everyone has a gun but me."

"I won this gun in a game of poker. Who else has a gun?"

"Mahlee. She has one. I saw it on Halloween. I did. It's in her tin can."

"You better leave Mahlee alone. She'll get you for meddling in her belongings."

Daddy put me down, and we stood by the fire. He pulled out a bumpy paper sack from his satchel. Inside, were oranges, apples, and a loaf of bread. "Happy Thanksgiving." Daddy tossed me an orange and an apple. He tossed two oranges to Mahlee.

I bit into the apple. "Is today Thanksgiving?"

Daddy nodded.

Now I have two things to be thankful for, spelling bees and Daddy. If Mahlee wouldn't make me read, I'd be thankful for her, too.

The ground rumbled. Daddy stood and motioned for us to follow. "Tie them shoelaces, girl. We got a train to catch. We can't stay around here. The cops caught Peg Leg for stealing and they're looking for a murderer, too. A man and woman were shot on lover's lane in town close to where the poker game went down. We need to move on."

Daddy and Mahlee kicked dirt onto the fire and we headed for the tracks.

Inside the boxcar, I tore the peel from my orange. Several hobos laughed and passed the whiskey bottle around. They offered me a drink. Daddy slapped the man's hand away. "She's too young."

Daddy tugged on my arm and pointed to the top of the boxcar. "Come with me. We're going to the top. These men are bound to get into a fight."

I peered out the boxcar door. The late evening sun hung in the sky like a giant orange. Daddy climbed first and pulled me by both arms to the catwalk. Mahlee followed. I sat Indian-style next to him, clutching my gunny sack with my fruit. Mahlee curled up next to me.

The wind rushed at us and I held onto my cap. I didn't want to lose my hat in the whipping wind rushing across the top of the boxcar. I moved closer to Daddy. I could see the reflection of the sky in the river below and the mountains with snow on them. I could see downtown Memphis.

The train rolled onto the Harahan Bridge. The bridge goes more than a mile above the Mississippi River and we're sitting on top of a boxcar. I shivered and Daddy climbed down between the two boxcars onto the knuckle. He pressed himself against one of the ends and called to me. "This gravel car is empty. It'll be warmer in there. I'm getting you out of this wind."

I have watched Daddy go between boxcars before but never above the mighty Mississippi. I moved down the ladder and Daddy held me close to his side. He pushed me into the gravel car. Mahlee made her way inside, too. I watched as Daddy stood on the knuckle between the boxcars. The strap of his satchel slipped down and wrapped around his leg. He couldn't get free and the wind flipped his hat off.

I reached for him, but Daddy's fingers came loose, one by one. He grabbed for the ladder with the other hand and caught the rung with two fingers. Daddy swayed. He swung like a tree branch bending in a storm. The boxcar jerked and his fingers slid off the rung. Daddy was tossed from the train toward the river below and I screamed.

As the train moved across the bridge, I ran the full length of the gravel car to look back. Mahlee shadowed my heels. From somewhere below, Daddy cried, "Annie Grace. I love you—tie them shoelaces."

I lost sight of Daddy as we chugged across the bridge. He must have landed in the Indian burial grounds by the cove. *Or did he plunge into the Mississippi River?*

"Daddy," I screamed, "I'm coming." Mahlee held onto me. I beat on her chest. "Let me go." We both fell to the bottom of the gravel car and she held me until I stopped hitting her. She clutched her trinket can, but Mahlee's gunny

sack and my reading book had toppled into the water. The roar
of steel on the iron bridge drowned out my screams and
Mahlee's prayer.

I pulled myself from Mahlee's grasp. "Let go of me. We
have to go back." I grabbed every one of my rocks from my
pockets. "I hope the rock I gave Skip brings him luck. These
are no good." In one swoop, I tossed the stones into the river. I
fell onto the car floor and cried until my eyes burned.

When the train found dry land across the river in Arkansas,
I jumped from the gravel car. After the last boxcar
disappeared, I ran across the bridge toward Tennessee. A mile
bridge wasn't keeping me from my daddy. A few feet onto the
bridge, my shoelaces hung on a loose railroad tie. I stumbled
and landed on my hands and knees. I was looking right into
the rushing water below.

I tied my shoelaces and stepped onto the ties with Mahlee
trailing me. Each time I glanced down, I got dizzy, but I kept
moving. I had to find my daddy.

Mahlee caught up with me. "No one could live through
such a fall. Girl, come back."

I screamed at God. "Daddy just returned to me. I didn't
read my poem to him. I didn't get to show him my rocks or
tell him I won the spelling bee with Skip. Thanksgiving Day
can't end this way. It can't." I shivered, but the hurt in my
chest wasn't from the cold anymore.

At the cove, I ran along the shore. The river swept by me.
A winter storm stirred death at the water's edge. If Daddy
died, I wanted to die, too.

I saw something floating in the river. It was Daddy's
satchel. I ran to the rocks and pulled the bag from the water. I
crawled up the hill as Mahlee yanked on my overall strap. I

buried my head in Mahlee's chest, her sobs and her shaking matched mine. "What will I do without my daddy?"

Mahlee spoke one word like an Indian chant into the wind. "Shoelace." She repeated the word, again. Not once or twice. But, again and again. "Shoelace."

My chest hurt and I yelled at Mahlee. "What are you doing? Stop saying the word shoelace. My shoelaces are tied."

"Your daddy gave you a gift today. He left you with your hobo name."

I stomped my foot. "He did not. He never gave me a new name. We've got to find him." I ran to the tracks. "He's not here. He's not anywhere."

Mahlee hollered to me from the bottom of the hill. "He's either hurt or he's dead. He's probably floating down the river."

"He's not dead. Not my daddy. You'll see. He always comes for me." I kicked the rocks by the tracks and sat down, rocking, and holding my legs.

Mahlee sat and rocked with her hands around her knees like a baby in her mama's arms. She talked to the shadows. Every few seconds she repeated, "Shoelace. Shoelace."

I ran my fingers across the canvas of my PF Flyers and remembered the last words from Daddy. The ones he cried as he fell from the train. *Tie them shoelaces.*

The rail hummed as another train rumbled in from the east. It's too cold to sit by the river. We had to move on. Mahlee and me hopped a train toward Little Rock. I held my daddy's satchel and rocked in the corner of a boxcar while Mahlee mumbled. "Shoelace. Shoelace. Who is Shoelace?"

I scooted closer to Mahlee. Tired and scared, I repeated her question. "Who is Shoelace?"

"You is. You've gotten your hobo name and your daddy gave it to you."

My eyes kept closing as Mahlee whispered "Shoelace," her words spun in my ears like a wheel rolling down the tracks. It's just Mahlee and me now. Guess it always has been. A sad poem fell from my lips.

> *"No more Annie Grace.*
> *Just a girl named Shoelace.*
> *Same face, Same hobo pace.*
> *It's Mahlee and me, Together, we'll be.*
> *But will we ever find a safe place?"*

I threw Daddy's satchel down at my feet and a soaked deck of cards scattered. I counted the cards. Fifty-one. There should be fifty-two. I flipped each card and placed them into piles. The ace of hearts was missing. Gone, like my heart. Gone into the Mississippi River.

CHAPTER SEVEN

NEW HOME, STUPID PEOPLE

IF ONE MORE PERSON TELLS Grandma Elsie I have a sweet face, I'm leaving for hobo camp. I haven't seen Tin Can Mahlee since we rolled into Texarkana three weeks ago. I wish Mahlee would come to the manor to sit with me because the people bombarding through the front door of the house were never going to call me anything except Annie Grace.

"You're a sweet thing." The lady with the round tummy tempted me to knock her hat off. I pressed my teeth together and smiled, instead.

Grandma didn't make me wear my new dress or the white hat she bought me for Daddy's memorial service. Thank goodness. The pea-green dress didn't match my red PF Flyers. I'm wearing my engineer cap. The one Skip gave me. My overalls and my red shoes make perfect funeral clothes.

I hid under the pedestal table using the tablecloth as a tent. The table held pies, cakes, ham, and biscuits. I sat on the hardwood floor hiding from the greedy hands who poured into the house. I wondered how many of these people knew my daddy. Or cared. The people grabbed plates as if they were eating their last meal. These people would never last a night with scraps of cheese and bologna.

Grandma Elsie's neighbors and church people came to Beech Street Manor, my grandma's boarding house, way before noon. They listened to this preacher man, Cody

Westside. He read from his Bible and told everyone my daddy would be missed. How can they miss Daddy? None of them know him.

Grandma said we were paying respect to the dead. I say, Daddy's not dead. He's missing. The story in the newspaper listed Daddy as dead, though. The paper had Gill T. Kree, 27, of Texarkana, Arkansas, died Thursday, November 22, 1945 in Memphis, Tennessee, because a train hit him. The paper is wrong. He fell. No train ran over Daddy. He got bumped from the train when his satchel wrapped around his boot. He tried to get free, but the *untied shoelace* on his boot got tangled in the satchel. No wonder Daddy kept telling me to tie my shoes.

He was a member of First Baptist Church. I wonder if he and Mama got married there? His papa was Otto T. Kree, an attorney. Grandma never told me that. Grandma asked people to send donations in Daddy's memory to Wheelock Academy in Millerton, Oklahoma, an Indian orphanage and school for Choctaw girls. Grandma and Grandpa have Choctaw Indian blood in their family. Guess I do, too.

Christmas is next week. Grandma Elsie has a Christmas tree in the parlor, strung with popcorn, tinsel, and red ribbons, but Daddy isn't here to see it.

Santa and God are mixed together in my mind. It's hard to think the guy in the red suit can bring presents to kids who have houses but not to hobo kids. If Santa isn't real, I wonder if God is? Mama's in Heaven. She has to be with God. He has to be real.

Good grief. The preacher sees me. I shouldn't have peeked from under the table.

Pastor Cody bent down and lifted the tablecloth. "Annie Grace. A friend of yours is at the piano in the parlor." He reached for my hand.

I crawled out ready to run up stairs. A quick escape waited on the second floor.

Pastor Cody smiled. "He says he's in town to get work at Red River Arsenal. He came to my church on Saturday morning by Swampoodle Creek."

I inched toward the stairs. "You have church by a creek? Can't you afford a building?"

He moved closer. "I'm the pastor at Church by the Creek for hobos. Well, for anyone who wants to come, even little girls. We have a Bible study, eat biscuits and drink coffee, too."

I moved up another stair step. "I don't like coffee. Your church sounds boring. No roof. No walls. Why come?"

Pastor Cody smiled. "The creek feels like home for some. It might feel like home to you, too. Besides, God loves to fish. You ever fish?"

"I used to fish with Daddy. Who's this person in the parlor?"

A skinny lady with cake called to Pastor Cody. He moved across the front room but turned back. "He calls himself Skip."

I tumbled down the stairs and rounded the fireplace to the front room where guests sat. I saw a curly black-haired man facing the piano in the parlor room. "Skip." He tapped the piano keys as I ran to him. "You play the piano? You know how to make music?"

He cocked his head. "My spelling bee champion. What are you doing here?"

"My grandma lives here. This is my daddy's memorial service." I could smell something coming from Skip. I sniffed his collar. "I smell cinnamon. What have you got on?"

"It's smell-good stuff Pastor Cody splashed on me." He stuck his neck out. "Take a whiff. I smell good."

"Yep. That's probably the best you've smelled in months."

Skip laughed. "Pastor Cody told me to take a bath, but I had one this month already. He picked me up in his ole jalopy and poured toilet water on me. I kind of like this smell."

"I'm glad you're here. I don't got many friends here. You don't have to wash to be my friend." I scooted next to him and waved a hand showing off the parlor. "We're having a funeral. We ain't got a body, but we're paying *respect* to Daddy. Grandma says we are. Where you staying, Skip?"

"I'm staying at Hobo Jungle." He put his foot on one of the pedals, touched a key near the middle of the keyboard, and played a ripple of notes.

I hugged him. To be close to someone who knows the rail feels safe. Maybe he'll stay in town for a while.

"Did you know Daddy fell from the MoPac into a river? Everyone says he's dead. I say he's playing cards in Memphis. Or hiding out from the law. I'm waiting for him to come for me. Daddy could use a bottle of good smelling cinnamon stuff." I sniffed his collar. "You do smell good."

Skip squinted at me. "Your pa met the deep water of the burial grounds under the Mississippi River."

"No. He's alive. He has to be." I leaned my head against Skip's arm. Tears stung my eyes and I brushed them away.

Skip tapped the keys lightly. "Pastor Cody heard me play at a tavern in College Hill. He met folks at the door and invited them to his church meeting. I figure this song fits."

His fingers flew across the keys as he sang, "I'll fly away, Oh, glory, I'll fly away."

I've never heard such good sounds. Nobody had played Grandma's piano since I got here. I could hear loud talking coming from somewhere. The parlor ladies were yakking louder than the music. They said my name.

Untied Shoelace

"I'm glad Annie Grace is living with her grandma. The rail is no life for a little girl, riding in boxcars and living with bums. Look, now she's sitting with that Negro."

I jumped from the piano bench and ripped through the room toward the lady with the bushy eyebrows. I could hear Skip playing faster and louder. The music bounced off the walls. I skidded to the lady. I couldn't help myself. I shoved her plate with the piece of three-layer chocolate cake into her chest. Frosting and pieces of cake stuck to her dress. "Skip's my friend. I'll sit with him if I want to." I darted under the pedestal table.

I could hear Grandma apologizing, smoothing things out. Most of the people weren't paying any attention. They were too busy grabbing free food from Grandma's table.

Skip played more hymns and sang words. My heart felt sad. The shoes strolling by at the bottom of the tablecloth made me want to trip them. A pair of men's brown shoes stopped right in front of me. "Gill's on the run. He's probably wanted by the police. I've heard talk of it downtown." A woman in shiny black shoes talked faster than I could listen. "Poor little Annie Grace. Hope she doesn't grow up and act like her daddy. He's always been crazy. Gill had something to do with his pa's death. My sister worked for Otto Kree. She heard them fight."

I barreled from beneath the table. The man and woman screamed and dropped their plates. "I'm not crazy and neither is my daddy." I bolted out the front door, as Grandma patted the lady on the arm consoling her for my bad attitude.

I marched around the porch in circles, huffing. I sounded like Mahlee when she gets mad. "Stupid lady. Stupid town. Daddy's not crazy. He does roam, but roaming doesn't make him crazy. He plays cards and loses nickels gambling.

Gambling doesn't make him crazy, either. Daddy loves me. He just comes up missing sometimes."

I plopped down in one of Grandma's rockers on the side porch. I could hear the chatter. No one missed me.

A girl in shiny shoes paraded up to me. "Want part of my orange?"

I stopped rocking. "Sure. Who are you?"

Shiny-shoes handed me a slice. "I'm Clara. I live on a plantation on Highway 67. I have servants. I have a bedroom as big as this entire house." She handed me another slice. "What do you say when a person hands you an orange?"

"Thank you." Juice dripped down my chin and I spit a seed on her fancy dress. "Sorry, sour oranges make me spit."

She wiped her dress. "I bet you ate beans before you got here."

I spit another seed near her shoes. "I like beans." My fist curled, ready to sock Clara, but the preacher came to the porch. Clara grinned at him and turned to go inside. I spit another seed at her back. The seed stuck to her sash. I grinned this time.

Pastor Cody moved to the open rocker. "Shoelace, do you mind if I sit down?"

He called me by my hobo name. He might be a nice man. Not sure, yet. I squinted at him. "Don't care. Free country." I swallowed the last bite of my orange.

He placed his Bible on the wooden table. "So, riding the rail is fun?"

"The best. It's a magic carpet ride." I rocked and nearly bounced out of the chair.

"I knew your daddy." His rocker stopped and he leaned toward me. "I played against him in baseball."

I screeched to a stop. "With my daddy?"

44

He nodded. "I knew your mama, Grace, too. They were sweethearts."

He had my attention. "Do I look like my mama?"

Pastor Cody has big teeth. You can see all of them when he talks. "She had the same reddish-blonde hair. And you've got her freckles. Did you know she loved to fly kites? She also sang in the church choir."

I let my imagination drift. I could see Mama in a light pink dress tied at the waist with a dark pink ribbon, singing in the choir. "I've seen a picture of Mama and Daddy sitting on a dock in swimming suits at Crystal Springs."

Pastor Cody nodded. "They loved to swim. I used to swim with them. Swimming always tuckered your mama out. She sat on the docks and watched us when she got tired." Pastor Cody touched my chin. "Your mama's heart tuckered out when you were born, too. Gill told me when Grace saw your pudgy nose she kissed you on the forehead, right before she went to Heaven."

I rubbed my hand across my forehead. "She kissed me?"

"Sure did. Special girls get kisses from their mamas."

"Did Daddy sing in the choir?"

"No, he never sang inside the church, but he'd watch your mama through the church window, smiling at her, distracting her as she tried to sing. Your daddy loved your mama and Grace loved him. On holidays, he'd sit with her in church."

Pastor Cody leaned in and looked at me. "I see you have her nose."

I smiled, and my fingers touched my nose.

He picked up his Bible. "I've got to run. Everyone's leaving." He headed to the group piling out the front door.

I slipped into the house as Grandma said goodbye to a man in a suit, the last to go except for Pastor Cody and Skip.

Grandma placed a hand on Skip's shoulder. "Good to see you, my friend."

"You, too ma'am. You still have your horse?"

"No. Sway Back died years ago."

Pastor Cody and Skip left and Grandma leaned her head on the closed door.

I tugged on Grandma's sleeve. "You had a horse?"

"Yes. A horse no one wanted except my pa."

"Can we get a horse?" I pressed my head against her tummy.

She sighed. "This is not a good time for a horse. Money's tight. Maybe someday." Grandma wiped her face and straightened her burgundy dress. "Annie Grace, you haven't eaten a bite. Make a plate and sit with me on the couch."

All the boarders were gone or upstairs in their rooms. I loaded my plate with pie, ham, and biscuits. I poured a glass of sweet tea and sat down with Grandma and she kissed me on the forehead. I smiled, bit into my biscuit, and grabbed a crumb from my plate, shoving it into my mouth. My glass slid from my other hand, hit the hardwood floor, and splashed tea on Grandma's shoes.

As I mopped the floor, I glanced at Grandma, who smiled at me with glassy eyes like a lake without ripples, calm and hopeful. *I hate to tell her I'm not staying.*

CHAPTER EIGHT

TO SKIP CHURCH

I'M LEAVING TODAY. CHRISTMAS IS over and the decorations are in the attic. I picked this Saturday because Grandma has signed me up for school. I'm starting next week on a Tuesday. I've got to find Daddy and I don't have time for school. I've packed my poems, his satchel, and a handful of biscuits in my gunny sack. One last glance at the two-story house and I'm gone.

I've tried to catch a train more than once, but Grandma would place a mop in my hand or have me hang clothes on the line. She's shadowed me, hugged me, and watched me. But today, Grandma Elsie left early for Piggly Wiggly to buy milk and butter. This is my chance.

Flup-flup-flup. A truck pulled up beside me in the alley behind the carriage house and Pastor Cody rolled his window down. "Get in. Your friend's waiting for you inside a church. He wants to talk to you."

"I've got a train to catch." I shuffled in my PF Flyers and hurried down the alley with the *flup-flup-flup* of the pastor's pickup singing along with a church bell chiming its gongs. The ringing of the bell on the steam engine on the MoPac told me that if I'm gonna make it, I better run. Freedom passes with each chug of the steam engine, with each gong of the church bell.

Honk. Honk. Honk. I tripped on the uneven Coffeyville bricks and hit the ground. I dusted off my overalls, picked up my cap, and turned, slapping my hand on the front of the hood. I wanted the last word. "Why are you following me?"

He stuck his head out the window. "You have to come with me. This could be life or death. Skip wants you."

"Skip? Why didn't you tell me?" I tossed my gunny sack over the wire fence in the alley, next to a group of bushes. I packed some biscuits in my sack and a jar of Grandma's homemade strawberry jam. I hope the ants stay out of my food. I'll catch another train later and get my bag this afternoon.

I jumped into the front seat and barely got the door shut before Pastor Cody turned the truck around. "What's wrong with him? Did he get hurt? Why is Skip at church?"

"My phone rang at the house as I was leaving for my service at the creek. He just wants you and I knew where to find you."

I leaned against the dash, watching each turn. We sped down dirt roads and Pastor Cody drove fast. Too fast. The truck skidded sideways and I dug myself from the floorboard as he rounded another curve. He braked to a stop in front of a small white church, tires skidding, and brakes squealing.

A crowd had gathered outside the double doors on the porch leading into the church. A cop stood guard like the steeple on top of the church and I wiggled passed the elbows and the wide rear ends, the skinny and the tall.

Pastor Cody and me were the only white people, except for the cops. I crept to the side of the church building next to the woods where the three-foot weeds nearly kept me out. I pushed on a window. It wouldn't budge and I tried another one. Then another one. I tried all five windows and they were all locked.

Pressing my nose against the last pane, I caught a glimpse of Skip sitting on the platform where the preacher stands on Sunday mornings. Skip wiped his brow, shoved his hand inside his shirt, and yanked out a small revolver. I've learned on the rail one bullet can end the pain, or create more.

"Skip. Skip." I slammed my fist on the glass and Skip's glassy eyes focused on me. "Skip, put the gun down." He laid the gun on the pulpit and shuffled toward me, his words muffled, his lips moving.

"Open this window." The crowd was hollering on the other side of the church. It sounded like they all wanted to be in charge. *Let's just go get him. He broke into the building after all.* I had even lost Pastor Cody, not that I cared.

Skip's mouth moved and I made out a few of his words. *I've got to tell you something.* He stepped backward, marched across the room, and picked up the gun. Skip tripped over the pew and the gun went off twice, one bullet lodged in the back of the piano.

"Skip, are you okay?" I smashed the window with my fist and the pane splintered. A sliver of glass sliced my wrist like a knife sawing ham from the bone and blood dripped like ice cream melting. *Ahh!* I held my breath and yanked the glass from my arm.

Saving Skip became all I could think of and I unlatched the window with my good hand, pushed it open, and crawled inside. I had to get to Skip before the grownups broke the doors in. I wasn't sure the people on the other side of the building heard the gun, but I couldn't take any chances.

I rushed to Skip and wrapped my good arm around him. "Put the gun down. It's me, your spelling bee champion." Blood dripped from my other arm onto his shirt.

Skip pushed me back. "You're hurt." He tore a piece of fabric from his blue denim shirt and wrapped it around my wrist. "I've got big trouble and now, you've gone and got yourself hurt."

"It's a small cut. Are you shot?"

"No. I'm fine. But you are bleeding."

The loud banging on the foyer doors got our attention and Pastor Cody crashed into the sanctuary along with men carrying sticks. The short round cop in the front tripped on something and they all fell over each other, like stacked firewood by the double doors.

I held out my arm with the cut, making a motion for them to stop. A waterfall of blood dripped to the floor from my wrist and my words ran together. I felt dizzy, but I was going to protect Skip. "Don't hurt my friend."

Pastor Cody rushed ahead of the others. He towered above them and stopped in the center aisle. He motioned for the mob to stay back. "Skip, let Shoelace go."

Skip grabbed the revolver and held it down at his side. "She's free to leave. Take her. Get her arm stitched up."

Pastor Cody reached out with one hand. "Shoelace, come with me. Let the police handle this."

"No. I'm not leaving. You brought me here. I'm staying." I moved closer to Skip and he slid his fingers into mine. Blood oozed through the denim rag on my arm and I leaned against Skip.

Movement by the broken window caught my eye. A shadow pointed a long gun at Skip. "No," I screamed. "Don't shoot him. He's not going to hurt anyone." I stepped in front of Skip, but he shoved me away. *Kaboom.* A bullet buried itself in Skip's body and a red stain appeared on his shirt and spread across his chest.

"Why did you shoot him?"

The mob came to life, running at us as Skip crumpled to the floor. He toppled near the altar and choked on his blood. I knelt beside him and he pulled me close, a tear ran down his cheek.

Skip whispered. "A murderer chased me here. He's gonna kill me and he's in the crowd outside. He knows, I know. This is his gun."

Skip handed me the revolver and I dropped it. "What? He's outside the church?"

"Yes, a murderer from Shreveport is now in Texarkana."

I leaned in to catch his words, he coughed, and he shook his head. "Be careful. The one who acts innocent might not be." Skip gasped for air. "I gotta tell you somethin' else. Your pa had a secret, one he told on nights when the whiskey did the talking. Folks told me about it when I played the piano in Memphis. It was Side Car Ace's treasure story." I got close. No one could hear Skip's last words, except me. He whispered again and time stopped.

I slumped backwards, dizzy myself. My blood and Skip's blood stained the floor. Skip's last words changed everything. If I had caught the train out of town this morning, I wouldn't have learned of Daddy's secret, and I would have been long gone.

A trickle of blood ran from the corner of Skip's mouth. He coughed and the blood dripped to the hardwood floor, a raindrop of blood fell with each twitch of his eye. Skip's mouth gaped open and he wrapped his fingers around my shoulder. He spoke one last time. "Get the lucky rock. It's in my back pocket. You're gonna need it."

The law-abiding crowd backed off and Pastor Cody gathered me in his arms, but not before I took the red rock from Skip's pocket. I tucked it into my overalls along with two secrets. A secret about a treasure. A secret about a killer.

Grandma Elsie met us at the hospital and ten stitches later, I went home. I cried all the way to the manor because I wanted to go back to Thanksgiving when Skip and me spelled those words on the tracks, to the place where Daddy got out of the car and picked me up in his arms. I need to find Mahlee. I need to sneak out and find her, to sit with her and rock.

CHAPTER NINE

FRIENDS IN TREE PLACES

GRANDMA MADE ME STAY INSIDE the house to let my arm heal. There's not much to do since the winter ice storm dumped six inches of snow on the ground. But late in the afternoons, I climb the oak tree outside my bedroom balcony. I found this huge knothole in the tree, borrowed one of Grandma's empty coffee cans, and hid my poems inside.

Tomorrow is my birthday. January 16. I'm turning ten. A perfect time to put my poems in one spot to save for the day Daddy returns. Or for the time I slip away to find him.

I search for Mahlee early in the mornings before the milkman makes it to our street and before Grandma gets up. I hope to find her today.

A freckled boy climbed out to a branch on the oak tree across the street. He straddled the branch and waved at me.

Oh no. He sees me.

The boy pointed at me. "Hey what are you doing in my tree?"

I held onto the branch above my head, balancing with the squirrel at the end of the limb. "This side is mine. Go away. I'm busy."

"I'm Thaddeus William Day, Jr. Who are you? And why are you using the tree instead of the door when you leave in the mornings? This is my fort. You're trespassing."

"I love to climb trees." I watched to make sure Thaddeus William Day, Jr. didn't see my can in the knothole. "I'm Annie Grace Kree. My friends call me Shoelace. My friend, Mahlee, is a hobo. We ride the rail. I've been looking for her."

"Good for you. Now get down. Stay out of my fort."

I pointed my finger at him. "Forts have walls, hidden doors, and traps. They have ropes to swing on. These are two giant oaks and they have wrapped their branches around each other. I'm in mine and you're in yours. You don't own my tree. My grandma does." I swung on a branch and jumped to a lower limb.

Thaddeus tiptoed across his branch, stepping carefully. "The tree on this side of the street belongs to my mama, Priscilla Day." He used both hands on a branch to stand up. "She's fixing my breakfast in our apartment on the second floor." He pointed at the window where a blue curtain dangled.

"I have bigger problems than deciding who owns which tree. I have to find Mahlee. Thaddeus, you stay on your side and I'll stay on mine."

"Call me Taddy. My mama and my friends call me Taddy. They would, if I had friends."

"Fine, I'll call you, Taddy. Stay in your tree and we'll get along fine." I worked my way down the trunk and hopped down to a few ice-covered patches of brown grass. Grandma's gray Persian cat, Chops, scratched his claws at the bottom of the tree.

Achoo. Taddy wiped his nose. *Achoo. Achoo.* "I'm allergic to cats. I'm going to my apartment." He inched his way across, sliding through the curtain into his apartment.

I whispered. "It's my grandma's cat." I wasn't glad Taddy sneezed, but I was glad he went home.

Untied Shoelace

I jogged toward the tracks, passing the Stone Bakery where the baker kneaded dough by the window. My mouth watered and I pressed my nose against the window drooling at the different kinds of donuts in the pastry counter. A soldier came from inside the bakery. "Would you like a donut?"

"Yes, thank you." In five years riding the rail no one bought me a donut. Not once. The man went inside the bakery and purchased not one donut but a dozen yummy donuts. He handed the box to me. I drooled and licked my lips. "Thank you. Thank you."

"Enjoy them. This is the best bakery in town."

At the tracks, I plopped down on the rail and munched on a chocolate and a lemon donut.

A shadow in the fog crept toward me on the tracks. A bumping *rat-tat-tat* followed by *thug-thug-thug.* The shadow spoke. "Shoelace? My Annie Grace? Could it be?"

"Mahlee? My Mahlee?" I ran and jumped into her arms. "Where have you been? When did you get a shopping cart? I've been searching for you. I've missed you." I hugged her tight.

In the cart, Mahlee's tin can sat next to a bed roll, empty soda bottles, and a pile of clothes. I touched every item and danced around her.

She swatted my hand. "Leave my stuff be."

We sat down on the tracks and I opened the donut box. "I have breakfast."

Mahlee ate three donuts and cleared her throat. "Shoelace, your daddy is gone. You know that, right?"

I shook my head. "He's not dead. He's coming for me. He is." I handed Mahlee another donut so she'd eat and not talk.

We made our way to Hobo Jungle and scooted down the slope to the camps. The morning sun peeked through the trees, a sign I needed to return before Grandma came hunting for me. She's been known to pop her head into my bedroom.

I moved closer to Mahlee to beg her to come home with me. "I have the largest room at my grandma's boarding house. You could stay in my room instead of here at the camp. My mattress has a heavy quilt. It's itchy and the bed sags in the middle, but the house has a roof. No raccoons. No snakes. And we have running water. If you won't sleep inside at the manor, will you sleep in the carriage house?"

"I'm staying at the camp. Your grandma doesn't want my kind there."

"I'm your kind. She wants me."

Mahlee shook her head.

I stood and headed up the trail. "Bye, I've got to go. Grandma says I'm starting school today. I told her I could read, but she won't listen."

Mahlee took my grandma's side. "You need to learn so you can do something great when you grow up."

"I am doing great things. I'm with you."

"Dream bigger, girl. Dream bigger."

I waved to Mahlee. "See ya tomorrow. If you need me, I'm at Beech Street Manor on Fourth Street." I hurried down the tracks and Chops had followed me. He scaled a fence, four trees, and sauntered in my shadow. He also bounced ahead of me. I shouldn't have given him a bite of donut. He thinks we're friends now.

Back at the manor, I pulled myself to the highest branch in the tree and jumped to the balcony. Chops raced me, prancing on the balcony rail, with his tail in the air.

Achoo. Twisting my neck, I saw Taddy climbing down his tree, dressed in brown slacks and a button-up white shirt with his hair slicked down.

Untied Shoelace

I balanced myself, pretending to be a circus performer, and jumped back to a branch. "Hey, why don't you use your apartment door?"

The brown slacks turned to me. "I love climbing trees, too."

I jumped to another branch. "Are you going to Central School?"

Taddy nodded. "Yes. And your cat is making me sneeze."

"It's not my cat. He simply follows me. My grandma's making me start school today. She says my arm's healed and it's time."

"Healed from what? You're not contagious, are you?"

"No. I cut my arm and had stitches." I rubbed the scar. "What grade are you in?"

"Fourth. I'm in Ms. Clarice Reece's class. You will be too, if you're in the same grade as me."

"I am. Wait for me. I'll go with you." I didn't mind starting school, too much, but didn't want Grandma petting me or going along. I'm used to doing things by myself. "Be right back."

Inside my bedroom, I pulled the cotton flowered print dress over my overalls and rolled up my pants legs. I kept my PF Flyers on and hollered down the stairs. "I'm going to school with the boy next door. We're in the same grade."

I jumped to the tree from the balcony following Taddy who climbs like he talks. Exact words. Exact steps. "Wait up. I'm coming with you." I jumped from limb to limb.

Chops pounced on a branch landing on Taddy's head. *Achoo. Achoo.* He swatted at the cat, lost his footing, and toppled backwards. He bounced off a limb and crashed to the grass.

I rushed down my tree and hovered above Taddy, who lay on the ground lifeless. Chops rubbed against my leg. I ripped off my dress and threw it at him.

Meooowww. Chops ran with his head stuck in a sleeve.

"Get out of here Chops. We're not friends. Look what you did. You've killed a kid. They're gonna blame me."

The dead boy sat up. *Achoo. Achoo. Achoo.* Taddy gave a belly laugh. "I'm not hurt. I was trying to scare you."

I slugged Taddy in the arm. "Don't pretend to die. I would have gotten blamed."

"It was funny. You were scared."

"I wasn't scared."

We ran the one block to the front of Central School. We were early and the doors were locked. We'd have to wait on the steps. I gave Thaddeus William Day, Jr. a glance. He straightened his shirt counting off the seconds until the front door opened. *Who knows, I might become friends with this Taddy if he'll stop pretending to be dead.*

I watched the other kids come to the school door, and I didn't like the way that one boy looked at me.

CHAPTER TEN

THE COLOR OF SCHOOL

MY NEW TEACHER, MS. CLARICE Reece made the morning fun, but she has a lot of rules. Stand in line. No talking in the hall. No whispering. No back talk. No walking around while she's talking. No sticking my tongue out at Taddy. No poem writing during history.

I recited my ABC's and read aloud for Ms. Reece. She made sure I could keep up with the other fourth graders. Thanks to Mahlee and Skip, I won the spelling bee contest with the word "fugitive." I could beat anyone in spelling.

Billy Joe, the boy who looked at me weird that morning got mad because he lost to me and mouthed fightin' words calling my daddy names. "Your daddy was a fugitive."

"Shut up, Billy Joe. You don't even know my daddy. He's not a bad man."

Billy Joe raised his voice. "You're a hobo girl. No mama. No daddy. An orphan. I have a family. My brother is coming home and he's a war hero. He can spell better than you."

My fist flew upwards aiming for his nose, but he ducked and my knuckles socked his left eye. Ms. Reece pointed to the door, sending me down the longest hall in the school to the room with the principal. The room where Mr. Meldrum kept a paddle on the wall. I'm not scared of him. Too much.

Back in class, Ms. Reece handed me a box of crayons. "These are yours. Put them in your desk and we'll use them in art."

I had never used crayons before. I lifted the lid to my desk, holding the top up too long looking at the box. When I lowered the lid, the kids were staring at me. The boys whispered, "Stupid girl." The girls giggled.

Taddy leaned across the aisle. "Have you never had crayons?"

I fidgeted. "No. I'm not sure what they're for."

"They're for coloring." Taddy pointed to the coloring pages on the bulletin board, pictures tacked to the wall on the other side of the room.

Ms. Reece grabbed a stack of paper and came my way. "Take these coloring pages. I have a few left from Christmas and you can color in these candy canes if you want."

I opened the box of crayons and Ms. Reece showed me how to stay in the lines. She told me candy canes were red and white. I practiced my coloring using those two crayons, but since I had never seen a candy cane, I colored the top half red and the bottom half white.

"Ms. Reece. Look at my candy canes."

She wrinkled her brow. "Those are pretty, but candy canes have red and white stripes." The other kids laughed.

I threw my coloring pages to the floor, darted from the room, down the hall, and out the front door. I sat on one of the branches in the oak tree on the playground and clutched my box of crayons, taking each color and marking on the branch until I'd used every one of them.

I sat in the tree until the other kids came outside for recess.

Untied Shoelace

Ms. Reece moseyed over to the tree and she surveyed my playground hideout, her eyes inviting me to class. "You've created a rainbow branch. Great work."

Ms. Reece is my favorite teacher. She sees me. She likes how I color.

I climbed down from the tree and smiled. "This is my first day. I'm bound to do better."

"You will. You have your father's spirit of adventure and your mother's smile."

"You knew my mama and daddy?"

"Yes, I played with your mama in the summer. I played hide and seek with your daddy and the Godfrey twins. We fished, chased trains, and went swimming."

Mr. Meldrum came to the steps. "Recess is over. Everyone inside." He was carrying a fancy leather satchel. Daddy's satchel matched the ones used in World War II, a canvas bag with a red cross on the top. I kept Daddy's satchel in my bedroom—

Wait. Where is his satchel?

I remember putting my cap inside the top drawer of the chest for safekeeping, but I don't remember seeing Daddy's satchel in the drawer when I got my socks this morning.

I darted through the playground gate and ran the long block to the manor. When I ran up the porch steps, I slammed the front door behind me and ran to my room. I pulled the drawer open. Daddy's satchel was gone.

I ripped through four drawers, tossing everything to the linoleum floor. White socks, panties, and T-shirts lay on the bed. I also threw my new overalls on top of the clothes. Nothing. No satchel.

I peeked under the mattress and pulled the three dresses from the wardrobe closet down, the ones Grandma bought. I'm sure we'll exchange them for more overalls at Belk Jones.

I bent down and searched under the bed. I found dust and the sock I lost two weeks ago. Nothing. Still, no satchel.

I ran to the railing at the top of the stairs. "Grandma, we've been robbed. Check the boarders. Don't let anyone leave. Search everyone's room. Daddy's satchel is gone."

Silence. She didn't answer.

A boarder knocked on the wall. "Quiet. I'm trying to take a nap."

Running down the stairs, I yelled for Grandma forgetting the sleeping man. Chops raced with me. "Grandma, where did Daddy's satchel go? I saved it from the river in Memphis. I put it in my dresser."

I found Grandma in the kitchen and she patted flour from her hands on the yellow apron tied around her waist. "Shoelace. What's on your face?" She pulled my head sideways, held my chin and shook her head. "Measles? You've got the measles."

"What? I'm sick? I've got to find Daddy's satchel. Am I going to die before my birthday tomorrow?" I stumbled to the chair at the table and plopped down. "I've got red dots on my arms." I pulled up my pants leg. "My legs, too."

Grandma inspected me. "You're not going to die. We may have to postpone your birthday party for a few days. You'll miss the next three days of school, but by next Monday you can go back. You're contagious." Grandma tilted my chin up. "Did school get out early?"

I changed the subject. "A party? I'm having a party?"

"We'll have to get over these measles, first."

"Grandma, I can't find Daddy's satchel. It's not in the drawer in my room."

She turned to her baking. "I'm sure it will show up. I'll help you look, but first, I'm finishing this cake. Your daddy loved chocolate cake. Last one I baked for him was right before your grandpa died. He enjoyed licking the spoon and the bowl." She poured the batter into two round cake pans and turned to me. "Wanna try?"

I licked the bowl following in my daddy's shoes. I wished he'd come through the door and wished he'd stride in carrying his satchel.

CHAPTER ELEVEN

DADDY IS BETTER THAN CAKE

I WIGGLED MY FINGERS. "CAN I uncover my eyes, now?"

"Not yet. Give me a second. Don't turn around."

Grandma made me face the opposite wall from her when I came back to the kitchen too soon. "Can I turn around now? This is my first birthday cake."

A deep voice behind me spoke. "Any sweet tea left from supper?"

I peeked from between two fingers down at the sock feet standing next to me by the ice box. I dropped my hands and saw a man sticking his finger in Grandma's bowl.

Grandma slapped his hand. "Yes, there's tea in the pitcher. Get your finger out of my frosting bowl. This is for my granddaughter's birthday cake."

I waved my arms. "I'm her granddaughter. I'm having cake when she finishes. Cream cheese frosting on chocolate cake. My daddy's favorite."

Grandma shook her spoon at me. "Turn around. I'm not finished decorating this cake."

"No one ever baked me a cake. This will be the best." I pressed my nose against the front of the ice box and leaned against my hands.

The man in brown socks squeezed by me. "Excuse me. I need an ice tray."

I peeked through my hands at the brown pants with the tiny stripes. His blue shirt needed ironing. It's probably the shirt he napped in.

"Hey. Mister. You been here all day?"

"Yes. It's my day off from the newspaper. I'm working the late shift tonight."

He roomed across from me. Maybe he saw someone coming or going, or anyone who might know something. "You happen to find a canvas satchel anywhere?"

"No, I slept most of the day." He held an ice tray. "I'll let you know if I do." He shuffled two steps, put the tray down, and gave me another glance. "What's with those red dots on your face?"

Grandma dropped ice cubes into a glass. "Ernie, this is Annie Grace Kree. She's staying with me. She's my joy. She's got the measles right now."

I showed Ernie my arms. "I'm contagious. You better watch out."

His sock feet shuffled faster as he left the kitchen with his tea.

"If you see my satchel, let me know."

He called from the stairs. "I will."

Grandma tapped me on the shoulder and gave me an eyeball-to-eyeball stare. "I hope Ernie Surratt's had the measles. I need all the boarders I can get." She twirled me around in a circle. "The cake is ready."

"You made white roses out of frosting?"

Grandma handed me a butter knife, motioning for me to cut the cake. "Yes. This is the best cream cheese frosting this side of the Red River." She turned to the counter. "Candles. I almost forgot."

Grandma put ten candles on the two-layer cake and lit them. "Blow them out and make a wish."

I blew out the candles with more spit than air and wished for my daddy to come back.

Grandma reached under the table. "I have a present for you. I wanted to get you a school bag and I already had this for you before you lost your daddy's satchel."

"I didn't lose his. Someone took it." I held the school bag close. "Thank you, this is great. Daddy's given me small gifts before like a penny and an old pair of gloves. One time, he gave me a blue marble, but I lost it the next day."

Grandma smiled. "It's real leather with a strap for your shoulder. You can carry your school supplies or whatever you tote around when you're climbing down the tree by your room."

I grinned and flipped open the flap. Buckled it back. Opened it. *Click. Click. Click.* I felt Grandma's eyes on me. I held the bag up. "Thank you, Grandma." I pulled the cake plate closer. "Can I can have two pieces?" I sliced the cake before she could answer.

I hugged my school bag with one arm while letting the chocolate cake melt on my tongue. I'd trade this cake for bologna with my daddy any day. I'd trade this new satchel, too. I walked to the bottom of the stairs and looked up toward Ernie's door. I couldn't help but wonder if that man knew something he wasn't telling me.

CHAPTER TWELVE

THE GRIM MISSING

TONIGHT IS MY BIRTHDAY PARTY at the Grim Hotel. The hotel is a few blocks from the manor and the building is eight stories tall. I bounced down the stairs from my room, sliding my hand down the rail. Taddy and his mama were in the front room waiting with Grandma.

At the bottom step, I stopped and stared at Taddy's mama. She was at Daddy's funeral helping Grandma with the guests. Priscilla is prettier than most mamas and several inches shorter than Mahlee. Her green eyes and soft face made me wonder if I would ever be soft or pretty.

I bailed off the step faster than a bullet. "Hey, Taddy. Have you ever been to the Grim Hotel to eat?"

"No. Mama says the building makes her sad."

Priscilla put her finger to her mouth, shushing Taddy. "We don't eat out much."

"Why? Is the food bad? I've eaten bad tasting food. I probably could stomach the taste."

Taddy slid next to me and whispered. "It's cause of Aunt Margo, my mama's twin sister."

Priscilla popped Taddy on his hind side. "Enough. No need to scare Shoelace with kidnapping stories."

"Kidnapping? My daddy kidnapped me. Kidnapping can be fun."

Taddy shook his head and disobeyed his mama. "Aunt Margo worked as a waitress in the coffee shop at the Grim Hotel."

Priscilla frowned. "You want a paddling? We don't talk about Aunt Margo."

Grandma ushered everyone out through the kitchen where Ernie sliced a piece of chocolate birthday cake. We went out the kitchen door and hurried to the car.

"I'm hungry. Are you hungry, Priscilla?" Grandma asked.

Priscilla smiled and got in the car. "Yes, thanks for inviting us."

"I'm hungry. What will we eat?" I kicked Grandma's seat.

"Order anything off the menu. They have everything at the Grim Hotel. This is your big night."

Taddy sat in the back seat with me. The tires bounced over the bricks in the alley. Sitting behind Priscilla, I mouthed to Taddy, "Tell me what happened."

Priscilla must have good ears. She gave Taddy a glance as if to say keep quiet. He scooted closer to the door and ignored me.

A few minutes later we stepped into a place made for rich folks. Inside the lobby, a boy carried suitcases for a man in a gray suit. The boy's shoes clopped on the stone-waxed floor. Grandma called him a bellboy. She explained every detail in the room and talked nonstop.

"Those two women are wearing fancy designer dresses." Grandma tapped Priscilla on the shoulder. "I may be pushing sixty, but I love keeping up with styles." They giggled like kids on a playground at school, even though Priscilla could be her daughter.

"Look at the furniture, nothing but the finest here." Grandma sat down in a fancy chair, so she could say she did.

"Look at those chandeliers and the beautiful ceiling. In the basement, they bake fresh loaves of bread every hour." She stood up and spun around. "On the roof they have grand parties with dancing and bands."

Grandma's joy spilled over and it felt as if I was getting another birthday present. Her laughter reminded me of Daddy's chuckles when he pokes fun at how Mahlee and me argue over everything.

Grandma announced to the three of us. "We're dining in the Palm Court Hall."

A server wearing black escorted us to a table. China. Crystal glasses. Shiny silverware. We had dishes in front of us too expensive to eat from. I slid my fingers across the outside of the glass. No crystal drinking glasses on the rail.

A lady in a white uniform trimmed in green, jotted down our order. Grandma ordered pork. Priscilla ordered chicken fried steak and Taddy and me ordered fried chicken.

No sooner than I'd take a drink of my water, the waitress refilled the glass. If we ran out of rolls in the basket, she brought hot ones. No one had ever brought me this much food. Grandma wiped her lips with a napkin. "We're having a feast."

I stirred my mashed potatoes waiting for Priscilla to agree with Grandma. I brought Margo up again to Taddy. "Is your aunt alive?"

"I don't know."

I scooted my chair closer to Taddy. "Spill it. Did Margo work there?" I pointed to the counter.

He bit into a green bean and gobbled it up. "No. She worked in the coffee shop on the other side of the building." He wrinkled his nose. "Mama's gonna paddle me."

"Not if you hurry."

Taddy tapped my arm. "Listen quick then. This part happened way before we were born. Bonnie and Clyde had robbed the National Guard Armory one day and Bonnie came inside and ate a sandwich while Clyde waited outside in their get-away car."

"He wasn't hungry?"

"I don't know. But when the cops showed up, he ran inside to get Bonnie and he snatched a hostage."

"You mean they kidnapped your aunt from the coffee shop?" I leaned closer trying to hear and bumped my glass, knocking it over. I dabbed the water up with two napkins.

Grandma touched the back of my chair. "Shoelace, move closer to the table and be more careful."

The waitress brought me a new glass and more hot rolls. Grandma and Priscilla chatted and giggled. They were focused on each other.

I nudged Taddy. "Keep talking."

"Bonnie and Clyde stopped in Grapevine. That's a town in Texas. After an all-night ride, they shot two cops and Margo got released. They made her hold the money. $1,865."

"How do you know the amount?"

"My daddy told me."

"Where is your daddy?"

"He died when I was little, but I remember everything like he did. He had a memory that never forgets. I have it, too. I remember numbers. I'm good at math, too. When I read words, I can retell the sentences without forgetting a word. I don't do this at school. The other kids make fun if you're too smart."

"So what happened to your aunt? Where did she go?"

Taddy leaned toward me. "Aunt Margo went sad. She was scared of everything and stayed with us. She also hid in the

70

closet. One day she ran off, right after my daddy died. Mama searched for her, but she finally gave up."

Taddy nodded toward his mama. "My mama misses her. She's cries for her late at night sometimes. At church, she has Pastor Cody pray for Margo to come home. That is, if she's alive."

Grandma tapped her fork on the plate. "Eat up. Seconds for everyone."

I squished more mashed potatoes in my mouth. "Yes ma'am." I wanted to ask Taddy more questions, but Priscilla eyed me.

Grandma pushed her plate back, "Dessert. I'm ready for cake."

"Me, too," Priscilla said.

Grandma and Priscilla stuck their noses inside the menu.

I turned to Taddy, to grill him. "So how does your mama know Pastor Cody?"

"My mama helps him at the church by the creek. She bakes biscuits most every Saturday."

"That sounds boring to me." I saw the pastry counter and jumped from my chair. "I'm checking out the pies and cakes.

Taddy followed me across the room. "Stop running. If you get in trouble, I'll get in trouble."

I pressed my nose on the glass case. "This is my first time at the Grim. It's my birthday." I turned to Taddy, nose-to-nose. "I just want to see what they have for dessert."

I had the entire pastry counter in full view. Pecan pie, lemon pie, and coconut pie. Chocolate cake, red velvet cake, and carrot cake. The lady pointed out every kind to me. So many cakes. Tons of pies, donuts, and sweet rolls. There were plenty of other pastries, most I'd never heard of.

The server lady put a bite-size piece of lemon pie on a napkin for me. One for Taddy, too. "Yum. This is tangy." The lemon flavor made my ears hurt but in a good way. Grandma's chocolate cake with cream cheese frosting tasted the best, but lemon pie made me say yum, too.

The side door to the restaurant flew open and a lady ran inside, bumping into a waitress who dropped a basket of steaming hot rolls. "There's a man on Stateline. He broke the window on a car." She wobbled in her high heels. "Police. Get the police."

The restaurant went from clicking dishes and people noises to shouting, confusion, and the men running out the door. Grandma ran to the window. Even Priscilla hurried to Taddy and me, to make sure we were not lost in the shuffle or getting in the way.

Dozens of people watched through the big windows and by the time the sirens rolled down Stateline, two men had already tackled the thief and held him on the ground between two cars. Taddy and me squatted down by the window and watched the wrestling match.

A cop marched up to Grandma. "Ma'am, the lady behind the counter said you own the car that was broken into. We need to talk to you for a minute, to make our report."

"Are you sure?" Grandma rushed out the door to the sidewalk.

I followed Grandma out to the street with Taddy and Priscilla.

A cop tried to move the people back. "Everyone move inside or go home. Show's over."

I know that face. It's the face from the church window. It's the cop who killed my friend, Skip.

My fists escaped and I pounded on the cop's chest. "Why? Why did you shoot? Skip never hurt you. He never hurt anyone."

Priscilla pulled me back, my arms waving. I was a wild bird caught in a trap. "Annie Grace. Stop. What are you doing?"

She held me close. I calmed down and stopped fighting her, hoping we'd go home soon. "You and Taddy wait by the wall. We won't be long, now." Priscilla showed us where to stand.

I wandered to Grandma's car to look around. I couldn't stay by the wall. There's nothing happening by the building. The cops wrote stuff down and I counted light poles on the street. Taddy followed me as I counted cracks in the sidewalk.

Clomp. Clomp. Clomp. Mahlee pushed her cart toward the alley and I waved to her as she crossed the street. "Mahlee. Wait up."

She stopped and the street light shined down on her. Dirt streaked her face. Her nails were yellow and her clothes worn. But to me, she was beautiful. Even the Grim dimmed in beauty. Mahlee needed a little polishing, but so did I.

Priscilla shouted from behind me. "Annie Grace, come back." I turned toward her and Taddy motioned with his hands. Mahlee took that as her cue to leave and pushed her cart on down the sidewalk.

"Mahlee, wait. Don't go." I ran to her cart and held onto it.

Priscilla and Taddy ran across the street and stopped beside me. "Do you know her?" Priscilla gazed at me. "Is she your friend?"

I wrapped my arms around Mahlee. "Yes. She rode with Daddy and me."

"I'm sorry. I haven't met her." Priscilla reached for Mahlee's hand. "It's nice to meet you." Priscilla's eyes grew big. "I know that ring. Where did you get it?"

"It's not Margo's ring," Taddy said.

Priscilla kept staring. "It could be Margo's ring. The ring has the same blue stone and the same band."

I took Mahlee's hand. "This old ring?"

Priscilla pointed to the blue stone on Mahlee's crusty finger.

Taddy shook his head. "Mama, you always think you're seeing Margo's ring. You saw it on the lady at church. At the store. Even in a magazine. Remember? You told me that Margo had the ring on her finger when she left."

"You're right. I know. It gets confusing. It's been too long. Seven years." Priscilla glanced at us and wiped her eyes. "I miss Margo. I'd give anything to find her, to know she's alive." She inhaled a deep breath. "Dessert. I need dessert."

Taddy whispered to me. "Mama eats sweets when she's sad."

Under the street light, I hugged Mahlee. "Are you still at the camps?"

"Yep. I'm staying with Slow Tom and Fast Tim. They're brothers. Tom is old. Tim is young. Tom runs slow and Tim runs fast."

As Mahlee talked, I stared at the ring. A few years back, she showed the ring to me after being gone for weeks. Daddy told her to take the ring off on the trains because someone might rip the band from her finger. Usually, she keeps it inside her tin can but not tonight.

Mahlee and me crossed the street and Taddy followed us. We moseyed down the sidewalk next to the Grim.

Grandma joined us. "All finished. I can get the window fixed." She glanced around. "Where's Priscilla?"

I pointed to the door. "She went inside the restaurant."

Grandma smiled at Mahlee. "Who is this?"

"This is Mahlee. She's the one who left me on your porch after Thanksgiving and then ran away."

"I did not run. I walked. I went straight to Hobo Jungle."

Grandma nodded and smiled. "Thank you for making sure my granddaughter got here safely. Any friend of hers is a friend of mine. Come see us at the manor. You're always welcome." Grandma looked at me. "I'll be inside. Don't be too long." She waved and disappeared inside.

I turned to Mahlee. "Are you hungry?"

She nodded. "Tom and Tim don't have much food to share."

"I'll be right back. Don't leave." I hurried inside the restaurant and tossed rolls and chicken into a cloth napkin. I raced out the door and handed Mahlee her supper.

Taddy had been watching like a statue and put his hand out toward Mahlee. "I'm Thaddeus William Day, Jr. My friends call me Taddy."

Mahlee grinned. "I'm glad to meet you." She pushed her cart down the sidewalk. Her smile added to my birthday party.

I cupped my hands to my mouth. "Mahlee, you can come to the manor anytime."

Mahlee called to Taddy. "Take care of my girl."

"I don't need no boy taking care of me."

Taddy laughed. "You can't keep your hands from making fists. You need me to keep you from hitting folks."

"Whatever. I can take care of myself."

We waved to Mahlee and skipped into the restaurant. We sat down at our table and the waitress served red velvet cake to us on a silver platter. I gobbled down my piece in four bites. I added red velvet cake to my list of favorite desserts.

On the ride home with the cold wind rushing in through the broken window, I shivered and wrapped my arms across my tummy. I've never eaten this much food in one night and

I've never been this full and felt so empty. *Daddy. I need my daddy.* Daddy's not like red velvet cake. Not too smooth. Not rich, either. He's a little tangy and a little sour. More like lemon pie, in a good way.

When I sneak out tomorrow, I'm gonna ask Mahlee if any of her friends know anything about my Daddy's satchel. Maybe someone has seen his bag or his cards. I'm sure the money is gone and his red flashlight that was inside, too.

On the rail, Daddy's satchel never disappeared. And now, when I come to Texarkana, a thief takes his stuff.

CHAPTER THIRTEEN

BUBBLES OF HOPE

MS. REECE TAPPED HER RULER on the desk. "Class. It's Friday, February 22. Your history reports are due today." Ms. Reece gave the morning announcements and then announced Taddy's birthday.

I whispered to Taddy from my desk. "No one told me it's your birthday. You're ten like me now." I plotted ways to celebrate. "Hey, let's go to the fountain right after school. We should party today."

"I will get in trouble."

"Fine. If you're chicken, go home."

"I'm not a chicken. You've called me chicken every day since I met you."

"I have not."

"Have to."

"Not."

Ms. Reece touched my shoulder. "Quiet, both of you." We nodded.

Talking Taddy into this became my challenge. He needed to see fountain bubbles on his birthday. At lunch, I slipped away from school and ran to the manor. I climbed the tree and hopped into my room, grabbed a paper sack, ran downstairs, and tiptoed passed a napping boarder on the sofa. I poured a handful of Grandma's soap powder into my sack and stuck it inside my school bag.

By the end of school, I had talked Taddy into going to the fountain for a bubble party.

But the fountain and bubbles party ended with sirens and now he's not talking to me.

I tapped on Taddy's window sill at his apartment. Even if I have to sit in his tree until morning, I'm staying until I apologize. It's nearly 11 p.m. I've been trying to tell Taddy sorry for ruining his birthday since after school.

I never counted on a cop driving his car through bubbles on the road. The cop slapped his stick on his hand. "Who decided soap in the fountain would be a great idea?"

"Me." I offered my best grin, the one that causes Taddy to give me ugly glances.

Taddy sighed and the cop moved closer to me.

I tugged on the cop's sleeve. "I never meant to turn the whole thing into bubbles."

The Ensign Fountain sat a block south of the post office on Stateline right before the Grim Hotel. The fountain has a tier for humans, one for horses, and another one for small animals.

The cop tapped his stick on the edge of the fountain. "So, what should I do with the two of you? I've got a couple of delinquents causing trouble."

Taddy broke down, crying and stomping. "You get me in trouble. We're not friends. I never want to see you again. I'm not a delinquent."

"But, we're in the same class. We live next door to each other. We're both ten. You have to be my friend. We're not delinquents. We simply had fun with bubbles."

The talk with the cop went downhill from there and Grandma picked us up. Taddy's mama made him go home. I don't know what happened to him, but I got sent to my room without supper. I've ruined his birthday and I've got to fix things. I'm in this tree, sitting outside Taddy's window until he answers. *Tap. Tap. Tap.*

Finally, Taddy peeked from behind the curtain. He opened the window. "It's nearly midnight. What are you doing? I'm already in trouble because of you."

"Please, I have to talk to you. It's time for a magic carpet ride."

"What?" He flared his nostrils and folded his arms.

"I can make it up to you. I promise this will be the best birthday ever." I pleaded as Chops pranced by on a branch beside me.

"You promised me the best birthday earlier. You see how the first part of the day went."

"Give me another chance."

Achoo. Achoo. "Not if the cat goes. You know I'm allergic. I'm beginning to think I'm allergic to you."

"Get dressed. I'll put Chops in my room. I'll wait for you on the porch."

A few minutes later, we headed out. As we neared the spot for the surprise, I wrapped a green scarf around Taddy's head, hiding his eyes. "You're not going to chicken out? Are you?"

"I'm not a chicken."

"I'm sorry. I won't say it again. Keep that blindfold on. Step over. Again. Step, one more time. Okay. Stop." I held his shoulders. "Take off your blindfold."

Taddy pulled the scarf down.

"We're at the railroad yard." His eyes grew wide and he glanced down the tracks. "We're near the bridge by the hobo camps." He backed up, his shoe getting caught between the rails. He stumbled backwards, bottom first.

"Do you see that boxcar? The one under the gorilla-arm tree? We're headed there. We need to cross a couple more tracks." I helped Taddy to his feet. "My daddy said if you

79

touch a nail in the railroad tracks before you cross over, you'll have good luck."

Taddy reached down and touched five nails. "If this gets us put in jail, I won't be your friend." Taddy whined, tossing the scarf to the ties.

"Please. I have a surprise. Let me show you. We're four blocks from home. Not far." I reached for the scarf and wrapped it around my neck.

Taddy sighed.

I climbed inside the boxcar. The train rocked and inched down the tracks. "Hop in." I reached for Taddy's hand. "Grab my hand." The engine shot steam into the night air.

Taddy's eyes grew as big as saucers. "What do you mean hop in?"

I bent down. "Take my hand."

A tornado sigh came from Taddy. "Don't drop me." He climbed the ladder and rolled into the boxcar. "Where are we going?" He moved to the door of the open boxcar and backed up, bumping into me.

I steadied my feet. "We're taking a short ride."

Taddy twirled around looking over the crates in the boxcar. "So this is where you used to ride?"

"Yes. It's the magic carpet ride."

A crate fell over. "Surprise! Happy Birthday. Happy Birthday, Taddy." A trio of voices, Mahlee, Slow Tom, and Fast Tim shouted and sang to Taddy. He toppled over the crates and landed on the straw in the rear of the boxcar.

Peering passed a crate, he stood. "Why didn't you tell me we weren't alone?"

"Happy Birthday, Taddy." Mahlee handed him a chocolate cupcake, the one I'd bought at the Grim Hotel earlier. I had cashed in Ernie's soda pop bottles at Hart Drug Store. I'll pay him back later. I had to buy a present for Taddy.

He bit into his cupcake and Taddy smiled a chocolate grin while I introduced my friends to him. "This is Slow Tom, you can remember him because he limps and he's wrinkled."

Slow Tom shook hands with Taddy. "I'm not wrinkled. It's trail dirt."

"This is his brother Fast Tim. He runs faster than most when catching a train but not faster than me. He's the younger of the two brothers. He has softer eyes."

"If you're… a… friend… of Shoelace, you're my… my… friend." Fast Tim stuttered. His words mix up when he's nervous.

"You met Mahlee last month. I sneak off to see her on Friday nights. I used to go in the mornings, but since I go to school now, I go at night."

Taddy grinned. "Thank you for the birthday party." Taddy scooted to the boxcar opening. "Has anyone noticed we're moving faster?"

The click-clack of steel rolling down the tracks sent the train north toward Spring Lake Park. If we pass the park, we have to ride five miles before we can jump off again. "It's time to drop and roll."

Taddy's eyes swam with tears. "Jump? I have to jump?"

"Yes. Watch me. Aim for the thick grass and roll down the hill. Keep your arms tucked."

I jumped first. The train inched along while Taddy stood in the boxcar door. Mahlee yelled *Geronimo* and gave Taddy the push he needed to get him off the train.

CHAPTER FOURTEEN

BLACK BOOTS BLACK NIGHT

I BRUSHED DIRT FROM MY clothes "Come on. We'll cut through the woods by the road. Mahlee calls it lover's lane. We'll see a few parked cars with boys kissing girls, but don't look at them or I'll tell." I helped Taddy stand, checking to make sure he hadn't broken a bone. A broken bone would have ruined the night for sure.

Taddy's breaths were deep. "We better hurry. It's getting late. Mama might wake up."

I saw the concrete street sign. "Let's go this way. This is Robison Road and it will take us downtown." I paused long enough to make sure Taddy came up behind me.

In the woods beside us, a wish-wash breathing sound swallowed the silence. "Mahlee? Slow Tom? Fast Tim? Are you there?" I figured they'd gone back to camp, but my ears tracked the steps of crunching leaves, sounds of panting and the ground crumbling under a shoe or an animal. The breathing and panting moved alongside us.

I stopped and Taddy ran into me. The breathing in the woods stopped, too. "Shhhh. We're not alone." I pulled him to the ground.

Taddy leaned on me. "What? What do you hear?"

"I'm not sure. Stay by this tree."

Untied Shoelace

He hid under a honeysuckle shrub next to the tree. *Achoo. Achoo.* Taddy wiped his nose. "I'm allergic to more than cats."

Even in the dark I could see Taddy's face. The moon was bright and the light sliced through the night. Taddy waited like a small tree in the forest and I could hear the huff-puff panting sounds, short and fast. The breathing came from something close by and I had this eerie sense of something grabbing me by the neck, which made my throat feel thick. My feet went numb and my hands were wet with fear. I tumbled backwards over Taddy.

I rolled onto my tummy just as a pair of black boots raced by me. The boots ran toward a parked car on the road, bouncing in the shadows with each step.

I stepped to the road to watch the boots. Taddy sat in the bushes with one hand pinching his nose, the other on his eyes. We were on the gravel road by the last row houses at the intersection of Richmond Road and Robison.

The huff-puff man spoke and shone a flashlight into the parked car. "I don't want to kill you, fella. You better do what I say. Get out of the car. Both of you."

A lady screamed and climbed out from the passenger side. "Please don't kill us. Take our money. Let us go." She held her purse out. "Take this."

A man got out from the driver's side and put himself between the lady and the huff-puff man.

The sound of a branch cracking made me stop in my tracks, but it wasn't a branch. The huff-puff man swung a pipe in the air, slamming it into the man's head. It made a crushing sound as if a hundred pecan shells broke at once. His girlfriend screamed.

I snuck closer moving next to a tree by the car, the girl's screams drowning out my steps. In the moonlight, I could see

the outline of huff-puff man. He wore a hood. It was a white
mask. The mask reminded me of the angel in Boone who wore
a sheet on Halloween. This was smaller, like a pillowcase with
eyes, and certainly, not an angel. The hooded man hovered
above the guy on the ground. He stood at least six foot tall and
kept swinging that iron pipe.

I gagged and flinched with each swing.

He turned to the girl whose hands were stuck over her
mouth. "Run. Run."

"Please, just take our things."

The hooded man stomped closer to her. "I told you to run."

She ran down Blanton Street, a gravel road leading away
from town. I wanted to tell her she needed PF Flyers so she
could run faster.

When the huff-puff man yelled at her, Taddy decided to
run, too. His feet padded on the dirt behind me. I barely heard
his whisper. "This birthday party is over."

I couldn't move. My feet were glued in place and I felt
dizzy. I couldn't leave the man on the ground. He moaned and
rolled around in pain, a pool of blood beneath his head grew
larger.

I started to pull him to the shadows, but I wasn't sure
where the hooded man went. I listened to the crunching steps
in the gravel, the panting disappeared. The hooded man must
be following the lady. She had screamed one more time and
now, silence has fallen, except for the moans of this man in
front of me.

"Help me. Who's there?"

I knelt above the man whose head was bloody and tied
Grandma's scarf around his wound to stop the gush of blood
pouring down his face. "I'll get help."

A light down the road lit the way. It was a car.

"Help me up. I've got to flag down the driver." The man staggered and ran into the road, holding the scarf against his head.

I shuffled to the shadows behind another oak tree looking down Blanton Street as the car pulled to a stop, its lights shined right into the face of the slumped over man. A man and woman jumped from the vehicle and ran to him.

The injured man collapsed to the ground. "Help me. I've been attacked and my girlfriend is out there somewhere."

The driver spoke. "Your head is slashed. You're bleeding. We're getting you taken care of first. Let's get you to Pine Street Hospital and I'll call the police." He helped the man tumble into the car and they sped off.

I plodded over to the parked car and touched the door handle. My knees buckled and I struggled to stand. The crickets held their breath. The silence was heavy and cold. It felt like there was no air left for breathing. I lost all strength in my legs and toppled to the ground like a limp rag. Only my hand propped me up as I sat in the blood-soaked spot on the ground.

"Oh no! I've got blood on me." I could see the red even in the dark. My clothes were coated and my shoes.

The faint sound of a girl whining and crying, rose and fell, and faded.

Where is the lady? Where is huff-puff man? What should I do next?

I have to get home. Have to get out of here. Have to get to a safe place. But first, I have to find the lady. I have to help her.

My cold feet ached. My heart drummed inside my body, pounding, and I could see my breath. I crept down the side of the street hiding behind trees. I ran through yards, cut passed the bushes, dodged fences, jumped a skinny bush, and crashed into the side of a car in a driveway.

Seeing at night became hard, even with the moon's basketball glow. Too many pine trees. The street went black, like the inside of a boxcar with no moon. But at least, I wasn't being chased by the huff-puff man. Since the lady's last scream, I hadn't heard anything else except my own steps.

At the end of the dirt road, I saw a porch light glowing like a lantern showing me the way. The last two-story frame house on Blanton Street. A couple of dairy farms were tucked behind the house near the fence at the end of the street. To get to those farms, I'd have to circle around and go toward New Boston Road. Huff-puff man could hide in a barn, so I'm not cutting through there.

"Help me … Help me … Open the door." The scream of the lady stopped me cold and my right foot slammed into a huge stone the size of a bucket, sending me to my knees. *Ouch!* The pain shot through my ankle and my toe throbbed. I listened to the lady cry and crouched beside the hedge between the two houses, and rubbed my toe.

No one came to the door. The lady limped from the porch. She tossed a pebble at the window upstairs and a light came on. She had lost the heel on one shoe and her dress hung behind her, torn as if someone used a machete, the sliced fabric dangled like a worn out flag.

She ran to the door and pulled on the handle. "Let me in. I'm Martha Long. My daddy works at the arsenal. I've been attacked. My boyfriend is Jack Hall. He's probably dead. Open the door. Somebody, please wake up."

The door to the house cracked opened and a man with a hairy chest stepped into the light. The lady collapsed into his arms, crying. He glanced around the yard. Thankfully, he couldn't see me behind the holly bushes, but I could see him.

Off to the side, I saw a body leaning against the house. Could that shadow be the huff-puff man? I bent down on both knees. My toe felt like mush, a raw feeling the way my finger felt the time I smashed the tip of it inside of the door at the manor. The holly bush had a hole and I could see through it. I could see a shadow.

"Ouch." The holly bush pierced my forehead and the needles stabbed my skin. But I saw him ... I couldn't take my eyes off the shadow-man.

The man crouched with both hands on the window sill. There was no light in the room and the shade was pulled down. If he broke the window, he could slip into the house.

I inched alongside the hedge, hoping the people at the house on my side slept through my being on their property, and hoping they didn't have a barking dog. I moved toward the rear of the driveway, which put me right across from the crouching man. I was close enough to want to run away, but not close enough to see for sure. The shadow had to be the huff-puff man. Who would be out this late snooping around a window? Besides me?

I had to make a break for the front porch to tell the hairy-chested man in trousers and slippers to watch out for a bad man lurking on the side of his house. I could wait inside with the lady until the cops arrived and then, I could sneak off when it's safe.

I had to get home, go to bed and pretend this Friday night didn't happen. I had to pretend I didn't see anything. I have gotten used to pretending my heart never hurts. It's easier to leave your heart without a beat, than to feel the ache. Plus, Grandma's not going to understand my slipping off with Taddy for a midnight birthday party.

I need to find a way to keep Taddy quiet, too. He remembers everything and he might talk. I have to get his word on being silent.

I rose like a deer, ran to the street, and rounded the hedge. I pounded on the door. "There's a bad man in your yard. You've got to stop him. You've got to catch him."

The hairy man pulled me into the house. Martha sat with a quilt around her body. She had melted into the cushions and sat, staring into the room with eyes that were frozen on one spot. Her face was marked with scratches and her eyes were purple and red. She could barely keep them open. Her fingers were wrapped around a small teacup, probably hot cocoa. Hot cocoa helps on dark nights.

The owner ran out the door to the porch carrying a long gun and flew from the steps. He ran around the house in pursuit of huff-puff man. He'll catch him now, if I didn't scare him off. I had to find out and followed him, stepping easy. I didn't want him to twirl around and shoot me. He stopped a boxcar length from the kneeling man and pointed the long barrel. "Who's out there? Give yourself up. The sheriff's on his way."

No response. My heart throbbed and kept pace with the heartbeat of my big toe inside my shoe. *Might be broken.*

Huff-puff man knelt by the window.

I hollered at the man holding the rifle. "There he is."

The man with the gun waved me off. "Get inside."

He didn't check to see if I listened and I moved so I could see. Two boys came up beside me. Brothers, I suppose.

"What's going on?" The wiry-haired boy asked.

"A man's attacked the lady in your house. He's hurt two people tonight."

The other boy nudged himself between us. "What's Papa doing?"

I answered for the wiry-haired boy. "He's catching a bad man who's hunkered down by the window." I pointed to the side yard. "You better go back inside."

The wiry-haired boy moved closer. "Papa, that's not a bad man."

Trouser man turned to his boys. "In the house. Now."

"But Papa …"

Their papa ran down the side of the house and tripped on his slippers. He toppled to the ground head first and the rifle shot into the darkness. He got his footing and raced toward huff-puff man, swinging his rifle like a sword.

The boys yelled duet screams. "Papa. Papa."

I choked on my spit. My toe throbbed.

The gun went off again and the trouser man hollered. "I've shot myself. The bullet ricocheted off something and now it's lodged in my hand."

The boys ran to their papa and propped him up.

Trouser man moaned. "Where's the attacker? Where'd he go?"

One of his sons answered. "I tried to tell you. That's a wheelbarrow. You knocked it over. We were playing hide and seek tonight and used it in our game. We put the wheelbarrow against the window. We hid under it."

Both boys helped their papa up and he waddled to the front yard. I couldn't make out the words he spewed at them, but I did hear them crying.

The sirens sent a shrill sound through the trees and lights came on at houses up and down the street. People wandered out on their porches. The sheriff's car skidded to a stop in front of wheelbarrow house, the one hiding Martha safely inside.

Standing behind the man, I tapped his arm. "Sorry. The shadows confused me. The wheelbarrow had arms in the dark." I'm not sure he heard me, since trouser man's wife came running to the porch.

"Tony, what happened to you?"

It was time to leave. My PF Flyers sent me out of the yard, around the holly, and away from the house. I ran down Blanton Street, south on Robison, and all the way to New Boston Road. I found the tracks and jumped in the middle of the rail and hobbled toward home.

The birthday party for Taddy ended with a huff-puff man attacking two people and with a trouser man getting shot in the hand after having a fight with a wheelbarrow. Texarkana had turned scary in the last few hours. I never figured I'd be afraid here. But tonight, I might be.

I passed the Presbyterian Church, the Baptist Church, and the Catholic Church. At the picket fence in front of Grandma's manor, I decided to whisper a short prayer to God, not sure why, since God never talked to me.

I glanced at Taddy's window on the second floor of the Bright Apartments across the street. "God, please let Taddy forgive me. I'll be nicer to him. He's my best friend at home and at school. He's gonna remember the details of tonight, too. God, if Taddy ever forgot anything, let this be the night his memory fails." I folded my hands together. "Amen."

I flipped the latch on the gate and the front porch light came on. Through the glass of the oval door, I saw the outline of Grandma. I wished for a tree to run and hide behind, wished for a wheelbarrow, but I didn't have one. "Dear God. This is part of my prayer, too. Make Grandma go to bed."

Untied Shoelace

Beads of sweat formed on my brow. The chill in the cold, February wind should have made me shiver, but not knowing what Grandma Elsie might do to me made me sweat.

So much for magic carpet rides. I glanced at my shoes and my overalls. My hands were filthy. Bloody, too. My hair felt tangled, my clothes were covered in grass stains and blood, and my toe ached inside my shoe.

I've got to get the blood off. I've got to get forgiveness. I've got to listen to the radio tomorrow and see if the cops caught the huff-puff man. I've got to swear Taddy to secrecy if he'll talk to me. Delinquents get sent away. I can't be gone if Daddy comes back, although he might not come. He might be dead. He might be …

I had to think of a story to tell Grandma, and I had to think fast.

Grandma bounded to the porch. "Annie Grace Kree. I've had it with you sneaking out. I've let you get away with it but no more. Enough is enough." She walked down the concrete path leading from the porch to the gate, wrapped her arms around me, and sobbed. "I love you. I can't afford to lose you, again. You're my baby-girl."

Chops pranced up to us, circled our embrace, and purred.

Maybe, I won't have to say anything. Maybe . . . I will simply let Grandma love me.

CHAPTER FIFTEEN

SCARY SLEEPOVER

I PEEKED OVER GRANDMA'S SHOULDER. "Who's in the window? Is that nosey Ernie?"

Grandma turned her head. "It's Taddy. He's waiting for you. He's been scared to death. He told me a man chased after someone. And now, Mahlee and Priscilla are out there searching for you."

"Priscilla? And Mahlee?"

"Yes, when Taddy ran home, he bumped into Mahlee and her cart in an alley. She brought him home." Grandma stopped and questioned me. "What in the world were you doing in the woods?"

"We were having a birthday party in a boxcar for Taddy. I wanted him to remember his birthday. We got off the train before it left town and cut through a field."

"You're a lucky little girl. He will remember this birthday, thankfully. You both will. You could have gotten hurt or killed. And you're covered in something. What have you been doing?"

"It's blood from a man's head."

"Whose head?"

"The man from the car."

"What car?"

Untied Shoelace

"I don't remember. It was too dark." My tears rushed like raindrops from my eyes. "The night went wrong after we jumped from the boxcar."

Grandma shook her head and sent me inside. "Go wash up. It's late. We'll talk in the morning."

Inside the front room, I held my blood-splattered hands over the fire to warm them. I glanced at my PF Flyers. They didn't look new. Not with blood and grass stains. Taddy lay on the couch, curled up, half asleep, shaking, and his were eyes heavy.

"Taddy. I'm glad you made it home. I'm sorry that I ruined your birthday." I glanced at my fingers and headed to the kitchen to wash.

Taddy rolled off the couch and followed me. "The bubbles at the fountain were fun, but I could have done without the cops. The cupcake in the boxcar tasted yummy tonight and your hobo friends made me smile." He tried to smooth away the night, even though his lips quivered. But he spoke with a strong boy's voice.

The glass door slammed against the wall at the front of the house. "We didn't find her. The police are searching for a man in a mask who attacked two people across town. We're unsure where to look. Shoelace could be hiding in an alley or in the woods." Priscilla shouted, as she rattled car keys in her hand.

I hurried to the front room. "I'm here. I'm safe. I'm sorry." I ran to Grandma Elsie, hoping to hide behind her fluffy robe that hung to the floor. Taddy scooted next to Grandma on the other side.

Priscilla put the keys on the end table. "There you are. I'm glad you're safe. What were you two thinking?" Priscilla reached for our hands, sat us down on the couch, and knelt in front of us. "No more sneaking out."

Pam Kumpe

I listened to Priscilla as she scolded us, but my mind talked to me at the same time. If I wanted to go out late at night, not even a masked man carrying an iron pipe could stop me. I have always done what I wanted, when I wanted. This bad man's not gonna stop me. And neither is Priscilla.

Grandma piped in. "Taddy, you and your mama stay in my room. It's the second door on the right by Ernie's room. I'll sleep with Shoelace. It's nearly two in the morning. I'm locking the doors and getting my shotgun. I'm putting it in the bed. To keep it close."

Priscilla waved her arm. "I don't want to be a bother."

"I insist. No bother at all." Grandma circled each room, checked windows, shut curtains, and pulled blinds. She locked the kitchen door and latched the front door.

I inched up to Taddy. "Do you know where Mahlee is? She was supposed to be with your mama."

"She walked inside with Mama. I saw her." Taddy looked around the room. "There she is. She's behind the door by the parlor, in the corner."

I swung around, my toe picked up a heartbeat of its own and I surveyed the room. The fireplace flickered and lights danced on the wall. In the corner, crouching and rocking, I saw Tin Can Mahlee.

I limped to her and wrapped my arms around her neck. "Mahlee, you're here. Stay with us. Stay here. Don't leave."

Mahlee rocked and her eyes mirrored the fear I felt running down Blanton Street.

"What's wrong? You're safe here." I wasn't sure I was telling her the truth.

Grandma ushered us toward our rooms. "It's late. We all need sleep."

Untied Shoelace

I tugged on Grandma's arm. "Can Mahlee stay with us? She needs a place to sleep."

Mahlee stepped from the corner. "It's been a long time since I slept in a real bed. If you let me stay, I can help watch the two youngins for ya." Her voice was tired and she mumbled words under her breath.

Grandma nodded. "Sure thing. I've got a roll-a-way bed. We'll put you in the ironing room. It's kind of a small room, but you can have it as long as you need it." Grandma rushed upstairs to make a spot for Mahlee.

Priscilla and Taddy disappeared upstairs behind Grandma.

Mahlee unlocked the front door and stomped to the porch. She returned with a *thud-thud-thud* of the wheels from her cart and bounced across the porch steps. She pushed her life through the door with all her belongings, including her tin can, right into Grandma's front room. She yanked the cart up the stairs, pulling, step by step, thud by thud. She made more noise than a cracking skull or a screaming lady, or trouser man fighting with a wheelbarrow.

Ernie pounded on the wall. "Quiet down. This is the noisiest boarding house I've ever lived in."

I slipped off my shoes, tossed my dirty clothes on the floor, and slipped into bed. I had a hard time staying on my side of the mattress. I tried to keep from rolling into the barrel of Grandma's gun by holding onto the outside of the mattress. But with Mahlee across the hall, I could sleep upside down if need be.

CHAPTER SIXTEEN

REMEMBER TO FORGET

"GRANDMA. YOU AWAKE?" I BLEW in her face. "Grandma."

I rolled over in the bed. I could see the sun shining on the balcony. I hung my head off the mattress and saw my PF Flyers stained from last night. My toe still hurts, but I have to clean my shoes. I don't think my toe is broken. It wiggles without making me scream.

I scooted around to Grandma's side of the bed and whispered, "Grandma. Grandma." Her eyelids didn't move so I found clean overalls, a shirt, and socks in my dresser. The kindest grandma snuggled with the barrel of a gun in my bed. She smiles in her sleep. She smiles when she snores, too.

I dressed and picked up my dirty shoes by their laces. I snuck down to the kitchen to scrub them and ran water into the plastic tub in the sink, hoping to get rid of the stains.

A tap on my shoulder made me hit my head on the cabinet. I spun around and saw Taddy in a long white shirt. He leaned into my face. "Should we tell Mama and your grandma what we saw last night?"

"No. When did you get up? What are you wearing?"

Taddy pulled on his clothes. "It's an old night shirt of your grandpa's."

"It looks like a dress on you."

Taddy sat down, tucking his shirt under him.

I moved from the sink and put my wet hands on Taddy's shoulders. "Don't say a word. If they think we have clues, the cops will bother us. And cops usually chase me."

Taddy frowned. "If we can help them catch the man, we should. He hurt two people."

I wiped my hands on my pants and got right in Taddy's face. "I've been thinking. Skip told me he saw a killer hide two bodies in the bushes, and the man saw Skip watching him. He chased Skip back to the camps and Skip stole his gun in a fight. That's why Skip hid inside a church. The cops came, but no one believed him. But I did." I released fear with my next question. "What if this is the same man?"

"Who is Skip? I've never met him. Is he a hobo, too?"

"Yes. He was a hobo. He played the piano for my daddy's funeral, but right after that a cop shot and killed him."

"Is it the cop we saw at the fountain? Is he the one?"

"Yes. It's the same cop. Same one at the Grim, too." I went to the faucet, twisted the handle on high, and splattered water with specks of blood onto the kitchen counter. "I don't like that cop."

"Do you really think the man who hurt those people is the one Skip told you about?"

"I don't know. It could be." I used the dishrag to clean off the counter top.

"My mama is going to ask me lots of questions. I have to tell the truth."

"You don't have to tell your mama." I tapped him on the forehead. "Try to forget. Erase everything from your memory. Not everything. Erase the part where we jumped off the train and saw the boots. Forget to remember that part."

Taddy stared at my hand. "Did you have blood on your hand?" He rubbed his hair. "Is it on my head?"

"Oops. Sorry." I wiped his face with the rag.

Taddy whimpered. "I can't forget. I remember everything. I wish I wasn't as smart as my papa. I'm always remembering stuff. Even if I don't want to." He sniffled. "Like the boots. Probably a size twelve. Big feet. See, my brain stores everything."

He strutted to the sink and stood beside me. "You should use soap. You need more than water to remove those stains. I know how to clean things because I've watched Mama. Put two scoops of powder in the tub."

I reached for the box of Dreft powder soap, put fresh water in the tub, and poured four scoops of soap in the water.

Taddy held out two fingers in front of my nose. "Two scoops. Not four."

I filled the tub with water and bubbles rose to the top, bubbling into the sink. My shoes were taking a bubble bath like we had at the fountain the day before. I swiped my hand through the bubbles. *Swoosh. Swoosh.* Bubbles floated in the air.

Taddy did the same. *Swoosh. Swoosh.* He blew them from his hand and giggled. It was a small laugh, but at least he wasn't whimpering or crying.

Taddy folded his arms and sighed. He leaned against the counter. "My papa died when I was two. He died in a plane crash in the war. His plane burned up. We have a pretend headstone for him at Rose Hill Cemetery." Taddy stuck his hand in the bubbles again, swirling his fingers around. "I wish he could be here. He could watch out for Mama and me, even though I don't remember him, much."

I blew bubbles in his face. "All this talk is making me want to forget you."

He grabbed a handful of bubbles. "I bet you won't forget this." He plastered my face with a pile of bubbles.

"I'll get you Thaddeus William Day, Jr." I chased him around the table five times before I slugged his arm and smeared bubbles on his neck. I didn't catch him right away. But I could have. I run fast even with a hurt toe.

"I wish I could be as brave as you. You're not afraid of anything." Taddy sat down at the table. "If I were a Boy Scout, I'd have courage. Two boys from the high school had their picture in Life Magazine because they earned more merit badges than any other Boy Scouts in the United States. I bet they're brave."

I put my hand in the bubbles, squeezing air from the soapy water. "You don't have to be in a magazine to be brave."

"A badge might help." He laughed, wiping his face with his hand. He rested his arm on the table in front of him. "Whose cigarettes are these?"

"Those belong to a boarder. They're Camels. Same kind Daddy smokes." I picked up the matches lying beside them. "I love to smell leftover smoke on Daddy's clothes."

"Not me. Smoke makes me sneeze."

I struck a match, lit a cigarette and puffed on it.

Taddy's eyes grew big like saucers, the same way they did when he had to jump from the train. "What are you doing? You can't smoke a cigarette."

"I'm lighting it for the smoke." *Cough. Cough. Cough.* "I'm putting it in the ashtray to let it burn."

"Why?" Taddy moved to the end of the table to get away from the smoke.

"So the room will smell like Daddy." I went to the sink to hide the tears in my eyes. *Daddy, will I ever be brave enough to live without you? I am afraid. Taddy thinks I'm brave. But I'm not. I need you.*

99

The *tap, tap, and creak* coming from the staircase meant people were waking up at the manor. Heavy steps shook the floor.

"Shoelace? Are you smoking? When did this start?" Grandma Elsie's high pitched voice vibrated the walls. Mumbling under her breath, Grandma put the cigarette out.

"I'm not smoking it, I'm smelling it. The smoke reminds me of Daddy."

"And what are these bloody shoes doing in my kitchen sink?"

"I washed my shoes. You say I don't help you enough." I danced beside her, smiling, putting my arm around her waist. "See. They're nearly clean."

"I'll finish it for you. Go wash your hands in the bathroom. Come right back. You and Taddy are setting the table for breakfast." Grandma finished scrubbing the shoes for me, rinsed them, and wiped down every inch of the counter with bleach. Now the room stinks. Daddy's smell is gone.

Grandma sent me to the back steps of the house to set the shoes out to dry. Outside, the fog lifted but not in the house. Grandma acted a little huffy-puffy this morning.

I twirled around her. "The table is set. I'm starved."

"No more cigarettes. Okay?" She held me close, grabbed Taddy, too, and squished us both, her rubbery body mashing our boney ones. I wasn't sure if a spanking or a kiss might be next.

Priscilla came down in time for scrambled eggs and buttered toast. In time to distract Grandma.

All four of us sat at the table. We were mostly silent, except for the silverware clanking on plates. The midnight birthday party and the attack on the couple were anything but silent in my mind. I didn't know how to hush the noise and jumped from the table. I grabbed a piece of toast, ate the center out of it, and ran upstairs to check on Mahlee.

I sat on the floor outside her door listening through the wood. Her sing-song nostril snore shook the wall.

Taddy tip-toed up the stairs and sat down with me. He whispered in my ear. "Do you think your daddy is alive? Or do you think he died in the river?"

"What's with all this talk about your daddy and mine?

Taddy's bottom lip quivered. "We just don't have any daddies to help us with stuff."

"We have Mahlee. She's stronger than two daddies put together."

I leaned on the door and put my feet straight out in front of me, wiggling my toes in my socks. My sore toe made me cry, "Ouch."

Taddy wiggled his toes copying me. "My papa would have been friends with your daddy."

I kicked Taddy with my good foot. "How do you know?"

"Mama told me how she met Papa at Church by the Creek." Taddy moved closer and put his hand to my ear. "My papa rode the rail before he married Mama. He came through Texarkana one summer."

I pushed his hand from my ear. "Your papa rode the rail?" I shook my head, not believing it could be true.

"Yes. He knew how to catch trains. When Mama handed Thaddeus William Day, Sr. a biscuit at the creek they fell in love. Daddy went to work at Buhrman Pharr Hardware Store on Third Street. They got married and moved into our apartment."

"You don't forget much, do you?" I sighed. "Taddy. I think my daddy would have liked your papa. And … your papa would have loved you."

I glanced at my socks, wondering if Taddy would ever forget to remember me. Wondering if we'd be friends for a long time. Wondering if he'd outgrow being allergic to me. Wondering if we'd have to talk to the cops.

CHAPTER SEVENTEEN

FROM NOTHING TO SOMETHING

BEFORE TADDY COULD SAY ANOTHER word, a man's voice rattled our ears. We put our faces between the slats and stared downstairs to the front room.

"Anyone here? Hello. It's me, Pastor Cody."

Grandma yelled. "We're in the kitchen."

Ernie cracked open his bedroom door. He was dressed in slacks and wearing a pressed shirt. "What are you two doing?"

I stood to my feet. "We're seeing if Mahlee's asleep."

"Who's Mahlee?"

"A new boarder." I ran down the stairs in front of Ernie. Taddy trailed me. We stood at the bottom and watched Ernie hop down every other stair.

"Does this Mahlee smoke?" Ernie wiped his nose and sniffed the air.

"I don't think so." I hoped Ernie didn't keep track of how many cigarettes were left in the pack.

Ernie stepped into the kitchen behind me and snatched a piece of toast. He stuck the pack of Camels inside his shirt pocket. "I'm off to the paper. I hope to make reporter soon. If I had a great story, I'd get promoted today."

Honk. Honk.

"There's my ride." The screen slammed closed as Ernie went outside.

I turned to Taddy. "Don't you tell him anything if he asks you."

Taddy sighed. "I'm not."

"He ate my last piece of my birthday cake. I'm not sure I like him. He's not in on what happened…"

"In on what?" Pastor Cody sipped on his coffee.

I looked his way. "Nothing."

Pastor Cody pulled something from his lap. "Does this satchel belong to you, Shoelace?"

"Yes. It does." I ran to the table, opened the flap on the bag, and a handful of playing cards tumbled to the floor. "Daddy's money is gone and his flashlight." I shoved my fingers into the small pouch inside. "My red rock. It's here. My poem, too." I unfolded the paper and read part of it out loud.

> *"Wake up and smile.*
> *It's been a while,*
> *Since you and me*
> *Rode a train for a mile.*
> *So hold on for a while.*
> *I'll find you, soon.*
> *Surely, by noon.*
> *Outside of Boone."*

I put my poem and rock in my pocket. "Where did you find my daddy's satchel? Who had it?" I bent down and gathered up the cards.

"Peaches rode her bike down the trail and her bike got away from her. A bunch of us ran to help her and Slow Tom found the satchel in the weeds." Pastor eyed the rest of Grandma's eggs.

"But, why did you think it was mine?"

Pastor Cody laughed. "I've noticed some posters written in crayon on the trees in town. The description of the satchel, saying you lost one, gave me a pretty good clue."

Grandma turned from the stove. "Are you hungry, Pastor? We have plenty."

Pastor nodded. "Yes, thank you."

Grandma scrambled another batch of eggs as Mahlee slipped into the kitchen.

I moved to give Pastor Cody a hug, but stopped and folded my arms, pulling the satchel to my chest. "Thank you for bringing my daddy's satchel back. I'm never gonna let it go."

Pastor Cody shoveled food into his mouth like I do when I'm starving.

Grandma pointed to a chair with her spoon. "Mahlee, sit down. I'll get you a plate."

"Thank you, ma'am."

"Call me, Ms. Elsie."

Mahlee brushed the satchel with her hand. "Looks like Side Car Ace's bag." She pulled out a chair and sat down.

The preacher shook Mahlee's hand. "Good morning, I'm Pastor Cody Westside. You've watched from the hill during services at the creek. I recognize you. It's nice to see you."

Mahlee nodded. "I like to listen to your talks about God. You make good sense." Mahlee yanked her hand from his grip and put it in her lap.

"Thank you. I love to teach. I'm glad to know I make sense."

Pastor turned back to me and picked up where he left off about my daddy's bag. "Fast Tim was at church this morning and he heard of trouble last night. A man and a woman were attacked. Were you and Taddy out late last night?"

Taddy and me looked at each other and answered Pastor Cody in unison. "We don't know anything."

I slipped the strap of Daddy's satchel on my shoulder and hurried upstairs to place the bag in my dresser. I hopped on the last three steps near the second floor and the strap slid down my arm, landing on the staircase. I tripped and fell, hitting my knee, and my sore toe.

I picked up the satchel and remembered that one night, when I snuck out with Mahlee, I carried Daddy's satchel with me. I don't remember returning to the manor with it. I must have lost it that night.

Inside my bedroom, I tucked the satchel in the drawer. *Miss you, Daddy. Miss you.*

A loud knock on the front door sent me to the staircase with my face between two slats. "I'm Officer Teacup. I'm investigating a case. I need to talk to Annie Grace Kree. Is she here?"

I ran to the balcony and jumped to the tree. I placed my poem inside my can, slid down the trunk, and toppled to the ground.

"Shoelace, come into this house." Grandma stood in the yard with her hands on her hips.

In the front room, I sat on the smaller sofa by the parlor door across from the officer.

"If it's not Little Miss Bubbles from the fountain. Tell me what you saw last night."

"Nothing."

"What did you hear?"

"Nothing."

"What were you doing in the Robison Road area of town?"

"Having a birthday party."

Officer Teacup pointed his finger at me. "Little lady, I suggest you tell me what you know." He stood, his hand swinging as if he wanted to paddle me, but Grandma appeared in the room.

"Shoelace, if you remember anything, you need to help the police capture this man who hurt those people."

I folded my arms. "I don't know anything." I wrinkled my nose at the cop who had shot Skip. Who also called me a *delinquent.* I'm not talking to him.

Officer Teacup tugged on a piece of cloth sticking out of his shirt pocket and pulled out a familiar green scarf. The one I used to blindfold Taddy at the tracks. A scarf stained in blood. "Does this belong to you? We found this scarf wrapped around Jack Hall's head last night. Would you happen to know his girlfriend, Martha Long?"

"No, I've never seen the scarf. I don't know either of them."

"Wait, that's my scarf." Grandma scrunched it in her hands. "Shoelace?" Grandma's eyes cut me in half.

"Ummm . . . I forgot. I tied it around Taddy's eyes to surprise him at his party."

The officer tapped his pen against his notepad. "So you do know this scarf?"

"Maybe."

The officer turned to Grandma. "I'm not getting anywhere with this child. If you can get her to talk, call me. We need clues to solve this attack. I need to find out if she can help us."

"I will let you know what I learn. I'll call you if she says anything."

Officer Teacup left in his squad car.

Pastor Cody, who had remained in the kitchen, came and sat down beside me. "You've gone and gotten yourself tangled in a mess. Before I leave, let me pray with you."

Taddy ran and sat right between us. "Will you pray for me, too?"

Pastor Cody called to Grandma, Priscilla, and Mahlee. "Let me pray with the whole family."

We all gathered together, but Mahlee stayed near the staircase.

"Mahlee, come stand beside me." I waved her to my side.

Chops jumped on the couch.

Achoo. Achoo. "Pray fast. I'm allergic." Taddy sniffled.

Pastor Cody laughed. "Are you allergic to prayer?"

"No, I'm allergic to cats. I think I'm allergic to Shoelace, too, but she did give me the best birthday party ever, even if I nearly died."

"You liked the cupcake." I knocked Chops off the couch and a loud meow called to the dogs outside.

Pastor Cody wrapped one hand around Taddy's hand and his other around mine. No one had ever prayed for me before or sat with me to pray. Pastor closed his eyes and Taddy did, too. I talked to God with my eyes open.

Pastor recited his prayer. "Dear God, help Taddy and Shoelace be strong. Help them to trust in you, to run and not grow weary. May they not be afraid. Amen."

As soon as he said amen, Chops pounced on Taddy's back. "Ouch." *Achoo. Achoo.*

"Chops, get out of here." Priscilla shooed the cat away.

"Mama. I'm not staying here. This cat jumps on me on purpose."

"We're going to stay a few days to make sure you and Shoelace are safe. We'll keep him outside."

Ernie burst into the front room. "Has anyone seen Officer Teacup? My boss told me he's coming here to talk to Annie Grace."

Untied Shoelace

I stood to leave the room. "You missed him. Officer Teacup left. You can call me, Shoelace. And I don't know anything. Nothing. Not one thing."

"But this could be my big break. I could become a reporter if I write this story." Ernie followed me to the kitchen, circled twice around me, and ran into me when I stopped at the screen door. "Please talk to me. Give me the scoop."

Earlier, having Daddy's satchel in my hands took my thoughts away and I nearly forgot to remember the attacker in the black boots. And now, I've got a boarder breathing down my neck to make him famous. "Talk to Officer Teacup. He knows everything."

I wish Daddy was here to light his Camel cigarette for real. I'd catch him up on the bubbles at the fountain, the green scarf, and the boxcar birthday party. I'd tell him about the night with Jack and Martha, the iron pipe, and those black boots. When it comes to my daddy, I tell him everything.

Although, Daddy's been known to keep things from me.

Ernie snorted and coughed. He rushed to interrogate Taddy, but Priscilla put a stop to his questions. "Ernie Surratt, I don't care if you are the Bowie County Sheriff's nephew. Leave my son alone."

CHAPTER EIGHTEEN

PLAYGROUND FIGHTS

MY FISTS JUMPED OUT OF my pockets before I could stop them. One hand hit Lester in the eye, followed by another one slamming into Gilbert's face. Ms. Reece watched by the school house steps and pointed her finger at me.

I called to her. "The Blanton Street boys started it. I finished it."

Ms. Reece marched up to me. "Fighting at school isn't permitted. Remember our talk? Help the boys off the ground. They're your neighbors and your schoolmates."

I kicked the dirt and reached down to help them. "They live across town on Blanton Street. They're not my neighbors. They blamed me for their papa getting shot in the hand. It was an accident."

Kids on the merry-go-round jumped off and sprinted to the other side of the playground. I put my hand out to pull Lester to his feet while giving Gilbert the evil eye.

When Lester balanced himself, I let go. "Gotcha. Help yourself up." One of my PF Flyers bolted forward, right into Gilbert's leg as Lester fell on him. I dove into the pile and we toppled and rolled on the ground, arms and legs flying.

Gilbert punched me in the arm. "Your daddy's a hobo. A no good bum."

Untied Shoelace

I spit dirt from my mouth. "Don't make fun of my daddy. He never shot himself in the hand with his own gun."

"You're the one who ran away in the dark. Scaredy cat." Lester patted Gilbert on the shoulder acting as if they'd won.

I wrapped my arms around Lester and Gilbert pulling them to the ground. Now they were in for it. Pretending to be the Lone Ranger in overalls, I walloped Gilbert tossing him like an empty potato sack and then Lester, who landed by the monkey bars. Gilbert crawled to the shade tree and coiled like a wounded snake.

I shook my fist at him. "Call me scaredy cat or hobo-girl, again. See what you'll get."

Wiping sweat and dirt from my face, the tornado-fight on the playground fizzled. Daddy taught me to stand up for myself on the rail, but my hands don't know when to stay in my pockets. Or when to stop. I can become a whirlwind of trouble if you make me mad.

"To the office. I've been patient with you, but this fighting has got to stop." A small girl whimpered and stood behind Ms. Reece as my *favorite* teacher pointed for me to go inside. "Mr. Meldrum is waiting for you."

I dusted myself off and shrugged my shoulders, watching the bugged eyes of the other kids, their gaze like a pack of hungry wolves. I've seen those eyes at camp fires with Daddy. They were probably happy I'd been caught by the teacher and the principal.

Taddy shuffled along with me. "Your grandma will have plenty to say when she finds out."

"She doesn't have to know."

Gilbert yelled with a girly tone. "Hey little smart boy, are you going to protect her?"

Taddy bolted up to Gilbert, who stood six inches taller. "Leave her alone. She's braver than everybody in this town, especially you and Lester."

Gilbert bumped his chest against Taddy, his wiry-hair springing like a wet sponge. "You're not big enough to save her. I could tie you in a bow and leave you on these monkey bars if I wanted to."

I bounced across the schoolyard to where they stood. *Whap. Whap. Whap.* The smack of my fist hitting Gilbert caused the kids who had circled around us to start throwing punches, too. The playground brawl at Central School lasted less than five minutes, but I got in a few blows on Gilbert before Mr. Meldrum blew his whistle.

This was my second trip to the principal's office in less than two months. I sat across from the man who carried a satchel like Daddy, a tall man whose eyes weren't devouring me. Mr. Meldrum tapped his desk with a ruler. "What am I going to do with you, Annie Grace?"

"I'm sorry. Maybe I could have a recess without any kids around me." I poured dirt from my PF Flyers onto the floor.

"Empty your shoes outside. Not on my office floor."

With the door shut, and Lester and Gilbert sitting in chairs in the hallway, Mr. Meldrum and I made a deal. He assigned me playground duty with the kindergarten kids to keep me away from the Blanton Street boys. To keep me from Billy Joe. To keep me from anyone who might cause my fists to swing. And I promised to work on my temper.

"Can Taddy help me on the playground? I don't want them to make a bow out of him."

"We'll see. Let's start with you."

Mr. Meldrum came around his big wooden desk carrying his ruler and sat down in a chair beside me. "I know you lost your father before Christmas. I also know the other night you witnessed something no one should have to see. I'm going to give you time to sort through this. But no more fights after today. This will end as of now."

"Yes sir. I can do better. I'm trying to keep my promises, but Lester and Gilbert make it hard."

Mr. Meldrum squeezed my hand. "I believe you will do better. Now get out of here."

I passed Lester and Gilbert in the hall, their tears told me they expected a paddling. I hoped they were right.

After school, Mahlee met Taddy and me at the front gate. Grandma Elsie had officially made Mahlee our babysitter. She watches us. She follows us and listens to our talks. She even sits in the tree with us. I'm tucking the secret of the fight in my pocket. No need to worry Mahlee. No need for Grandma to know. No need to tell them everything.

CHAPTER NINETEEN

PEANUTS FOR ALL

PASTOR CODY TOSSED HIS PEANUT shells to the table. "I'm off to the train station. My cousin, Reed Gordon, is coming home today. He's a Navy Seal. You'll like him." Pastor turned to me. "I believe you've met Reed's brother, Billy Joe, at school."

"I know him. We're in the same class. He's a good speller. He also has a good left hook."

Pastor Cody smiled and left through the front door.

Taddy slugged my arm. "You better become friends with Billy Joe. He's related to a pastor. He'll tell God on you."

I flipped a peanut shell at Taddy. "No way. I don't like Billy Joe."

"Those peanuts smell. Yuck." Taddy made a throwing up sound. *Yack. Ack. Yack.* "They stink like nasty socks boiling in salty water." Taddy shuffled from the kitchen to the front room.

Mahlee cracked three peanuts with her fingers. "I worked on a farm that had peanuts. First time I tried them, I thought I was eating raw pinto beans. The more I ate, the better they tasted."

On the table sat a bowl with a batch already drained and ready for eating. On the stove, another batch bubbled away in the water.

Untied Shoelace

Taddy yelled from the other room. "Peanuts are for elephants. I don't like how they look even after you shell them."

I mouthed back. "You don't even know what they taste like. You won't try anything new. You eat your eggs over-easy and your toast burnt. Same ole. Same ole."

Taddy stomped across the hardwood floor and slid into the kitchen, nearly joining Chops on the floor under the table. *Achoo. Achoo.* He wiped his nose with his arm and grabbed a peanut, tossing it back. He then grabbed a handful and sniffed them. "They smell rotten to me. I'd rather have vanilla ice cream or chocolate chip cookies."

For the last three weeks, the man on the radio repeated his story about the bad man. The cops have no suspects and they keep saying they are hoping for leads. Nothing too much going on, except Mr. Daniel Darnell moved in with us and brought peanuts in his suitcase. He wears the same brown suit and matching leather shoes every day.

Mr. Daniel Darnell cracked open a peanut. "I love peanuts. Boiled. Roasted. No matter. I'll eat them anyway I can get them." He cracked more shells and left them in a pile on the kitchen table. Ernie and Mahlee were having a contest to see who could crack and eat the most peanuts. They gobbled them faster than I could grab one.

"Shoelace, check the water on those peanuts on the stove, will you?" Mahlee asked.

My PF Flyers slid to the stove. The floor was littered in peanut shells. *Crunch. Crunch. Crunch.* I turned on the faucet, put more water in the pan, and dried my hands on the towel by the stove.

Mr. Daniel Darnell popped a peanut into his mouth. "I've been trying to meet with the Four States Fair President. I hope to convince him to have my family's hot roasted peanuts at your fair in October."

Taddy skipped into the kitchen and leaned on the table, grabbing peanuts simply to drop them one by one, not tasting a single nut.

Mahlee cracked another peanut. "Where is Priscilla? I haven't seen her much today."

Taddy pointed to the second floor. "She's sick. Her tummy hurts. I bet it's the peanuts." He dropped another handful to the table, peanut-raindrops, and went back to the couch.

I chomped down on a mouthful of peanuts and moved closer to Mr. Daniel Darnell. "Can I call you Mr. Darnell? Or do I have to say your first name every time?"

"Call me Mr. Darnell."

He used whole sentences with verbs and nouns. Ms. Reece wants me to use them, too. They sound nice coming from him. Mr. Darnell must have made good grades when he was a kid.

He rattled on. "Our hot roasted peanut wagons travel the circuit with PT Barnum's circus, but we're growing our business. Hope the phone rings today. A meeting would be great."

Grandma plowed through the kitchen door. "What's this? Peanut shells on my clean table?" She scooted them into her apron and dumped the shells in the trash can. We're used to Grandma cleaning around us. No one moved. We simply cracked more peanuts.

Mr. Darnell stood and put a hand on Grandma's shoulder. "Ms. Elsie. Can I drive you to the store?"

"Mr. Darnell, I've told you time and again, we have a pantry full of groceries."

"I have pretty big appetite and can eat my weight in your home cooked meals. My father raised five boys and taught us

Pam Kumpe

This is the day the Lord has made.

to do to others the way we want to be treated. Since th
has ended, there's no more rationing. Let me fill your j

"Not necessary. We always make it through." Gran
swished the next round of peanut shells from the table,
them in the trash.

Mr. Darnell jingled change in his pants pocket, read
show kindness for no reason. "A few extra items won't

Grandma untied her cat apron and hung it on the ho
the icebox. "We could use some flour and eggs."

I jumped from my chair. "I'm going, too. Taddy, con
with us." I ran to the screen door, one foot in the kitchen
the other out the back, holding the door open. "Taddy, y
coming?"

"No. I'm staying here."

Mahlee inched to the front room. "I'm listening to the
radio in the parlor. It's time for *Muffin the Mule*."

I laughed at Mahlee. "That's a kid's show."

Mahlee put her hands on her hips. "He's a talking puppet.
He kind of reminds me of you."

I slammed the screen. "Taddy, come on. We might get a
cookie at the bakery." I sat down on the bottom step to tie my
shoelaces and pressed my nose on the mesh. "Mahlee, you're
not funny at all. I'm not a mule. Or a puppet. I'm a real kid."

A freckled tornado pushed by me at the door, knocking me
off the back steps. "A cookie does sound good."

I jumped up and ran with one shoelace left untied. I
toppled to the ground. I could almost hear Daddy saying *Tie
them shoelaces.* I sat in the grass, tied the other shoe, and
wiped the tear off my face.

Grandma climbed into the passenger seat and Mr. Darnell
was behind the wheel. I jumped into the back seat next to
Taddy. Grandma turned around in the seat. "Run back to the

house. Ask Ernie or Mahlee to watch the peanuts on the stove."

I ran into the kitchen, sliding on the floor, and Ernie's voice rattled the wall by the stairs. "Thank you. You won't regret this. I'll do my best to make a great reporter."

I stood on the opposite side of the wall in the kitchen. I forgot why I came back inside and listened as Ernie told the person on the phone to run his story. I started to bolt around the wall, but Taddy ran into me. "What are you doing?"

"Keep your voice down. I'm listening to Ernie. He's made reporter."

Taddy threw his hands up. "You always dilly-dally. I came to get you."

Ernie raised his voice and we pressed our ears to the wall.

"Yes, run with it. It's a firsthand account of the attack last month."

Taddy and me scooted around the wall as Priscilla appeared at the top of the staircase. "What's with the noise? Why are you shouting? Did I hear you correctly? Did you write a story about Taddy and Shoelace? They're children. We don't want the attacker to know their names." Priscilla bolted down the stairs, skidding off the bottom step, bumping into him.

Ernie hung the phone on the receiver. "I'm sorry. I didn't mean to wake you. It's a small news story for the paper. Nothing big."

I marched up beside Priscilla and turned to Ernie. "You can't put me in the paper." I placed my hands on my hips mocking the way Grandma scolds me, only this time I scolded Ernie.

His face went pale. "I'm trying to break into the business. This story would change my life. They have no leads in the case. The article could help them find the attacker." Ernie backed into the corner.

Priscilla pressed her finger against his chest. "Call the paper and take the children out of the story. If you don't, I'll get Ms. Elsie in here." Priscilla turned to me. "Where is she?"

"She's in the car with Mr. Darnell. They're going to the store. She sent me inside for something."

Ernie sighed deeply. "I'll call my editor back, right now. I'm dialing the number. I should have talked to you. I'm sorry. I'm new at this. My background is in circulation, I didn't mean any harm."

"You better take care of this." Priscilla put her hand on my shoulder and guided Taddy and me out the door. We ran into Grandma by the sheets on the clothesline.

Grandma raised her voice. "I've waited in the car for ten minutes. What's taking you so long?"

"Grandma, you won't believe what Ernie has done. He's written a story on the person who hurt the man and woman last month. He put Taddy and me in there, too. He's a reporter for the paper now. He's getting his big break. But I think Priscilla's gonna break him first." I spouted out everything I learned eavesdropping.

Grandma Elsie rushed passed us and stormed into the kitchen. She swiped the rest of the peanut shells to the floor and screamed at Ernie. "What were you thinking? This is my granddaughter and her friend. Don't put them in jeopardy. Do you hear me? Now, get the paper to stop the story or change the names."

Ernie scratched his head. "They won't use their names because they're children. Besides, it may be too late to stop the story."

"You be careful what you write. If anything happens to them, you'll deal with me." Grandma stormed out the back door.

I ran to the screen. "I'm staying here at the manor." I didn't want to ride to the store with an angry grandma.

She called back to me. "Keep watch on the peanuts, then. They may need more water."

Before I could answer her, Taddy scooted up beside me. "I've never seen your grandma this mad. I'm staying here, too."

Mr. Darnell would calm Grandma down on the ride to Piggly Wiggly.

Repeating Grandma's warning to Ernie, I added mine. "Ernie, you better not get me hurt. I've wanted to tell you this since January. I've been mad at you for two months. You ate the rest of my birthday cake when we went to the Grim. And you didn't ask me."

Ernie sat down in a chair. "I'm sorry. Chocolate is my favorite. Your grandma is a great cook. Her kitchen's always open and she tells boarders to help themselves. I'm sorry."

Mahlee came into the kitchen and her face told me what I suspected. She's falling for Ernie. The other day, I saw her wink at him. He winked back. They were standing under my oak tree talking in the shade one afternoon. I sat on a branch above them and tried to ignore the winking, but now, Mahlee's wrapped her arms around his neck. I couldn't ignore that.

Mahlee whispers loud and shouted her not so soft words to Ernie. "We have to keep the children safe." Mahlee pulled a chair next to his and placed her hand on his chest.

Priscilla shook her head and went upstairs to her room. Ernie and Mahlee moved to the wooden rockers on the front

porch to talk. Yuck. Rocker talk. And more hugs. I had to do
something else.

I turned to Taddy. "Hey. Let's plant peanuts in Grandma's
garden before she gets back."

Taddy wrinkled his nose. "I could care less about your
peanuts, but I'll go out to the garden with you."

I dug holes in the ground using a shovel I found in the
carriage house. Planting handfuls of peanuts, I tossed a bunch
inside each hole and watered them with the garden hose. If
they grow, I can show them to Mr. Darnell in the fall if he gets
the contract. Taddy and me washed our hands with the water
from the garden hose and went inside to the front room.

Priscilla came downstairs and sat on the sofa.

I touched her hand. "Are you still sick?"

Priscilla rubbed her tummy. "No. I'm much better. I
shouldn't have eaten a bucket of peanuts these past few days."

I moved next to her. "I planted peanuts in the garden.
Maybe I can sell hot-roasted peanuts at the fair, too." I crossed
my fingers. "I've never been to a fair. I've seen Ferris Wheels
from trains, but Daddy and me never had the money to go."

Priscilla put her arm around me. "This fall, we'll take you
with us to the fair."

I bounced to the big chair by the window. "I could ride the
Ferris Wheel and see all the rides."

Taddy rushed to me and pointed. "Did you see them?
Mahlee kissed Ernie two times."

I got on my knees in the chair and peeked over the top of
it. "No, I didn't see them kiss. Are you sure?"

Taddy put his hands on his hips. "I've seen people kiss
before."

Priscilla glanced out the window. "You two, leave them
alone."

Ernie and Mahlee were breathing in each other's face when Priscilla screamed and jumped from her seat. "The stove's on fire. I see flames." Priscilla tore into the kitchen and yelled from somewhere inside the smoke. "Taddy, get on the phone and dial the operator. We need help."

I panicked, my heart pounded inside my chest, and I cried. "I forgot to put more water in the pan on the stove."

Priscilla ran out of the kitchen with gray soot on her face. "Outside. Everybody out. The stove and the cabinets are burning."

Two red fire trucks with sirens blaring stopped out front and another truck parked beside the house. We stood in the yard and watched the smoke billow from the manor.

A crew of firemen carried hoses into the house and doused the fire. They sprayed water everywhere. The stove and the cabinets were a mess. Gray soot covered most of the downstairs walls, too. I couldn't stop the tears from rolling down my face. Grandma's house is ruined and it's my fault.

Mr. Darnell drove into the driveway. Grandma stuck her head out the passenger window. "What happened? Is everyone okay?"

"We're fine," Priscilla said.

Grandma Elsie thanked the firemen for saving the manor, but she cried when she staggered into the kitchen, her favorite room in the house.

"I'm sorry, Grandma. I left the peanuts boiling in the pan and the water boiled out. A hand towel caught fire. It's my fault." Telling Grandma *sorry* unleashed the other things I'd done wrong since I came to live with her.

I couldn't save Skip. I had a fight at school with Billy Joe and the Blanton Street brothers. I can't keep my promises to Ms. Reece. I disappoint Grandma. Daddy wouldn't be proud of me if he were here. I put bubbles in the city fountain. I held a midnight birthday party for Taddy. I had him hop a train. I saw a bad man hurt two people. And now, I nearly burned down Grandma's boarding house. Maybe I should go ride the rail.

I tore up the stairs to my room and pulled off my PF Flyers. "These shoes are no good. They run fast, but they run me into trouble." I plopped down on the bed and my body bounced on the mattress. Grandma's gun lay in the middle of the bed. I wondered if I should touch it.

CHAPTER TWENTY

KITCHEN'S CLOSED

"GERONIMO. I'M A FIREMAN AND I've got the fire under control." Taddy pretended to hold a water hose.

"You're not a fireman. You're a fourth grader who is smarter than everyone and no one knows it." I waved for him to leave my room, but he stayed and plopped down on the bed on my feet.

"Sorry."

"Get out. Go."

He bounced on the springs, pressing his loafers on the floor. "Did you know my best friend is a famous poet and she doesn't know it?" Taddy stood and stumbled on my shoes, knocking my school bag to the floor. He fell against the bedroom door, slamming it shut.

"What are you doing? You're the noisiest fireman in town." I laughed and my whole body shook. I picked up my school bag from the floor.

Taddy, the earthquake boy, handed me a cookie. "Mr. Darnell brought us sugar cookies from the bakery. I brought you one."

"How many have you eaten?"

"Four. I love sugar cookies." Taddy danced and pounced around like a Slinky toy. "Mama said the kitchen's closed. Mr. Darnell is ordering your grandma a new oven from Sears &

Roebuck. I brought you a cleaning rag. We're wiping soot from the walls."

"Okay. I'll be there in a minute." Taddy sounded way too excited. "Shoo. Leave my room. Shut the door on your way out."

Taddy stopped jumping. His lip turned upward. He held back, but a quivering bottom lip told me he might cry. He probably would tell on me for hurting his feelings. I'll deal with him later. He shut the door and I leaned against it. I could hear the sound of breathing like the exhaust from a car rattling.

"I can hear you breathing. Go downstairs. I'll be there in a second." His muffled response made me ask. "What? What are you saying?" I opened the door. "What?"

"I'm here. I'm waiting for you."

I slugged his arm. "Will you leave me alone? I caused the fire in the kitchen. I mess everything up. I cause trouble."

"Not for me. You're my best friend. I'd pick you, even if you wouldn't pick me." Taddy pulled out an acorn and handed it to me.

"Why do I want this?"

"It's an acorn."

"No kidding."

"Put it in your pocket. Keep it with you and you'll have good luck."

I held the acorn and shook my head, not sure Taddy told me the truth. But I could use a little luck. "So you keep acorns in your window sills at your apartment? For good luck?"

"Yes. You'll notice nothing bad has happened there. No fires. No fire trucks. No trouble. There's nothing going on over there."

"It's because no one is there." I repeated the words slowly and Taddy realized what he'd said.

He changed the subject. "I need to put acorns in the window sills at the manor since we've kind of moved in." He ran to his room, the one he shared with his mama.

I could hear him across the way, talking to himself. "I've got to put these last three acorns in the window. Three acorns will keep lightning from striking and trouble away."

He came and stood beside me. "Got your rag?"

"I do. It's right here." I hopped down the stairs, not sure I'd met anyone as odd as Taddy. Or as smart.

**

After a week of wiping, dusting, washing, and having no time to hang out by the tracks, the manor sparkled. Even more than before the fire.

Pastor Cody had brought in Slow Tom and Fast Tim to work on the cabinets. They nailed, cut wood in the yard, brought in pieces, and hammered. The cabinets were brand new, the finishing coat of white paint drying, which is why Grandma told me to stay out of the kitchen no matter what. The kitchen would reopen soon, but Grandma had to wait for the oven to arrive.

Thankfully, Ernie's first newspaper article didn't say anything different than what the radio said. Both said the attack might be a freak accident. Nothing on me. Or Taddy.

Grandma joined me in the garden. I had no sign of any peanut plants, but I kept watering the dirt.

She patted my arm. "Thank you for helping me this week. You worked harder than any of us to get the boarding house cleaned up. Ernie told me you pitched in with any task he gave you." She took the water hose from me, went to the faucet by the house, turned it off, and dropped the green plastic hose to the ground.

"We've had a rough start, and we've gone through a lot of changes, but we'll always have each other." Grandma pulled me into her rubbery body, her folds of fat cushioning me. She's warmer and nicer than a cushion on a couch.

"I'm sorry. Trouble follows me."

"Tomorrow morning, I want us to have a fresh start. I'm taking you out for breakfast to the Stockmen Hotel. It's on Highway 67, a mile out of town, just west of here. There's a restaurant and they cook as good as your grandma." She kissed my cheek and headed into the house. I followed her through the kitchen, which came with another warning that the paint was still wet.

Since the fire, we've eaten lots of sandwiches and cereal. Not any hot meals. A few months ago, I'd settle for cheese or bologna on the rail. Now, I miss my grandma's cooking and her baking. My tummy growled like it did when I ate my birthday dinner at the Grim. The chicken made me lick my fingers. I'm sure this meal will be grand, too.

Bed time came early and Sunday morning even faster. "Grandma, get up. I'm hungry. I'm dressed. I've got my shoes on and pulled my hair in a ponytail." The ponytail hung loose and fell. My blonde hair doesn't keep pulled back very good.

I blew in Grandma's face. She snored. I swooshed more air at her, this time in her ear. She simply swatted her face. I stayed clear of the shotgun in the bed, since Taddy had told Grandma I touched the barrel of her gun the other night. He saw me yank my hand away when he yelled Geronimo and busted into my room.

I got a hard talking to by Grandma. She cried, saying she didn't know what she'd do if I got hurt or went missing. But she keeps the gun in our bed because she wants to protect us if she needs to. *Taddy's such a tattle tale.*

After a half-hour of me blowing in her face, Grandma woke up. She got dressed in her flower print dress and jingled her keys. "Hop in the car. I'm craving coffee and pancakes."

"I'm hungry, too." I jumped down each of the three steps leading out the kitchen door. It was barely eight o'clock and Mahlee, Ernie, Priscilla, and Taddy were still asleep. They'd have to eat cereal, but not me.

As Grandma drove, the rain fell from the clouds and soaked the streets. I would have waited to water my peanuts yesterday if I had known the rain was blowing into town. "Are we there, yet?" I pulled myself to the dash.

"Nearly, but I'm stopping for gas first. There's the Stop Agan Service Station. We don't want to get stranded." The gas attendant filled the car, and we headed to the Stockmen Hotel.

I glanced at the sign as we pulled out. "Grandma, they spelled *again* wrong."

She patted my leg. "The owner spells it that way. It's an old family name."

At the restaurant, our table sat next to the front window. The waitress brought milk and juice for me and coffee for Grandma.

Grandma added cream to her coffee and looked out the window. "Weather's letting up. The roads will be muddier than ever."

I sloshed juice around in my mouth and held the tangy drink in my jaw longer than I should have, pressing my nose on the window pane by the table.

"Swallow your juice," Grandma said.

Gulp. "My throat loves the burn." Sirens squealed outside the restaurant. "What's going on?"

A man sitting at the table beside ours turned to us. "There's something going on by the railroad spur by that parked car."

I pressed my nose on the glass. "Where? What's happening?" A car drove up and parked on the side of the road and Ernie got out of the passenger seat. "I see Ernie. He's with the fat reporter. They must be writing a story." I waved, but he didn't see me.

"Sit down, and act like a lady. Don't call people fat." Grandma watched the people gathering outside. A patrol car parked behind Ernie and the other reporter, and a familiar face with the square jaw got out of the car. Officer Teacup stomped in the mud to the parked car on the road.

My PF Flyers sent me out the door of the restaurant and across the muddy road. Officer Teacup put his hand up like a stop sign. "Get back. This is a crime scene. Two people have been murdered."

I strutted around Officer Teacup and tapped on Ernie's arm. He made notes on his pad while looking inside the parked car. I snooped and asked, "What happened?"

He motioned for me to move. "It's Reed Gordon."

I moved back a few steps.

Ernie wandered around the car to the other side and talked to another cop. "Can you believe this? Reed just came home from the war and now, he's dead. His hands are crossed, and his pockets are turned inside out. The poor girl in the back seat is Patti Malvern. She's sprawled face-down."

Officer Teacup joined them, and I leaned on the car listening in. "Reed was shot twice, and they both have wounds in their head. Patti's purse was beside her in the seat."

Ernie wrote the specifics. "I've got this photo of her. I'm running it with the story in tomorrow's paper. I found this picture on the seat."

Drops of rain soaked my hair, and breakfast with Grandma got swallowed up in death. I removed the lucky acorn from my pocket and tossed it to the ground. My heart was as heavy as my wet shoes stuck in this muddy road.

Grandma called to me from the restaurant parking lot with her matter-of-fact, come now or get punished voice. "Shoelace, come inside. Your eggs are cold and your pancakes soggy. Leave Ernie alone."

I ignored her and watched another man in a police uniform drive up. Ernie went to the man. I shadowed him and Ernie shook the man's hand. "Can I get a quote for my story from Bowie County Sheriff Haskell Surratt this morning?"

He slapped Ernie on the back. "Hey, nephew. How's Ernie Surratt doing these days? Writing for the paper, I see." He gave him another hearty handshake. "I'll help you with whatever I can release to the community. We have two dead people. It's unclear what happened, but we know two innocent people lost their lives. I hope Officer Teacup didn't tell you any confidential details."

Ernie shook his head and jotted more notes on his tiny pad. I raised my head and tried to see what he wrote. Officer Teacup's voice made me jump. "Young lady, you're standing in a tire track. You've ruined part of the impression. Get back to the restaurant. Let us do our work."

My foot was stuck in the mud and the rain caused my hair to cling to my face. I ignored Officer Teacup and listened to Ernie double-check facts for his story. "Reed is wearing his Atlanta High School class ring. There's blood throughout the car, and blood is dripping from the bottom of the car door."

Officer Teacup moved to Sheriff Surratt, and I stood close enough to eavesdrop on him, too. "I found a blanket in the car and a .32 cartridge shell. It may be from a Colt."

Untied Shoelace

Grandma's screams for me escalated, and she came across the road like a tractor plowing a muddy field. "Shoelace. Inside, now. Let the police do their job. We need to get out of their way."

Back in the restaurant, Grandma sipped on coffee. I drank four glasses of orange juice, gulping, while watching out the window. I gobbled my food and tried to read lips through the glass, but the words were garbled.

After Grandma drove us home, I slipped off to my room. I felt numb. My first breakfast at a restaurant with her was now stained with two murders. Taddy tapped on my door, but I sent him away. I lay on my bed facing the shotgun, and I was afraid I'd have a nightmare if I fell asleep. So I just cried and held my lucky rock most of the afternoon.

**

The last few days of March kept Ernie busy writing stories and follow-up pieces. The radio talkers announced updates. Mostly, the same thing. "March 24, 1946. Texarkana lost Reed Gordon and Patti Malvern. Investigators are growing weary, but everything points to robbery. Sheriff Surratt believes the attack came from a transient."

"What's transient mean?" I asked Taddy.

"Transient is another word for hobo. Turn the station. The Mickey Mouse Theatre Show comes on in a minute."

I ran my hand through my hair. "My hobo friends don't kill people." I scratched my head. "Touch the dial and I'll beat you up." I pushed Taddy away from the radio.

Taddy put his hand on mine and helped me turn the radio dial to the children's show. "I want to sing. They play fun songs. Listen. They're singing, *Who's Afraid of the Big Bad Wolf?*"

I talked over the singing. "Did you know the police have talked to 200 people and now, there's a $500 reward?"

As the "big bad wolf" song repeated the chorus, I listed the clues in my mind from what I saw or heard at the restaurant. Details of the gun. Details in the car. Important clues. I wished Taddy had been there to capture the details in his mind.

Taddy snapped his fingers in my face. "Didn't you like the song? You'll find yourself singing it. Are you listening to me?"

I nodded, not paying attention to him. If I won the reward money, I could pay Grandma back for ruining the oven. If I had a few more clues, I could solve the murders. My feet tapped the floor with a new song, *Old MacDonald had a Farm.*

Grandma called to me from somewhere in the manor. "Shoelace, time to go. The memorial service is starting. We've got to go to Pastor Cody's house to pay our respects."

I ran toward her voice. "Coming."

Reed had moved in with Pastor Cody when he got home. They were more like brothers than cousins. If I have to watch people eat Pastor Cody's food like they ate at Daddy's memorial, I'll yank their plates from their hands. I hope the round lady stays home. Safer for her, safer for me.

Too bad Skip's not here to play the piano. He's in Heaven with Mama. I don't want to go. I don't want to see Billy Joe. I'm sorry his brother got murdered, but we're not really friends. I'd rather sit in my tree and write a poem. It's been four months since Daddy fell from the train, and my heart aches like it was yesterday.

I hurried to the carriage house, and my heart raced. I put my hand to my chest and stopped in the yard. I heard a voice. It was a sound like Daddy's voice and I twirled around. It wasn't him. Just a kid walking by on the road laughing with his pa.

My heart pounded with sadness all the way to Pastor Cody's house. Funerals are no fun. People just eat and talk and cry. Billy Joe will miss his brother more than ever today, an ache that will never quite go away. I will try and be nice. But it won't be easy.

CHAPTER TWENTY ONE

PEACE PIPE

PASTOR CODY'S TWO-STORY HOME sat on a big corner lot a few blocks from Rose Hill Cemetery. I counted three chimneys and two bathrooms. The memorial lasted for a million minutes or at least thirty. After the speech part, food appeared on the table, and people chewed on fried chicken and fluffy biscuits.

In the parlor, people cried and talked to Reed's mama and daddy. Their talks caused more sobs and hugs.

I shuffled through the hallway to the back porch. I saw Billy Joe sitting crossed-legged on the grass under the oak tree. He wiped his face, looked around, and lay down on his side. He bawled like a baby. Clara, the girl with fancy dresses who shared her orange with me at Daddy's funeral, reached him first. "Hi, Billy Joe. Can I sit with you?"

Billy Joe shrugged and wiped his eyes. "If you want to sit on the ground, I can't stop you."

I jogged to them, my overalls flapping on my legs. "Hi, Clara. You're wearing a bright yellow dress today. It's pretty." I used my good manners and my squeaky voice when I spoke to her. I sat next to Billy Joe.

Clara turned up her nose at me. "Annie Grace Kree. How do you know Billy Joe?"

Untied Shoelace

"I go to school with him. Did you know he's a great speller?"

Billy Joe squirmed and sat up. He crossed his legs. "Winning spelling bees is what you do. I come in second now."

Clara sighed. She dusted her dress off making sure the wrinkles on the yellow cotton got smoothed out. She pointed her finger at me. "Her daddy died a hobo, and she's a hobo."

Her words stung and I jumped to my feet. I moved inches from Clara's face, breathing like a steam engine. "My daddy may have lived on the rail, but he loved me. You have servants taking care of you." I spouted the words at her like the day I spit orange seeds on her sash. My hands formed into fists, and I swung a right hook at her nose.

Billy Joe jumped up and grabbed my hand. "Stop fighting. Peace. We should smoke a peace pipe like the Cowboys and Indians and become friends. My brother Reed would want us to."

Clara wrinkled her nose. "I don't smoke."

"We can pretend to. I'm Wolf-Reed Indian Chief and both of you, sit down, cross your legs and bring your peacemaking faces. You're the cowgirls."

Clara turned her nose higher and tip-toed toward the house, but she turned to dish out a few more remarks. "I'm not smoking a pretend peace pipe with Annie Grace. Besides, I'm no cowgirl. I'm a lady." She changed her face to sad and looked at Billy Joe. "I'm sorry your brother died. But I have to go. I don't care for hobo girls."

She galloped like a wild horse clomping on the porch stairs. My shoes ran for her, my arms waving in the air. "You're bratty and mean. I don't care for you, either." I grabbed her curly hair and twirled her around. "I'm gonna knock your teeth out."

"I'm telling on you. You should go back to your hobo people." Clara screamed.

Pastor Cody appeared. He stepped between Clara and me. "Shoelace, I have cake for you. Want a slice? You like chocolate. Your grandma told me."

I choked on spit. "Pastor Cody, I do like chocolate, but I have to do this first." I socked Clara in the jaw and then circled around Pastor Cody like a wild Indian. Clara crumpled like wrinkled cotton and cried for her mama.

"Come inside right now." Pastor Cody held my arm and ushered me into his house across the scuffed hardwood floors. He escorted me to a room past the parlor, a double door entrance to a library.

Billy Joe rushed to us. "I'm coming with you. Clara's mama might say I hit her if I stay out there."

Pastor Cody stepped into the room with Billy Joe and me. "You might enjoy this room. It's my thinking and praying room." Pastor Cody handed me the chocolate cake. "Stay in here for a bit."

He moved to Billy Joe, who sat in a large chair by the window, and squeezed in beside him. Billy Joe's eyes were gushing again. "I miss my brother. What will I do without him?"

Pastor Cody reached for Billy Joe's hand and cupped it in his. "Your parents told me you could stay here anytime you want. I can't fill your brother's shoes, but I can be a friend to you." Their talk was meant to be private, but I sat too close not to listen in.

"Why did my brother have to die? Who wanted to shoot him and Patti? They were getting married." Billy Joe pressed his face into Pastor Cody's chest.

Untied Shoelace

I stumbled to the book shelves and stared at two entire walls filled with books. I ran my fingers across the spine of several books. A couple smelled stale and damp, others were coated in dust.

The chatter in the other rooms grew quiet. Billy Joe and Pastor Cody's shoulders shook and their sobs grew louder than my ears could stand. Their moans turned to sniffles and I sat in the corner of the room holding my knees and rocking like I once did, months ago beneath the Harahan Bridge in Memphis.

"Billy Joe. Where are you?" A kind voice called for him.

"I'm in the library."

A woman peeked in the door. She held a cloth hanky and her face revealed red eyes. "We need to go home. Your papa's waiting in the car."

Billy Joe gave Pastor Cody a hug. "I love you. See you soon."

Billy Joe strode up to me and held out his hand. "Peace. Let's be friends. My brother would want me to follow in his footsteps."

I rose and clasped my hands around Billy Joe's neck, and he wrapped his arms around me.

He ran to the door. "See you at school. I'm going to win the next spelling bee."

"I bet you will." I stumbled backwards into the books as Billy Joe shut the door to the room.

Pastor Cody sat motionless. "Life is hard. Reed and I were best friends. We swam at Crystal Springs, fished at Spring Lake Park, and played baseball. I played first base. He played third on his team. At twenty nine, Reed became a hero in the war. He will always be my hero."

Pastor Cody strolled over to me. "Did you know heroes come in all sizes? They even wear PF Flyers." He ruffled my hair and peeked at my shoes.

"I'm no hero. I'm a hobo girl."

Pastor Cody moved to the books. "Reed loved to disappear inside the pages of books." He touched a brown cover and pulled a book from the shelf.

I peeked at the cover. "I used to read this book with Mahlee. She made me read on the rail, even though I argued with her. I lost my book in the Mississippi River."

Pastor Cody sat Indian style on the floor. "I love to read. This is the book my parents gave me for my eleventh birthday." He touched the wall, his gaze leaving me for a second.

The wood carvings made the permanent cases on the walls look like strong arms. Like Billy Joe's hug. I sat and crossed my legs, too.

Pastor Cody hugged the book. "My mother and father left this house to me. The fever got both of them when I was a teenager. Father was a pastor like me. Mother cooked for everyone." He wiped a tear from his cheek. "When my father wrapped his arms around the hobo, he became the arms of God. This is a big old house, and many of the hobos stay here." He put his hand under my chin and smiled. "Your daddy would have been welcome here, anytime."

"Me, too?"

"Absolutely. This house is for special people, like Annie Grace Kree." He tousled my hair. "You know, God loves you and He's made you to last."

He sounded like he meant what he said, but in my ears question marks flooded in. I wondered if God did love me. Or could. I glanced at my PF Flyers, happy they were mine, but I was sad that I took them. Could God love a borrower?

"Here, take this book. *Hero of Strange Hill* is yours, but it'll cost ya."

I pulled my pockets out. "Empty. I have nothing to pay you with."

"Actually, the book will cost you two things. Taddy needs help passing out hymnals at Church by the Creek on Saturdays. I need you to promise me you'll quit fighting. Your fighting is getting in the way of your living."

"Okay. But girls like Clara don't make it easy. She's mean."

"You might want to show Clara a little kindness. Behind her bossy ways, there's a nice girl lurking."

I rubbed my fists together. "I'll try. I'll do better. I promise." I wished I meant what I said. I've promised Ms. Reece, promised Grandma Elsie, promised Mahlee, and promised the principal, Mr. Meldrum. Now I've made a promise to a pastor. I'm bound to get in big trouble for lying to a pastor.

Pastor Cody stepped to the double doors leading from the library. "When you think of people as family, you treat them differently. Billy Joe thinks of you as a friend now, kind of like family."

Grandma Elsie stuck her head in the room. "It's getting late. I don't want to ride in the car after dark and make ourselves a target. Let's get going."

I ran to Grandma's side. "I've got a new book. A little boy becomes a hero for his family in here." I hollered at Pastor Cody, who disappeared down the hall. "Thank you for the book. I'll see you Saturday."

CHAPTER TWENTY TWO

MORE THAN A TOOTHACHE

MY TEETH CHATTERED, BUT I stayed in the water. "Hey, Taddy my toes are slimy. The bottom of this lake is gooey." I splashed water on Taddy and Billy Joe. I slipped when my right foot turned sideways, leaving my other foot stuck in the mud. With my overalls up at my knees, I stomped in the shallow water.

Taddy tossed his fish hook in the water. "Stop splashing. Don't get my clothes wet. Mama will get me if I get sick."

"Spring and water go together. See, those ducks like water. I can hear the lion at the zoo roaring. He likes this time of year, too. Even the flowers are blooming. I like yellow flowers. Don't you?" I pointed to the stone bridge that connected a small island to the main part of the park. "I'll get you a flower if you want."

"I don't like flowers. I'll just sneeze."

Taddy's allergic to cats, and if he keeps talking, he'll be allergic to lake water, too. I flapped more water his way. "Quack. Quack. Quack."

"Stop it. If you don't stop, I'm going to …"

I stepped in front of him. "Going to do what?" His short legs dangled over the edge of the stump. Billy Joe hopped in the water. He winked at me. We grabbed Taddy and yanked him head first into the lake.

Taddy wiped his face. "I'm soaking wet. Look at me. If my calculations are correct, I won't dry off before I get home."

I splashed water on his face. "Talk like a kid, not a grownup."

A water fight followed, along with the laughter and the dunking. Taddy first. Billy Joe second. Then they ganged up on me. Thankfully, we played in shallow water.

Pastor Cody moved from the shade where he read the newspaper. "You three are soaking wet. If you get sick, I'm gonna lose my hide." He tucked the paper under his arm, sat down, and removed his socks and shoes. "Water's not too cold."

Taddy and me grabbed Pastor Cody and pulled him into the lake. Billy Joe laughed hard and he fell backwards. A second water fight with Pastor Cody sent the four of us to the shore to catch our breath.

Pastor Cody picked up his shoes. "We better get going. The sun's going down, and we'll freeze. We look like wet dogs in a rain shower. Besides, see the 'no swimming' sign? We aren't supposed to be in the water."

I shivered, my teeth chattered, and my ears hurt. "We're not swimming. We're wading. Besides, I can't swim."

Taddy moved to grab the string of fish on his pole. "This is a good haul."

"Stop counting your fish. If you count them, you won't catch anymore."

Taddy shook his head. His grin looked like a catfish whose hook got loose from its gill. "We're going home. I can count them if I want to. Seven good ones. They will make for a good fish fry one night."

Billy Joe wrung out the water from the bottom of his shirt. "I'm cold."

"Me, too." I unrolled my overalls and they weighed my legs down. My shirt clung to my skin like moss on a tree. "Pastor Cody, I need dry clothes. I'm freezing. This wind hurts my bones."

Pastor Cody stepped to the dry grass. "I'll start the truck." His long legs sprinted across the playground to the parking lot.

I fell into the grass. The sun shone low, but the wind caused chill bumps to race up my arms. I waited for Billy Joe and Taddy to put their shoes on, and shook.

The last three weeks, Taddy and Billy Joe passed out songbooks with me at Church by the Creek. I only handed out two songbooks, but at least I showed up. I kept my promise to Pastor.

During the week, after school, I also watered my plants hoping for peanuts in the fall. Mr. Darnell caught the train to Georgia last week. He'll return in October for the fair. He got the contract.

"Load up. It's getting dark," Pastor Cody called.

I ran with Taddy and Billy Joe to the truck. We piled in like sardines and I sat next to Pastor Cody. Pastor Cody hums when he drives. Which made me hum, too.

Pastor Cody stopped the truck in front of the manor and let Taddy and me out. "See you both tomorrow at my old home church for the Easter program. Nine o'clock sharp."

"Thanks for taking us to the park." I waved a penguin goodbye and waddled to the porch.

Taddy ran past me. "Bye Pastor. See you tomorrow. Drink orange juice and take vitamins. Stay well." Taddy handed his fish to Grandma and went to change his clothes.

I peeked into the kitchen, dripping water on the hardwood floor. I smeared the puddle with my toes, hoping the water dried before Grandma saw the mess.

Untied Shoelace

"Shoelace, you're getting the floor wet," Grandma said. "Why are your clothes soaked?"

I didn't answer and licked my lips at seeing the meatloaf and mashed potatoes on the table. Grandma had cooked the meal at Priscilla's apartment since the kitchen at the manor is still closed. Thankfully, Priscilla's kitchen is open.

Ernie placed knives and forks on the table. From behind me a *tap-tap-tap* on the stairs came closer. Mahlee sauntered down the steps, not even saying hello, going right by me. She was a clunky ballerina in her old boots clumping across the floor. She had tucked her hair behind her ears with bobby pins and I could tell she wore one skirt, not three, on this day. She also wore one top. On her finger, the blue ring sparkled, matching her eyes.

"Ernie, let me help you with those plates." Mahlee sang.

Her goo-goo talk caused me to shiver. Mahlee and Ernie acted mushy, like teens who sit together at the movie theater. What she sees in Ernie I'll never know.

Grandma squinted at me. "Shoelace, change your clothes and dry off."

I disappeared for dry overalls, and then flew downstairs and sat at the kitchen table. I gobbled up four biscuits and ate all the potatoes on my plate. I had room for a small piece of meatloaf. I'd get more later on. Cold meatloaf is great.

Mahlee leaned close to listen to Ernie, her hair draped on his shoulder. He whispered stuff in her ear, and she giggled.

Chops meowed.

Mahlee bent down to look under the table. "Sorry, Chops. Didn't mean to kick you." She turned her face to Ernie and Chops waddled from the room.

"Has anyone noticed that Chops is getting fat?" No one heard me.

Grandma turned to Priscilla. "The Easter play will be one to remember. The folks at this church do everything big."

Priscilla hummed a tune under her breath and leaned against her chair. "I love this time of year. I'm looking forward to the services in the morning."

Taddy's head drooped and his arm lay in his uneaten potatoes.

I crept up behind Taddy and knocked his arm off the table. He jerked awake. "More potatoes, please." He wiped his eyes.

Priscilla's grin popped out. "Son, time for bed. We've got a big day planned for Sunday. Head on up. I'll be there in a second."

"Goodnight. I'm going to bed, too." I raised my eyebrows, glancing at each one of them. No one noticed me or listened. They were busy talking and I shuffled up to my room, tired from a day of Saturday church and swimming.

I blinked my tired eyes and tucked my hand under the pillow, ready to give in to the night.

Grandma joined me in the bed. "Dishes are done. I'm exhausted." Her shotgun was our dividing line. "Night, Shoelace. Sweet dreams." Grandma kissed me on the head and tucked the quilt under my chin.

Things changed as soon as I closed my eyes. I'm unsure of why I ran beside the train. Or how I got there. My surroundings changed … everything changed … and the gravel shook. My PF Flyers slid across the ground and an earthquake rumbled below me. I ran behind Skip and Daddy as we planned to catch the train out of Texarkana.

"Skip, pull me up. Daddy, take my hand." Skip and Daddy climbed the ladder to the boxcar ahead of me. They stood like statues in the open boxcar door. Skip grinned, while Daddy laughed a wicked cry. One-by-one their teeth fell out of their mouths dropping to the gravel in front of me.

"Daddy what's wrong with you? Pull me up. It's Geronimo, ride-the-magic-carpet time. Skip, your teeth are on the ground. Your teeth are too, Daddy. What's happening? Daddy, pull me up."

Daddy's hand reached for me, his fingers broke off at the knuckles, and blood dripped from them like water faucets running in a kitchen.

I rubbed my face, pinched myself, and screamed. "Daddy, save me." I ran beside the train. Skip's face blurred like melting butter on top of a hot muffin. His face formed into a new face with new skin and he looked like Jack Hall, the man attacked by the huff-puff man. Daddy's face melted away and re-formed into the face of Martha Long. He held a cup of warm coffee, the steam rising into his nostrils like smoke from a steam engine.

Daddy's and Skip's grins faded and their faces became ghostly glares as their bones got new skin with new cheeks, eyebrows, and lips, without teeth. Daddy looked like Reed Gordon this time. Skip looked like Patti Malvern.

"Daddy, where are you? Skip, come back."

I rubbed my eyes. They stung. I shook my head. I plunged to the gravel as the train clacked on the rail. Surrounded by the teeth, I picked up a handful of molars. They dissolved in my hand like ice melting, and turned to ash.

I rose to my feet and lost my footing when a giant tooth the size of a coal car knocked me down the hill. My body became a wheelbarrow without wheels. My untied PF Flyers slipped off my feet and my shoes floated to a shoreline by a lake, a pond filled with fish swimming in mid-air. An oak tree shaded my shoes from the moon's light and the clock struck midnight off in the distance.

The Blanton Street brothers stood at the top of the ravine, laughing. They pointed at my shoes and ran for them. "No, those are my PF Flyers. I found them in St Louis." I bounced like a rubber ball, saw the sky every other bounce, and the moon. A man sat on the crescent moon, and his black boots dangled. He waved at me.

The cliff … I sailed over the edge losing my sense of balance. Everything turned dark, and I crashed with a THUD.

I awoke to Grandma's voice. "Shoelace, did you have another nightmare?" Grandma leaned over her shotgun, reaching for me on the floor.

"I think so. I don't remember any of it." I wished the floor felt softer and less gritty. "I'm going downstairs to get a drink."

Grandma resumed her snoring before I even shut the door.

In the kitchen, I cracked the door open to the ice box and scoured the shelves for leftover meatloaf. A full tummy might keep me from dreaming and falling out of bed. "Where is the meatloaf? We had plenty left from supper tonight."

"I ate the meatloaf." The shadow spoke from the kitchen table.

My socked feet went opposite ways, sending me to the floor, and my head slammed into a rack in the ice box. "Ernie, you scared me to death." I tottered to the table, pulled out a chair, and Chops squealed.

Sitting down, I folded my hands on the table. "None left? No meatloaf? Did you eat the biscuits, too?"

"Yes. Working these odd hours at the paper, I eat at the wrong times. I get hungry at night."

In the shadow of the light coming through the kitchen window, Ernie held a cloth to his face.

"What did you do? Did you cut your face shaving?"

"No, I have a toothache. I made a dentist appointment for Monday, but when I eat, the tooth hurts."

"So stop eating." I patted my face wondering if I'd ever have a toothache.

Ernie rubbed his jaw again. "I hope I can tolerate this shooting pain in my jaw till Monday. Hopefully, this ice will help numb it." His red eyes made my eyes water.

"Hurts bad, huh?" I rubbed my face again thinking how bad he must feel.

Ernie put the rag on the table. "Makes me want to pull my teeth out and toss every single tooth to the ground."

I remembered that my dream had teeth falling, a giant tooth, and PF Flyers by the shore. Oh no! I left my shoes at the park today with Grandma's keys in them. I tore out of the kitchen, stepping on Chops' tail.

Hurrying to Mahlee's room by the circle window upstairs, I stepped inside without knocking.

"Mahlee, wake up." I shook her, turned her chin toward me, grabbed her nose, and pinched it. She snorted but slept on. I whispered faster than Ernie chewing food. "I accidentally put Grandma's keys in my pocket and I stuck them inside one of my shoes when I played in the water. I left my shoes at the park."

She snored.

I slapped her face. "Mahlee. I have to get my shoes and those keys. Grandma's gonna need them for Sunday church in the morning. I can't wait. I have to go now. This won't take long."

"Not now. We'll go in the morning." Mahlee rolled over on her cot, her tin can held close to her side.

"I'm going alone. I'll go without you if I have to." I threatened, hoping she'd get up. "I'm leaving. Going. Gone." I shut the door and stood outside her room.

She cracked the door. "Are you waiting on me?" She tapped me on the head. "Why did you have your grandma's keys?"

"My hat was in her car and the car was locked. I wanted my hat to wear it to the park, and I forgot to put the keys back. The park is just down the tracks. We can see to get there. The moon's full."

I motioned for her to follow me to my room. I slipped on my Oxfords, and we climbed down the oak tree since Ernie was nursing his tooth in the kitchen.

Mahlee yawned most of the way. I pulled on her hand. "We're almost there."

She yawned again, but with an owl this time. "I'm sleepy. Why did I let you talk me into this?" The frogs kept time with Mahlee's mumbling.

"There's the lake. I left my shoes by the oak tree where Taddy caught his fish." I ran ahead, the moon lighting my way.

I called to Mahlee, who was snorting and yawning. "I found my PF Flyers." I put Grandma's keys in my pocket and my socks. I had one shoe on when Mahlee caught up. I slipped the other one on.

Mahlee tapped me on the shoulder. "Who's in the shadows over there? I see a reflection of someone in the water. See? Look there." Mahlee grabbed my hand and yanked me to my feet before I tied my shoes. She moved us behind the oak. "Look. Near the swings."

"You're trying to scare me. I'll hurry." I laughed at her, but the gaze she held on the object across the water caused me to shiver. I stopped laughing.

She pulled me close to her. "Someone is wearing a white mask. We've got to go. Run as fast as you can to the tracks. Now."

We sprinted like deer in the woods, cutting by the dirt road near the park entrance. At the bend in the road, my foot slammed into a hard blob. I tumbled and plummeted to the ground as Mahlee kept on going along the road toward the tracks.

"Mahlee . . . Mahlee . . ." My arm throbbed from the fall. My shoulder had slammed into a leather case and it popped open. "What is this? A horn?" The case had stickers on the outside and velvet on the inside.

Dazed, I stood and tripped again. This time, on a soft, warm blob. A wheezing came from the blob and made a gurgling noise. Was it a sick deer or a hurt dog?

Mahlee came back for me, yanked on my arm, and tugged me along. "If the hooded man saw us at the park, he could be following us." Mahlee pushed me, her breathing quick and heavy, echoing with another sound in the woods. As we moved along the tracks, the echo faded and the moon shone brighter.

At the manor, we climbed the oak tree in giant leaps and snuck into the house.

I sat by the wall next to the bed. Grandma's breath was the lone noise in the house. I put my hands around my knees and cried, trying to be quiet.

Mahlee sat next to me, rocking, taking my hand in hers.

After a few minutes, Mahlee slipped off to her room and shut the door.

I went downstairs and hung Grandma's keys on the hook and raced up to my room. I fell into my bed and dozed off with my pillow wrapped around my head. My dreams took me back to the park with running, screaming, and someone pushing me under the water in the lake.

When Grandma hollered for me from downstairs, my body ached from staying up too late and from fighting off someone in my nightmares. "Shoelace, what are your Oxfords doing on the front porch?"

I stepped part way down the stairs and peeked over the rail. "What did you say? What's on the porch?"

Grandma stood at the bottom of the stairs looking at me, the morning paper in her hand. "Come see for yourself. You left them on the porch. A dog could have carried them off. Shoes are expensive."

I dashed down the stairs to the front room and headed to the oval door. Through the glass, I saw them. My Oxfords. The ones I left behind at the park last night when I put my PF Flyers on.

Grandma marched up behind me. "Are those your shoes?"

I coughed and rubbed my face with both hands, as crusty things crumbled from my eyes. "Yes, they are."

"Better bring them in."

I opened the door, knelt down, and touched the black and white leather. "The laces are tied in perfect bows." I stood and glanced down Beech Street. To my left, I saw the train leaving town. The lone whistle blew three times. To my right, the church bell chimed a hollow dong and a few birds chirped in trees.

Who brought my shoes home? Who would bring my shoes to the porch? And who would take the time to tie the laces?

Mahlee joined me, and we stood with our mouths open. Mahlee used her mumbling voice. "The masked man knows where we live." She turned her head every which way, and whispered, "Dear God. Why is it always so dark? Please roll away the darkness. Send us your light."

The door slammed against the wall and Taddy rushed to the porch. "What are you doing out here? We've got to get ready for church. Today is the Easter program."

CHAPTER TWENTY THREE

BIG BAD WOLF

"PASTOR CLINE LOOKS LIKE LUMPY mashed potatoes in his suit. He needs a bigger size." I whispered to Taddy from my seat in the pew.

"Shhhh. This is where you sing and stop talking for a minute." Taddy's words kept beat with the music bouncing off the walls in the church.

I pointed to the stained glass window on the side wall. "Look, the light coming through the window is shining a rainbow on my lap. I can take the rainbow home." I cupped my hands and guided the beam of rainbow colors into my overalls pocket.

Taddy handed me his songbook. "Stop talking and sing."

I opened my mouth and gave Taddy what he asked for.

Taddy turned to me. "What are you singing?"

Taddy continued in the group sing-along before I could answer. "Tell me the story of Jesus. Tell me the story of Jesus. Wonderful, wonderful story of Jesus, the crucified One."

I sang in Taddy's ear again, tossing my less than churchy song straight into his eardrum. My song caused him to slam my songbook and smash my finger in the pages.

"Ouch." I gave Taddy the elbow.

"Sing a church song." Taddy chimed at the top of his lungs. The voices around us drowned out his voice, but I could read his lips.

I whispered. "I'll sing what I want. I'm singing my new favorite song to you. You taught it to me a few weeks ago when we listened to the radio in the parlor."

"What? When? Give me the exact time."

"The song goes like this. Who's afraid of the big bad wolf, the big bad wolf, the big bad wolf?" I sang right into his ear.

Grandma tapped my leg, a firm pat to be quiet.

Taddy whispered, "You need to sing church songs in church."

I wrinkled my nose and howled like a wolf. "Ooweeee…" I pursed my lips and copied the sounds the lady in front of me sang, squeaky ones, shrill.

The man behind me leaned forward. "Slap that woman. Make her stop."

Taddy slugged my arm. "Stop your howling. We'll get in trouble. Pastor Cody invited us, and you need to act right."

"I can sing if I want to."

"But if you keep howling and singing 'big-bad wolf,' we will have our first fight."

"Will we? You would get your dress pants dirty, and I would win."

Priscilla leaned forward on the other side of Taddy and put her finger to her lips. "Both of you. Shhhh …"

I flipped through the pages of my songbook, glancing past Grandma to my right. Mahlee's fingers wrapped around Ernie's fingers and they grinned at each other. *Yuck.* Their singing blended with the soprano lady, although they missed most of the words since they were making goo-goo eyes at each other.

The song ended, and the music man spoke from the stage. "Let's prepare our hearts to celebrate the resurrection of Jesus since Easter is next Sunday."

I scratched my leg, bent over, tied my shoe, and nearly fell off the pew. Clara had perched herself on the same row but across the aisle. I caught her watching us. I tapped Taddy's leg. "Clara has Oxfords like mine. I should give her mine. Oh wait, she probably has six pair."

"Leave her alone." Taddy sat tall, nudging me to do the same. "The play is beginning. Pastor Cody is playing the part of Jesus."

Kaboom. The double doors in the rear of the church building swung open, crashing into the wall. Heads turned. I got on my knees and turned to see if the characters for the play entered the building. Four people were dressed in sheets, a couple carried swords, and one group wore gold helmets.

"Did they have cops in the Bible?" I pointed to Officer Teacup, who hugged the wall in the back.

"No, no cops." Taddy craned his neck. "Where?"

I turned Taddy's chin in the right direction.

"Back there. By the lady in the purple hat with a bow the size of a boxcar. He's moving along the wall and now he's talking to the pastor at the side, next to the stage." I twisted around and sat down. I wasn't watching Jesus anymore, but I was keeping my eyes on Officer Teacup. I wanted to wave and let him know I came to church. He might not call me a delinquent if he saw me.

Pastor Cline ran to the front, interrupting the play. "I hate to do this. We have an emergency in town. The police need our help."

Officer Teacup stepped in front of the sheet people and the gold helmets. "I need you men to come with me. A man was murdered last night. This one happened in our backyard." The ladies gasped and the men asked questions.

Chatter rose like a funeral song. My ears hurt. Listening to the people howl in fear confused me. *Tell us what happened? Should we get our guns?* My ears blocked out the noise, and I went numb as the nightmare of last night flashed across my mind. I remembered touching the warm blob and the shadows raced passed my eyes, and I remembered how the blob moved, how it whimpered when I toppled over it. I remembered the hand . . . a woman's fingers with red nail polish.

"No. No. No. No." I held my head and twisted from side to side. I slid from the pew like a worm trying to get off a fish hook, grabbed my knees, and wailed. "No. No. No. I want my daddy. I want to go to the camps. To the rail. To go back before the dead bodies."

I grabbed my ears, the memory of last night howled in my heart and shouted at my mind like a pack of wolves circling me. I wanted to scream, to ask this nightmare to leave. I rocked … the ache ran deep. I could hardly breathe.

Officer Teacup kept talking despite my outburst and Grandma patted my head while listening to the officer. "The murder happened behind the church at Spring Lake Park. Peyton Mars is dead. His body was left on North Park Road. Someone found him early this morning around six. We found his Ford Coupe, but Bay Jo Baxter is missing. He gave her a ride from the VFW after she finished playing at the dance last night."

I rocked and cried, and Taddy crawled to the floor to sit with me between the pews. "What's wrong? Dead bodies? What's going on?"

I glanced around. "I have to tell you a secret." Clara watched me from across the aisle. The grownups talked murder, and I pulled Taddy in closer to block Clara from my view. "Mahlee and me snuck out to get my PF Flyers during the night. I left them at the park after coming home barefooted yesterday."

"Why go at night?"

"I had Grandma's car keys in my pocket and tossed them inside my shoes when we waded in the lake. Last night I remembered the keys, and I begged Mahlee to go with me. She hiked to the park with me."

My throat tightened. I had to tell him the rest. "When I found my PF Flyers and the keys, Mahlee got spooked saying she saw a masked man across the lake."

Taddy's breath became shallow. "Did she?"

"Yes. I saw the white hood in the water, too. And we ran away. When I was running, I stumbled over something. It was a horn and I saw a woman's hand in the dark."

Taddy wiped his eyes. "How do you know it was a woman's hand?"

"Because her fingernails were painted red."

"Are you positive?"

"Pretty sure. I didn't remember seeing the hand until a minute ago." I coughed and gagged on the fear burning inside my throat. I rose to my feet and plopped in the pew.

Taddy reeled himself up and did the same. He sighed with a gasp. Inhaled. And sighed, again.

The chaos and shouts, the screams and talking, and the rattling in my head sounded like a dozen radios all on the wrong station.

I grabbed Taddy by the neck. "The woman sighed like you just did, when I rolled across her. And now, she might be dead."

Taddy wrapped his arms around my neck. "It's not your fault."

I sobbed, my breaths jerky like I might run out of air. I followed Taddy to the rear of the church behind the last of the people leaving the building.

A sticker caught my eye. It was stuck on the seat in the pew where the lady with the purple hat once sat. I picked the paper up. Part of it was torn, but I could still make out the words, *Texas High School*. I held my breath and plummeted to the floor.

Taddy touched my shoulder and I jumped.

"See this sticker? It's like the one on the music case." I folded my fingers and put it in my pocket.

Taddy pulled on my arm. "Let the police figure this out. Mama said to get you."

In the car, I held my hand on my chest checking the thumps. I waited for my chest to cave in or for my heart to stop. Out the window, I watched a group of men join the other cops. Pastor Cody ran to Officer Teacup and disappeared into the woods.

Ernie kissed Mahlee on the cheek, leaving her. Another news story would have his name on it in the paper tomorrow. He joined the search party with pen and paper in hand.

Women and children piled into cars and engines roared. They left, tires squealing.

Grandma Elsie, Mahlee, and Priscilla made speculations and talked nonstop on the drive home. Taddy sat up, listening to every word.

At the manor, Mahlee slipped upstairs to her room. Priscilla and Grandma fixed a meal, and Taddy and me found a chair at the table.

Priscilla chimed in. "I hope they find the girl. Her mother works at Belk Jones and Bay Jo goes to Texas High School. She's plays saxophone with the Tonenaires on the weekends at the VFW. Poor thing. She's a young girl with her whole life ahead of her."

I touched my pocket, the one with the sticker, and wondered if I had really tripped over a person last night. I nearly threw up, held my breath, and gagged on snot that ran down the back of my throat.

Grandma hugged me and handed me a tissue. "In February, we had an attack by Robison Road. In March, we lost Reed and Patti and now, we have another crime. I hope the police figure out who is loose in our town."

"Meowwww ... Meowwww..."

"Where's Chops? He sounds hurt." I bent my neck, listening for which way the meows came. I followed his cries to my bedroom. "Oh no. Grandma, hurry. Quick."

Grandma, Priscilla, and Taddy rushed up the stairs. Mahlee called from across the hall. "Shoelace, what's wrong?"

"Out here, on the balcony. Chops is bleeding. Help him."

Mahlee ran to the balcony and cradled Chops. She placed him on a quilt, wrapping him in the folds of fabric. "Shoelace, I hate to tell you this."

"No. he's not going to die, too." I hit the wall.

"Shoelace. Chops is having kittens. Chops is a girl."

Priscilla bent down. "Awe. Look at the white one."

Grandma stood behind me. "Chops is having kittens?"

Taddy pushed me aside. "Kittens? We have more cats?" *Achoo. Achoo.*

I pushed him back. "Get off the balcony, and go sit on my bed. You're scaring Chops."

Taddy moved clear across the room. "I'm allergic to girl cats, too."

During the next hour, Chops meowed and meowed, and she gave birth to three more kittens. Three gray kittens to go with the white one.

Grandma, Priscilla, and Mahlee wandered downstairs. I talked to Chops. "You will need a new name."

Taddy answered from across my bedroom through the open door. "We should call him, I mean her, Cleopatra."

"Cleopatra? Pick another name."

"Let's call her Prissy."

"No. Think of another name." I pulled open my pocket and let a piece of the rainbow add color to Chops and her kittens.

"What are you doing?" Taddy asked.

"I'm letting the rainbow shine on Chops. Hey, we can call Chops, Rainbow."

Taddy nodded. "I like Rainbow. She's gray. She could use a colorful name."

Downstairs, the screen door on the kitchen slammed and Ernie's voice rattled off words. Taddy hopped up. "I'm going to see what Ernie found out."

"Wait. I have something else to tell you about last night."

He came across the balcony sneezing six times in a row. "Go to my bed, away from the cats. I'll come to you." I closed my pocket saving part of the rainbow.

We sat on the bed. "When I put my PF Flyers on at the park last night, I left my Oxfords behind by a tree. I forgot them. Remember how you came out to the porch this morning?"

"Yea. What were you doing?"

"My Oxfords were on the porch. Someone brought them to the manor and the laces were tied in bows. Weird, huh?"

Before Taddy answered, the screams and cries from downstairs sent us running to the kitchen.

Ernie held Mahlee's head against his chest. "Bay Jo Baxter's dead. She was found two miles from Peyton Mars' body on Morris Lane. They were both shot."

Ernie's face turned red. His words backed up in his mouth. His hand went to his face, he swallowed, and the tears dropped with each word. "Bay Jo wore a buttoned overcoat. Her right hand was put in her pocket. Her left hand was outstretched on the ground. The police are saying the weapon used is the same as the first double murder, a .32 automatic Colt pistol." Ernie paused and rubbed his chin. His eyes red, he blinked. "One more thing. Her saxophone is missing."

"How do they know? Maybe the horn is in the woods or on the side of the road." I closed my mouth before I let out more than I should.

"They're searching for it."

I listened to the grownups talk about murder, talk about how this happened right before Easter, and how scared everyone is to leave their homes.

I made my way to Rainbow on the balcony and rubbed the tiny paws of her kittens. Taddy came to the bedroom door. "If you're going to play with the cats, I'm going back downstairs."

"I'll be there in a minute." I cuddled the white kitten. "I'll call you White Beard after my hobo friend in Memphis." The names of the three gray kittens would wait until I could tell them apart.

For most of the afternoon, I watched the wiggly fur balls. Taddy returned to the top of the stairs singing. "Who's afraid of the big bad wolf, the big bad wolf, the big bad wolf?"

I whispered to the white kitten. "I am."

CHAPTER TWENTY FOUR

THE PHANTOM KILLER

ERNIE PARKED THE CREAM-COLORED car with the red rims next to the manor and I watched him step from the car jingling the keys, whistling. I was watering my peanut plants trying to see who was with him. He was alone.

Ernie rocketed over the fence and ran to the screen door of the kitchen. "Come see my new car."

I ran toward him and accidentally squirted him with the hose.

"Girl, put the hose down."

"Sorry." I tossed the hose to the ground. "What kind of car is that?"

"A 1946 Studebaker Skyway Champion. Cost me a pretty penny. Mahlee will look nice sitting in the front seat with me."

"You're a big time reporter with your own wheels."

The screen door creaked, and I glanced to see who came outside. Mahlee jumped toward Ernie's arms from the top step, knocking him to the ground. Ernie's a small man and Mahlee's too big for catching.

"What's going on out here?" Grandma carried a bucket of nails, a roll of string, and a pan.

Ernie pointed at the Studebaker. "I've bought my first car by saving all my extra money from this past year. I'm making enough to get my own place, too."

Grandma dropped a pan. "Your own place? This is your home. You're welcome here as long as you'll stay."

Taddy barreled from the house with Priscilla behind him. "Who has a new car? Ernie?"

I pretended to have facts filed in my brain. "It's a 1946 Studebaker Skyway Champion."

Taddy climbed the picket fence. "Cream. Nice color." He ran his hand along the curves and opened the door on the passenger side of the car to look inside.

I joined Taddy and ran my hand along the side panel. Ernie hopped the fence. "Hands off. Let's keep the scratches off for a few days."

Grandma shuffled to the picket fence. "We'll need a gate since you're parking on the side of the house. Slow Tom and Fast Tim will need to get to work before one of you falls."

"Yeow." Mahlee caught her skirt on the fence and hit the dirt, a puff of sand flew into her eyes.

Ernie helped Mahlee to her feet. "Darling, are you hurt?"

I whispered in Taddy's ear. "He's calling her darling. They talk silly to each other. Like boyfriend and girlfriend."

Taddy shook his head. "They like each other. You must be blind."

I bumped my shoulder against his. "They should stay friends. Ernie's not her type."

Mahlee smiled at Ernie and slipped her arm around his waist. "Take me for a ride."

Ernie blushed. "Sure thing. Let me get the door for you."

"I want to go. Taddy and me can ride in the back seat." I wanted to make sure I got the first ride, too.

"Shoelace, this is Ernie's car. Let them ride alone first. You can ride tomorrow." Grandma shook her head and put me to work. "I've got more pots and pans and string in the house

162

on the kitchen table. Buhrman Pharr sold me their last bullets earlier, too. Hope I don't need them."

"What am I doing with the pots and pans, and all this string?"

"You're in charge of making an obstacle course in the yard, around the house. Loop the string through the handles of the pots and hang them on the fence, on tree limbs, and on bushes. In the dark, if an intruder hits the string, the clanking noises will wake us and I'll get my gun." Grandma tossed me her do-it-now, do-it-right-look.

Grandma and Priscilla returned to their barricading inside, looping string and pots together across every window in the front room and the parlor. Grandma had nailed the windows shut upstairs. Hope we don't need to escape through a nailed window.

I ran to the kitchen and caught Grandma with a load of pots in her hand. "If you hang pots on the balcony door watch out for my White Beard and the Three Stooges."

Grandma laughed. "Three Stooges? Are you calling the gray kittens Larry, Moe, and Curly?"

"Yes. Taddy and me saw the movie at the Sanger Theatre two times one Saturday. The names fit. That's the movie place where the usher shines his flashlight in my face when I talk during the show." I ran to the yard and crashed into Taddy on the way out.

"Watch where you're going."

"Sorry."

Grandma left my stack of pots and pans and string by the steps, but I had to finish watering if I was going to have peanuts growing by the fall.

She stuck her head out the door. "Shoelace, I see you over there. Get to work."

I hurried to the screen door with the hose in my hand and stuck my head inside calling to Grandma who had gone back inside. "I just need a few more minutes."

"Get that hose out of this house. You're watering the kitchen." Grandma took the hose from my hand and tossed it to the yard.

"Sorry. I'll wipe this up." I grabbed a cloth by the sink and Grandma went back to her nails in the front room.

Taddy peeked in. "Why are you on your knees?"

I tossed the rag at him. "I hosed down the floor by accident. You could help me."

Taddy crossed one foot over the other and leaned against the wall, rubbing his chin. "So tell me how we're going to get the reward money. The radio announced that it's up to $2,000."

I wiped the floor with another dry rag, sat down, and crossed my legs. "Let's team up. We can split the reward. We'll need Ernie's help to get the scoop."

"You have a problem keeping your word. You break promises."

I stood, moved to the back door and saw the pots and pans. "I've got to booby trap the yard. By the way, you tell anyone we're investigating the murders, and I'll tell the kids at school how smart you are."

Taddy followed me out the door. "So this means we're in business?"

"I guess so. I'm the sheriff and you can be my deputy."

"I want to be the sheriff."

"I'm older than you by a whole month. I'm in charge. Deal?"

Taddy held the string to help me with my chore. He whispered, "Deal. But I would make a better sheriff."

164

Untied Shoelace

Ernie drove up from his drive with Mahlee as I hung a frying pan from a limb. I barely let him get out of the car before rushing to him with questions. "Hey Ernie. How did you come up with the name Phantom Killer in your story? Do the police have a bunch of leads? Is it the preacher's son? Kids at school said it's the preacher's boy who lives out on a farm near Maud. A teacher told another teacher a crazy man did it. Or is it the sheriff's son who stays at the sanitarium?"

Ernie shooed Mahlee into the house before answering me. "Leave the sheriff and his family out of this. He's my uncle. His son is not involved."

I pressed on. "Did anyone find the saxophone? Do they have any idea who took it?"

Ernie raised one eyebrow and squinted at me. He backed me against the fence. "What do you know?"

"Nothing. I'm seeing what you know."

Taddy interrupted our conversation. "I love your car. Does it drive smooth? Can we go for a ride? The sun's still up."

"Sorry kiddo. I'm running across town to do another story. There's too many cars being stolen in town. I'd rather cover the murders, but I have to do these stories, too." Ernie hopped into the driver's seat, waving bye to us.

Taddy shook his head. "You nearly told him you saw the saxophone. You keeping a secret is like Ernie not writing a story. You spill your guts. I should be the sheriff in our investigation. You talk too much."

"Not gonna happen. I'm the sheriff." I jumped over the fence, picked up the water hose, and squirted Taddy from head to toe. "Remember we're a team. But I'm the boss."

"Stop it. These are my school clothes."

Taddy grabbed the hose from me and soaked my overalls. We laughed and watered the entire yard making a puddle the size of a small pond by the back door.

Grandma showed up. "You're soaking wet. You get wet more than anybody. What am I going to do with you?"

"Taddy is wet, too." I pulled him in front of me. "See. Wet."

"She hosed me down," Taddy whined. "I paid her back."

"Turn the hose off, and both of you put on dry clothes."

I wandered upstairs leaving little puddles on each step. I called from the top. "Where's Mahlee? I want to see if she likes Ernie's new car."

Priscilla moved into view at the bottom by the railing. "She's resting in her room until supper."

Grandma called to me from the kitchen. "Dry clothes. Now."

I stopped by Mahlee's door. She used to cry late at night inside boxcars as we rode across the country. She would mumble and pray, and cry and sway. She always ended her spells by asking God, *why is it always so dark?* I put my hand on her bedroom door. "I hope she's okay."

"Young lady, hurry and change, and get back to hanging pots in the bushes." Grandma ordered.

Before I went to my room, Grandma told Priscilla. "These are nightmarish times, and I'm scared. What if the murderer is someone we know?"

Back in the yard, I finished hanging pots and pans on the fence and Taddy hung a few on the hedge by the front porch. The booby traps were set. We finished in less than an hour. I celebrated by beating a pan with a stick and shouting like an Indian announcing to the world my chores were finished.

"You sound like an Indian Chief, not a sheriff," Taddy mouthed.

Thubalup. Thubalup. Thubalup. A horse trotted down the road and Taddy and me ran to the fence.

Untied Shoelace

Taddy pointed at the man in the saddle. "Who's that?"

CHAPTER TWENTY FIVE

THE LONE RANGER RIDES AGAIN

"I'M LOOKING FOR ERNIE SURRATT. Do you kids know him?" The Spanish man wearing a ten-gallon hat sounded like the judge in Boone, Missouri. But this man had two guns and both of his arms.

I rushed to the porch, opened the door, and called for Grandma. "This man wants Ernie."

The horse kicked at the fence and the pans clamored. The clashing sounds caused the horse to buck. Dust swirled from the ground like little whirlwinds and settled in clumps as the man pulled on the reigns. The horse snorted and neighed.

"Is this where reporter Ernie Surratt lives? I'm JJ Ross, Texas Ranger. I'm staying at the Grim Hotel. I'll stay in Texarkana until I catch the Phantom Killer. Mr. Surratt can interview me and his story in the newspaper will let everyone in town know I'm here."

I leaned on the gate and pointed my stick at the Texas Ranger. "Ernie drove away a few minutes ago. He's writing a story on stolen cars. He'll be gone for hours."

JJ Ross climbed off his horse and tied the reigns to the fence. "I'll wait. Mind if I sit on the porch?"

Grandma invited him inside instead. "Supper's on the table. Won't you join us?"

I stepped between the Texas Ranger and Grandma. "I'm sure he ate supper at the Grim."

The man in the khaki suit and boots strutted across the porch and into the manor. "I'd be happy to join you for supper."

JJ Ross winked at me. "You better help your grandma pull the blinds when it gets dark, and I'd suggest you sleep on the floor on pallets. Stay away from the windows. You might get shot. And keep the doors latched."

JJ Ross gobbled Grandma's food like hungry folks at a funeral. He bragged on how he captured bad men, and Priscilla kept watching him, devouring every word. She smiled and thanked him for being in Texarkana to protect us. I wish he'd protected the lemon pie, but instead he ate two slices and asked for three cups of coffee.

Thirty minutes later, which felt like four days, Ernie jogged into the kitchen. He put his hand on Mahlee's shoulder and kissed the top of her head. Then he reached out and shook the ranger's hand. "Are you JJ Ross? My editor told me you stopped by the office."

"You're looking at him. I'm known for getting my man. I want to put a bulletin in the paper to get the word out regarding the gold-plated saxophone."

I moved my chair next to JJ Ross, who looked like the Lone Ranger. He kept his hat on through our meal. Grandma makes me take my engineer's cap off at the table. She should have knocked his hat off for being disrespectful. "Are you going to catch the killer?"

JJ Ross winked at me. "This is grownup talk, little girl. Best you leave us to it."

Standing, JJ Ross tipped his hat. "You made one fine dinner, ma'am. Thank you."

The Lone Ranger followed Ernie into the parlor. Before the door shut, the 'big-hat' man described the horn. "The saxophone was in a new black leather case with blue plush lining. The horn was in perfect condition. The saxophone is a vital clue."

I ran into the parlor. "Do you think anyone saw the horn? Peyton and Bay Jo were at the park after the dance in the middle of the night. Maybe, she left her horn behind."

The lawman twirled around in his boots leaving marks on the hardwood floor. "I'm JJ Ross. I'm leading this investigation. We know she carried her horn. Finding the saxophone may give us the murderer's fingerprints. What do you think you know, little girl?"

"Nothing. Only asking."

Taddy pulled me out of the parlor as Ernie pointed to the door. "Some sheriff you'd make. You talk too much. Try listening." He followed me to the porch. "Why don't you like JJ Ross?"

"He thinks he's somebody important. He thinks he knows everything. This is our investigation, not his. I'm the Lone Ranger of Texarkana. He should go home." I neighed at JJ Ross' horse.

"I thought you were the sheriff?"

"I can be both."

Priscilla came to the porch, brought her sweet tea, and sat in the rocker beside mine. Taddy hung a leg on the porch railing and watched her. And I watched him.

Priscilla sipped her tea. "The newscaster on the radio said 150 police units are patrolling the streets. And now JJ Ross is here. This murderer will be arrested soon." She bounced in her chair, her voice keeping time with the rocking.

Untied Shoelace

Taddy kicked the railing like the horse kicking the picket fence. "Are we safe? Do we need more pans?"

Priscilla stood and rustled his hair. "Taddy, if anyone tries to break into the manor, we'll hear them. Grandma Elsie has a gun. And Ernie has a gun. We're safe."

I started to tell them Mahlee has a gun, but Mahlee would get mad at me for sharing her secret.

I sauntered to the railing beside Taddy. "Did you see the revolvers the Lone Ranger had on his hips? Those handles are pearl. They're the same color as Ernie's new car." I pulled out a small pad of paper and a pencil from my pocket.

The door creaked, and JJ Ross paraded down the steps. He opened the gate and let it swing shut. He mounted his horse, fixed his hat, and nodded. Before he kicked the horse, he gave one last instruction to us. "Never forget. I shot two ex-convicts at the Crazy Pond Hotel in Mineral Swamp, Texas. I'll catch the Phantom Killer. I'll shoot him, if I have to."

JJ Ross rode his horse east on Fourth Street passed Ernie's Studebaker, the wrong way. In a few minutes, his horse galloped by the manor going the other way. The Lone Ranger tipped his hat to make sure we saw him. Tonto could help him find his way around town.

Mahlee and Ernie danced onto the porch and Grandma Elsie two-stepped behind them, smiling. Ernie grinned like a possum being chased by a cat. Mahlee held out her hand. "We have an announcement." She touched the new ring on her finger. "Ernie and me, we is engaged."

Ernie kissed her cheek, and his loafers danced around Mahlee in a big circle. She's broader than him and stronger. "She's my bride. I've waited a long time for her."

I jumped from my rocker. "No. You can't get married."

Mahlee giggled and waved me off. She held her hand out for Priscilla, the 'let me show you the ring' smile brought Grandma closer for a look, too.

Grandma Elsie and Priscilla rushed into the house holding onto Mahlee. They hugged her and cried, and Ernie followed behind them like a puppy without his tail, a smiling puppy, though.

Back in the rocker, I wrote a new poem with sad, mad, and lonely words. Words about bologna, too.

Taddy shuffled to me. "Are we friends?"

I scratched my nose. "Sure, we are."

"Then it's not just you and Mahlee."

"But it's been Mahlee and me for a long time. Now she loves Ernie. You have a mama." I wrinkled my eyebrows. "Mahlee has a man with a Studebaker. I just have Grandma."

Taddy sat by me in the other rocker beside the small round table. "I'm Thaddeus William Day, Jr. You're my friend. The only one I have."

"I am glad we're friends. It's just that I'm not used to sharing Mahlee." I waved my paper in the air. "Do you want to hear my new poem?"

"Sure. I love poetry. I have your poems memorized."

"You do?"

"Yes."

"Well, here's the latest.

> *The Lone Ranger rode into town,*
> *Which only made me frown.*
> *Mahlee and Ernie have a new car,*
> *And I just want to go far.*
> *Taddy is the deputy and I am the sheriff.*
> *We're the Vest-i-gators.*

Untied Shoelace

The best detectives in town,
So don't ya frown."

Taddy ran inside the house, dancing and singing my poem. "The best detectives in town."

Having a friend who sings my poems is a first.

I climbed my tree and put my poem in the can. I jumped to the balcony. Grandma had four pans and lots of string on the door leading to my bedroom. To get into the house, I had to use the front door.

When I came inside, Grandma Elsie chatted to an empty room in the parlor. I inched across the floor, made my way to the staircase, and sat on the first step, leaning my face against the slats. I listened in.

"Otto Kree. I wish you were here. I would give anything to know what made Gill run away after the horse kicked you."

She stopped talking, came to the front room, and plopped on the sofa. The cushions bumped into a bunch of pans on string and Taddy came running into the room.

"What's all the noise?"

Grandma held a pan. "It's me. Sorry to scare you."

Taddy saw me spying on Grandma. I put my finger to my mouth and he joined me on the stairs.

Grandma talked to the photo in her hand. "Gill came to your law office to get paid for his chores. Why did everything have to be an argument? The horse got spooked, you fell, and Gill ran. What happened? Wish you could talk to me from the grave." She held the picture to her chest and wept, rocking like I do when folks die.

I tried to stand, but my face became wedged between the slats on the stair case. "Grandma, Grandma. I've got my head caught. My ears are hung. I'm stuck."

Grandma came over, knelt, and bent my ears back. "What have you done now?"

My head popped free and I rubbed my ears. "Thanks. My head gets stuck in stuff."

Grandma grinned.

I stood next to Grandma. "Did my daddy like his pa?"

"They never seen eye to eye. Your grandpa made his money defending crooks. Hard times made Grandpa bitter, but he loved Gill. Gill had trouble seeing that. They had lots of fights."

I have a hard time with fighting, too.

"Time to lock this house. We need rest," Grandma said.

Taddy gave me a pat on the arm and skipped up the stairs. "Night. You know, I should be the sheriff. My ears don't get caught in things." He laughed, jumping away before I could slug him.

The pots and pans were in place and the loose nails were on the window sills. Priscilla pulled the blinds and Ernie locked the doors.

Grandma decided we could sleep in our beds upstairs. Taddy and Priscilla shut their door, and Priscilla shoved a piece of furniture against the door. Ernie told Mahlee he had a loaded gun and he'd keep her safe and I've gotten used to having a shotgun between Grandma and me.

When my head hit the pillow, Rainbow scampered in my dreams. I relived how she got her new name and how she gave birth to gray kittens. In the dream, the kittens were as big as the train station with faces like Grandma's frying skillets. Three skillets. With cute eyes.

Creak. Creak.

I sat up in bed and whispered. "What? Who's there?"

Grandma snored, hugging the gun. I pulled the scratchy quilt to my neck and closed my eyes.

"Meow..."

I leaned over the edge of the mattress and pulled White Beard into bed. He crawled around my neck and purred.

Creak. Creak.

The iron hinge on the gate in the alley made a squeaking noise.

Creak. Creak. Clack. Clack.

The sharp snapping noise grew louder and the hollow sound rushed up the stairs to my room. I had to see if it was the gate.

I shuffled in the dark downstairs holding White Beard against my chest, sliding in my socks. I peeked out the window, pulling the blind open a little. Ernie's car was parked on the side of the manor. No shadows. Nothing moving there.

I moved to the kitchen door. It had a small window without a blind. Grandma had nailed a towel over the glass. I pulled a corner up to look out in the yard. A shadow. I saw white. I saw more than one thing of white. I counted five. I stopped counting at eight and screamed, causing White Beard to meow like her tail was caught in the door.

I screamed with all I had in me. "Grandma, there's hooded men in the yard." I sat on the floor, wrapped my free arm around my knees, and rocked. I held White Beard to my chest with the other hand.

Grandma came running down the stairs with Priscilla on her heels. She held her shotgun above her head like a wild woman. Priscilla dialed the operator asking for police assistance.

Grandma barreled out the door, getting tangled on the pans strung around the knob. She charged like a bull as I watched from the open kitchen door. She stomped in the mud puddle, the one made from the water hose earlier, and raised the barrel. "Leave us alone."

She fired the shotgun into the darkness and the neighborhood dogs howled. After the kaboom and my scream, she yelled. "Get out of here. Leave us alone." Her words fell like vapor, stopping mid-sentence.

"I've fallen in the mud. Can it get any worse? What's in my yard?"

Moo. Moo. Moo.

The echo of cows singing in the night made me shake my head.

Grandma cried out. "No way. We have cows? Where did they come from?"

I scuttled down the steps, my feet sliding in the mud, and I joined Grandma on the ground in the puddle. A cow plodded in the muddy water. *Moo. Moo.*

Police cars surrounded the house, and the sirens woke neighbors as lights came on across the street. Four patrol cars parked beside the Studebaker, and their headlights shone on my imaginary hooded men – which turned out to be black and white cows grazing in our yard. Oversized Oxford cows roaming in the dark.

From inside the house I thought I saw hoods. They were short though. I didn't think about it then.

The officer walked up to Grandma. "Ma'am. A train jumped the tracks two blocks from here. When the boxcars toppled over, dozens of cows got loose, scattering behind homes. We've gotten most of them corralled."

Ernie showed up with his revolver, rubbing his eyes. "What's the commotion? A gun blast woke me up."

Mahlee stumbled up behind him, asking for me. "Shoelace. Where's Shoelace?"

"I'm right here." I hurried to her side. "I'm right here." Her hug felt like warm syrup on the pancake of my heart running through my veins.

Grandma turned to Ernie. "We're fine. A bunch of cows trampled the fence on the side of the yard. Guess we'll need Slow Tom and Fast Tim to repair the fence now."

Good thing the shadow on Ernie's Studebaker hid the pellet holes on the side panel of his new car. I'm staying out of his way tomorrow, he might be repeating words he spouted the time he slammed the ice box on his fingers.

We went to bed, and I cuddled White Beard listening to the wind blow the pans in a *ting-ting-thud* outside on the balcony. I wondered if the Phantom Killer lay in his bed plotting his next move. I also wondered if JJ Ross lay in his bed at the Grim Hotel plotting a way to catch the murderer before anyone else got hurt.

I planned to hide Grandma's shotgun from her. She's a crazy woman with that barrel in her hands. A boxcar of cows and a bucket full of pellet holes in Ernie's car brought Mahlee and me back together. Tomorrow, listening to Ernie mouth and scream when he sees the damage will simply remind me of Mahlee's late night hug.

Maybe, it's time I learned how to shoot a gun. But who would teach me?

CHAPTER TWENTY SIX

THE SHOOT OUT

"AH. AH. NO. NO. I can't push anymore."

The piercing sound coming from my bedroom reminded me of Ernie yelling at Grandma for shooting holes in his new Studebaker. But this hollering came from a lady whose tummy pooched out with a baby trying to get born.

Rebecca and Harmon moved into the manor after the Spring Lake Park murders, three weeks ago, afraid to stay at their apartment with the Phantom Killer loose in town. Now Rebecca is having a baby in my bedroom, on my bed. Even Rainbow and her kittens were kicked out of the delivery room.

I'm sleeping in Mahlee's room on a cot next to hers, which I love. Grandma is sleeping in the parlor on the velvety couch by the piano. Since the cow incident, she now keeps her shotgun by the kitchen door. Ernie leaves his hand gun in the drawer by the ice box. Maybe he plans to help Grandma protect us.

Ah. Ah. Ah. Ah.

"Grandma, does the doctor know how to stop the screaming?" I looked toward my room upstairs. "Rainbow meowed when she had kittens, but not like the pregnant lady."

The next holler caused Priscilla to twitch and Taddy to jerk in his seat on the couch. Priscilla's tea glass slipped from her hand, she caught the glass on her lap, and balanced it with both hands, for a second. Then the glass toppled, and she spilled half of her drink on the floor.

"Shoelace, grab the mop please?" Grandma Elsie asked.

"Yes ma'am." I unrolled myself from my place in the big chair. "You two leave my spot alone." I pointed at Taddy and Billy Joe. "I'm sitting there."

Taddy popped up from beside Priscilla and jumped into the chair. "I can sit wherever I want." He smiled a crooked grin.

I hurried to the kitchen and wet the mop in the sink, wringing out the webbed cloth. Back in the front room, I slapped the gray threads of the old mop across the sticky tea on the hardwood floor. "All done. Floor's clean."

Ah. Ah. Ah.

The yells came faster and more often.

Pastor Cody and Billy Joe picked a great night to join us for supper. This noise makes it tough for Pastor Cody to plan Ernie and Mahlee's wedding. Not that I mind.

Mahlee admired her engagement ring. "Next year is too long to wait. We could have a small wedding right here in the front room of the manor. I'm thinking around Christmas."

Mahlee changes the date with the second hand on a clock. She picks a new date and new time every other day.

Too bad Ernie left to cover a story about a robbery. He's missing out on all the wedding plans. Not that I care about that, either.

Grandma offered her an idea of what to do. "Mahlee, you could elope."

I leaned on the mop. "Where's Eeelope? Is it in Texas?" Everyone laughed at me before I finished my question. It made me feel bad.

"Elope means they would run off to get married." Billy Joe called from where he sat Indian style.

"I was seeing if you knew." I wiped my brow and held my temper inside. I didn't want to hit him tonight because I needed his help. I motioned to Billy Joe to follow me to the kitchen.

We stood by the new stove where the lemon pound cake tempted us on the cake platter. "Want a piece?" I put the mop in the corner.

Billy Joe's eyes got big. "I ate a huge slice at supper. Would your grandma mind?"

"Naw. She loves for us to eat her food. She bakes every day. I'll get you a piece." If I reached Billy Joe's stomach, I could talk him into teaching me to shoot the shotgun.

I shoved a plate with cake on it toward Billy Joe who pulled out a chair and sat down. Upstairs, Rebecca sang a solo of birthing pains.

"She better have her baby soon. She's gonna run out of breath." I sat across from Billy Joe. "Your paper on the bulletin board at school says your brother, Reed, taught you to shoot like him. Will you teach me to shoot my grandma's gun? You heard what Grandma did to Ernie's car."

"I could show you. It will cost you a trade though."

I moved past the pile of baby blankets at the end of the table. "What? Anything."

Harmon yelled from upstairs. "The baby's coming. The baby's coming."

The chatter and talk in the front room bounced off the walls while Billy Joe and me planned a lesson with the gun. Right under their noses.

I grabbed a couple of shells from the drawer and the shotgun from the corner. "Come on."

Billy Joe shoved the last bite of cake into his mouth and we trooped outside, careful to let the screen door shut easy.

The weather felt more like fall, rather than May. A few birds fluttered over us. Rainbow and Moe, Larry and Curly pranced up, meowing and rubbing our legs with their fur. White Beard slept in the garden, curled up.

We moved under the oak tree on the side of the house by Ernie's car. "So what's the trade?"

"At school next week, during the spelling bee, I want you to let me win."

"Win? You want me to lose on purpose?"

"Never mind. I'm going inside the house." Billy Joe pounded around the front yard by the fence.

I yanked on his shirt. "No, wait. I can lose. I can. I will. I promise." I hoped my promise became a *real* promise, since losing is hard for me.

Taddy danced an Indian pow-wow around us. "What are you two doing? Why do you have the shotgun? Grandma's gonna wail the fly swatter at your back side if she sees you."

He's becoming a Taddy-Tonto boy every day.

"I'm learning how to shoot. You saw Ernie's car. Grandma's aim is off."

Taddy parked himself on the steps by the front of the house. "I'm staying. I want to watch." I nodded. Turning Taddy away meant he'd go tattle. I cocked the gun and put a bullet into the barrel.

Billy Joe put his hand on the gun. "Hold the barrel here with this hand, the other here. Put the gun against your shoulder, aim, and fire." He stepped away from me.

Taddy jumped up waving his arms. "Put the gun down. You can't just shoot a gun in town. I don't want to watch this after all. It's dangerous."

"I can shoot at the Harrison's tree in their front yard. The trunk is four-feet wide. I'll aim for the bark." I was confident I could hit the tree. The loud kaboom we'd hear never crossed my mind.

Rainbow raced under my feet as I held onto the loaded gun. And Taddy sneezed when the three little gray kittens caused me to twirl around.

Billy Joe hollered. "Watch out. A white kitten is behind you."

Taddy sneezed. *Achoo. Achoo.*

I stumbled and pressed the trigger. *Kaboom.*

The window pane glass shattered like a hundred tea glasses crashing to the floor. "Oh no! I've shot the window out of the manor." I dropped the gun to the grass by the porch steps and, wouldn't you know it, Ernie drove up just in time to see it all.

The front door flew open and, in the commotion with the yelling and screaming, Grandma held my arm tighter than she will remember. "Young lady, I forbid you to touch this gun. You've shattered my picture window and those pellets grazed our heads. The chandelier is in pieces and the books have pellets in them. You could have killed someone. What were you thinking?"

"I wanted to protect us from the killer." I ran to the rocker on the porch and fell into the seat, holding my knees, and I cried. I mumbled like Mahlee and put my hands to my face wishing I had the guts to tell Grandma how I landed on Bay Jo Baxter at the park. How my Oxford shoes were laced up. How I had touched the saxophone. How I had the sticker.

Billy Joe touched Grandma on the arm. "Ms. Elsie. This is my fault. I bragged on knowing how to shoot and how my brother Reed . . ." He broke down, running to Pastor Cody's side. "I miss my brother. Why did he have to die? Why was he murdered?" Billy Joe's tears and sobs tore at my heart. His tears became mine, and I ran into the house, running past Harmon on the stairs, as I headed to Mahlee's room.

I skidded to a stop at the top and turned to Harmon. "Are you holding your baby?"

"Yes. A baby girl. Isn't she beautiful?"

I inched to his side and peeked in the folded blanket. "She's pretty. A little red and wrinkled. Needs more hair."

"Her hair will grow in." He stepped down a stair. "What's the noise outside? Did you hear a gun?"

I swallowed hard. "Billy Joe gave me a shooting lesson. It became a shoot-out of Grandma's window in the front room. The kittens tripped me, and I accidently pulled the trigger. Grandma's ranting in the yard. She'll want to get rid of me."

"Rid of you? She's the proudest I've seen her in years. When your pa snatched you, she lost her smile. You've given her smile back." Harmon kissed the head of his little baby girl.

"Well, she's lost her smile tonight. I nearly shot her."

"Thankfully, you missed her. But no matter what, your grandma loves you."

"Ya think so?" I turned around, stepping alongside Harmon, going downstairs.

"Love you?" Harmon paused, looking me right in the eyes. "Your grandma would give her life for you. She nearly did the year your pa took you. She rode train after train hunting for you. She returned to the manor with sad eyes and was sick for months. And now . . . now she has you and you have her heart."

"But I cause her trouble. I break promises. I mess up. I start fires and shoot out windows."

Harmon stopped on the step and scrunched me with his free arm. "Your grandma believes in you. She sees you … sees the Annie Grace Kree potential."

I sat on the bottom step to think. "Hey Harmon? What ya gonna name your baby?"

"Rebecca wants to name her after your mama."

"My mama? Why?"

"They were best friends. Your mama taught Rebecca how to play the harmonica. And they sang in the choir at church. They even played a duet with their harmonicas in the high school play. She loved your mama."

"A harmonica? I never knew she played music." I smiled at Harmon. "So will the baby have my mama's full name?"

Harmon patted my head. "Yes, she will. Especially since your mama protected Rebecca in the fifth grade when four boys made fun of her stuttering. They locked her in a shed and made threats. Your mama showed up with her papa's shotgun."

"Mama used a shotgun, too?"

"Yes. She pointed the barrel and told the boys she might miss one of them, but she was going to hit someone. They ran home like scared rabbits. She was a tough one."

"My mama? Tough? Am I like her?"

"Exactly. Same eyes. Same ways. She would be proud of you."

"You think she would be?" I pumped Harmon for more details.

"Absolutely. Want to know a secret from the day at the shed?" Harmon shifted his baby girl to the other arm.

"What? Tell me."

"Your mama forgot to load the gun, but the boys had no idea she could bluff."

"No way. She forgot her bullets?" I laughed, thinking how brave Mama acted, even though I'm sure she would have walloped them boys with the barrel of the gun if they'd caught on.

Harmon stepped into the front room, his shoes crunching on broken glass. Everyone came in the house and followed Harmon to the kitchen where Priscilla made silly eyes over the baby's toes. He showed the sleeping baby to Ernie. Taddy tiptoed to the baby to get a look, and I watched from the doorway.

Pastor Cody walked up to Harmon. "Mind if I pray over this little one?"

"Not at all," Harmon said.

Billy Joe hung on Pastor Cody's side as he prayed. "Lord, watch over this little girl. May she know how fearfully and wonderfully made she is."

Mahlee sighed and shambled out the door. Ernie glanced her way and moved to the screen, pushing it open. Mahlee cried and mumbled. "The baby's missing. She's missing cause of me."

Pastor Cody stopped praying and we all looked at the door. Grandma pushed it to and motioned for Pastor Cody to finish.

"In Jesus name, amen."

Grandma asked Harmon. "May I hold your little girl?"

Harmon handed his baby to her. "She's sleeping. She has the cutest nose."

I leaned on the folds of Grandma's pillow body and peeked at the baby. Grandma kissed my head. "Love you, missy. Leave the guns to the grownups."

I nodded, although I'm not sure my nod told the truth.

Harmon beamed and announced, "We are naming her Grace Lucille Fallbrook after Annie Grace's mama.

Grandma gave a 'Praise the Lord' shout as new noises leaked from her insides, those hiding behind the apron of her sadness. Her smile lit up the room and her bouncing shook the house. She kissed the fingers of the baby and whispered, "Grace Lucille Fallbrook. Such a pretty name."

The kitchen became a room full of boxcar friends. To think, my mama saved Rebecca's life without using any bullets. Maybe I'll use an unloaded gun next time.

Mahlee's voice turned shrill, and we all looked at the kitchen door. I listened to her words as they pierced the night. "Stop telling me I'll be fine. You don't understand."

I could hear Mahlee crying in the back yard, and Ernie trying to help only made her sadder and madder. Their talk sounded like a cat fight and Mahlee was winning.

I started to go help Ernie when the phone rang.

Ring-a-ling. Ring-a-ling.

He almost knocked me over running inside, pushed me out of the way, and grabbed the phone before anyone else could get to it. "A shooting? Hwy 67? Ten miles out of town. Got it. I'm headed there, now."

CHAPTER TWENTY SEVEN

THE CHICKEN HAWK

BAM. BAM. BAM. BAM. PASTOR Cody and Billy Joe boarded up the front window and Grandma handed me the broom. It came with instructions to sweep the glass from the floor and to find pellets embedded in the books. I had to make the front room spotless. *What a way to end a Friday night.* Taddy and me better solve the murders and win the reward money. I need to buy a chandelier and pay Grandma for the broken window.

Crunch. Crunch. The baby doctor stepped on pieces of glass. He squinted at me, shaking his head. He carried his little black bag out the front door. Harmon disappeared with Grace Lucille upstairs to the delivery room to check on Rebecca.

**

I crawled into my cot after a night of chores and fell asleep with the pillow molded around my head.

Waa. Waa. Waa.

I toppled off my cot and landed on White Beard, who meowed at me. He sniffed my breath. "Come here sweet baby kitten." I cuddled White Beard to my chest and crawled back onto the cot.

Baby Grace cried across the way while Mahlee said her prayers. "Why is it always so dark? Where is my … where is my … I want her back. God, please give her back."

Who does she want back?

I listened as long as I could, but the purring of White Beard sent me to my dreams. Every time I nodded off, Grace Lucille squealed. This baby found her scream, a pitch sharper than the squeal of metal on rail. "Yikes." I covered my ears with my pillow and blocked out the noise.

The next morning, tired and cranky, I carried White Beard with me downstairs. I cracked open the screen in the kitchen and shooed him outside.

"Food smells good, Grandma. I'm starving." I hugged her side to see if she had gotten over being mad. "Eggs? Yum."

Grandma patted my arm. "Will you take the trash out to the alley? I smell a sour odor coming from the can. Be sure and empty the trash that gets stuck in the bottom."

"Yes ma'am." I grabbed the heavy metal can and marched to the barrel where Grandma burns the trash.

Taddy followed me as if we were lining up in the hall at school. "Where ya going?"

"I'm taking out the garbage. Wanna get in." I held the can out. "It's not too full."

"Not funny." Taddy sprinted behind the old well at the side of the yard and ran up behind me. "Tag, you're it."

"Not playing. I'm too tired." I pretended to be tuckered out, but I was waiting for Taddy to move closer to trick him.

Taddy jogged to me. "You're no fun."

I galloped and pretended to be a horse let loose from the barn. "Tag, you're it."

"Not fair." He tripped on the trash can, the one I tossed at his feet to slow him down.

Untied Shoelace

We jogged around the clothesline and the oak tree, playing tag. I hopped over the tomato plants, careful to step high enough to clear them. When I raced to the big double doors at the carriage house, I stopped and fell into the wall, out of breath. Taddy slammed into me.

"Watch out." I pointed to the sky. "See the chicken hawk? He's circling us. They carry off baby pigs, rabbits, kittens, and even kids." I leaned on the white wall as the plaster crumbled around me.

"There's nothing in this yard a chicken hawk wants." Taddy pretended to do an Indian dance. "Ke-mo sah-bee. We're safe. Chicken hawks might eat the Blanton Street brothers. Or Clara. But not us."

I breathed a sigh of relief when the chicken hawk flew away. I sighed another big breath when Ernie drove up. He parked his Studebaker on the side street after being gone all night. He stepped through the new gate and wobbled with each step. His eyes were sunken, his face drawn.

He waved. "Hey kiddos."

I ran to him. "What happened last night? At the farm?"

"There was another attack and murder. It's been a long night at the paper. I fell asleep at my desk and have ink on me from the typewriter keys." He wiped his face with his fingers. "But I finished my story for this morning's Saturday edition."

Taddy pulled on Ernie's arm. "Is it a big story? Are you going to be famous? Maybe you'll write a book from these stories." Taddy's pitch in his voice told me how important Ernie's articles were to him. He does save every story.

Ernie tousled Taddy's hair. "This might be the biggest story, yet. The Phantom Killer may have murdered, again." He stepped to the screen door at the kitchen. "I smell bacon. I could eat a slab of bacon this morning."

I stopped at the bottom of the steps. Taddy bumped into me and I turned to him. "Will they ever catch the Phantom Killer?" I sighed and wished a chicken hawk would carry off the bad man and drop him in the Red River.

Taddy hopped up the steps. "He'll get caught. Or he'll leave town."

I had to run back for the trash can. When I came inside, I moved to a chair beside Ernie.

Mahlee ran to the other side and pulled her chair close. "What's on your face? Is that ink?" She spit on her fingers and wiped his skin. "You look beyond hungry."

"I am exhausted. I need food and then sleep."

I played with a fork in front of me. "So what happened? Who got murdered?"

Grandma flipped the bacon and wiped her hands on her apron. "Another murder? Last night?" She turned around, sighing like a steam engine running out of steam.

Ernie nodded at her. "Victor Stamps was shot twice in the back of the head through the window in his living room. He was reading the newspaper when his wife heard breaking glass."

Grandma turned to Ernie. "I know that farm. It sits a few miles down the road from the airport." Grandma went back to stirring the eggs and beat the yoke out of them, shaking her head.

Ernie kept rattling off details. "His wife, Kacey, had given him a heating pad for his sore back and he was sitting in his armchair when the shots hit him." Ernie tried to swallow, but the food got hung and he coughed.

"Did he kill her, too?" I licked my fork, although I had not taken a bite of food, yet.

"No. She's in stable condition in the hospital." Ernie sighed like his heart ached from writing stories on death.

Taddy stuck a butter knife into his milk glass, swishing. "So this story is in the paper?"

"It should be."

Taddy left the knife in his glass, darted across the front room, and turned the handle on the door. "I'm getting the paper …"

Ernie ate breakfast and Mahlee propped her elbows on the table. She appeared to be somewhere else and stared at the ceiling. She mumbled to herself. Grandma handed me a plate with three crisp pieces of bacon and swirled beaten eggs.

I kept saying the name Victor Stamps again and again to myself. I had heard that name somewhere and the secret Skip told me before he died tingled in my toes. My fingers went numb and my mouth screamed, "Victor Stamps. That's it. Victor Stamps."

"Girl, calm down. You're safe here. You are safe at the manor." Grandma held both my shoulders.

I crammed eggs and bacon in my mouth as fast as I could to keep from spilling the beans. I had to hurry and catch the next train. I had to leave. I had to find a way to slip off.

More words slipped out and I spit egg onto the table. "How did Ms. Stamps get away?"

Ernie dropped his fork to the floor, his hand shaking. He looked like he had to share what he knew or he'd bust. His face got red, his eye twitched, and the ink on his face looked purple like a bruise. Mahlee picked up his fork and got him another one.

Priscilla shuffled into the kitchen. She tossed a slab of butter in a pan for a new batch of eggs, helping Grandma with breakfast.

Ernie tapped his fork on his plate and kept talking. "Ms. Stamps ran from her house to get help and escaped through the corn field. When will the murders stop?"

Priscilla spun around from the stove. "What? Another murder? Say it's not so."

Ernie nodded. "Yes ma'am. Out on Highway 67."

Priscilla shivered. "This is getting scary. No one is safe. Do we have to talk *murder* in front of the children?"

Ernie stabbed his bacon. "Sorry ma'am. I'm so used to writing these stories, and I forget they can be troubling to little ones."

I scowled at Priscilla when she turned to the stove to crack the eggs. I tapped Ernie on the arm. "So Victor died in his chair?" I hoped Ernie would bite and keep talking.

"Yes, right in his chair. Then the killer chased Kacey and shot her. A bullet grazed her cheek. A second bullet lodged in her jaw."

I hoped Taddy might make mental notes of what Ernie said, but he wasn't paying any attention.

Ernie asked for the newspaper, but Taddy glanced at it first.

I moved closer to Ernie. "How did she get away?"

"Kacey left a river of blood running to another house. They carried her to Michael Meagher Hospital."

Taddy jumped at the break in our talking. "Hey, the story is on the front page. Whoa. Look at this headline: Murderer Loose. Texarkana Husband Dead, Wife Lives."

Priscilla held her hand out. "Give me the paper and change the subject."

"Save the paper, Mama. I'm cutting the stories out. In fifty years, Ernie will be famous and I'll have his articles." Taddy paraded behind Ernie running his fingers across Ernie's shoulders like touching precious gold.

Ernie ignored Priscilla and tossed out a few last pieces of the story. "JJ Ross said it's a wonder Kacey Stamps didn't bleed to death. The gun used in this murder is different than the .32 caliber used in the first four murders. This gun was a .22 caliber and the murderer left smudged fingerprints and full hand prints."

Mahlee buttered a piece of toast for Ernie. "You need a bath and sleep."

"You're right. I may have to return to my desk and write a follow-up. I need rest."

He stood, taking a bite of toast. "One more thing. The cops found a red flashlight by the hedge near the window where Victor got shot."

Priscilla shook her spoon at Ernie. "Ernie Surratt. No more talk of murder. You're scaring the children."

Taddy shook his head. "I'm not afraid."

I nudged Ernie's arm. "I'm not scared, either. Where's the flashlight?"

Ernie inhaled a deep breath and his throat jiggled. "The FBI sent it off for prints, but I've got a color photo of the flashlight in the paper."

Priscilla took a peek at the photo in the newspaper. "Do they think the flashlight belongs to the killer?" She waited for an answer, but we were all staring at her. "Stop looking at me. I just wanted to see the flashlight." Priscilla broke down and tears rolled down her face. "It's not safe to sit in your own home. Who's next?" She wiped her nose with her hand.

Grandma agreed and hugged Priscilla. "Shoelace and Taddy, you two stay in the yard. Don't leave the manor. Or better yet, remain inside." Grandma sat down to drink her coffee, the mood in the kitchen sadder now, but at least my shooting out the front window was old news.

I pumped for more details, breaking the silence. "What's the reward up to? Is it going higher?"

Taddy rolled his eyes at me.

Ernie chewed on his toast. "The reward money has reached $7,000."

My toes danced in my PF Flyers. My hands itched and my head plotted. I motioned to Taddy to follow me to the parlor. I grabbed his shirt. "Come with me."

"What do you want?"

In the parlor, I whispered, "I have to go to the Stamps farm. I have to go now. You have to cover for me. I've got to hop a train and ride out there this morning. I have to find the treasure." I let the word *treasure* slip from my mouth hoping Taddy missed the word.

"Treasure? You can't go off looking for a treasure. You have to stay at the manor. Besides, the cops will be watching the house. What are you up to?"

"I'll tell you later. Right now I've got to see if I can find something. If I'm right, I'll tell you tonight."

"How will I cover for you?"

"Your job is to keep Grandma happy. Tell her I'm in my room or in the carriage house. Wherever she is, make sure you tell her I'm in another spot in the manor. Just cover for me."

"You're gonna owe me if we pull this off."

"I know. Hey, will you water my peanut plants while I'm gone? Watch out for the chicken hawk."

"Sure. But that's a double-owe me." Taddy peered around the door making sure no one heard us. We shook hands like grownups and skipped from the parlor. We were 'vestigators on a mission.

Untied Shoelace

Harmon came to the kitchen to get Rebecca's breakfast. He carried Grace Lucille in a pink blanket in his arms. Taddy and me scooted into the kitchen behind him peeking at the baby.

Grandma Elsie and Priscilla used their baby gurgle voices and Priscilla reached for Grace Lucille. "I'll hold her for you. Take your wife her breakfast tray."

"Thank you." He spooned eggs onto a plate, added four pieces of toast, and a handful of bacon. He chewed on a piece of bacon while Grandma poured two cups of coffee, one for him, one for Rebecca. Harmon disappeared to the delivery room with a tray of food.

Priscilla hugged Grace Lucille. "She's so cute. I could eat her up."

I hurried up the stairs and grabbed Daddy's satchel from beneath my cot. I made sure my lucky red rock was inside and pulled out my engineer's cap. A treasure search at the Stamps farm requires a cap. I might even yell *Geronimo*.

Taddy met me outside Mahlee's bedroom door. He blocked the stair case. "I've changed my mind. You have to stay here. You'll get shot. That Officer Teacup doesn't always look before he pulls the trigger." He planted his hands on his hips.

"Move out of the way. I'll let you be the Lone Ranger and I'll be Tonto. You can be the sheriff and I'll be the deputy. Besides, I'll be home for supper." I twisted my words around to convince him and gave Taddy my girly smile, the one I try not to use, except in emergencies.

Taddy frowned and then he hugged me. "Don't take too long."

I pushed him back. "Don't' worry. I'll hurry."

I became a whirlwind and jumped on every other stair. I went out the front door and around the side of the house.

Pam Kumpe

White Beard meowed and rubbed against my shoes when I peeked around the back of the house. The ole chicken hawk circled above my head and swooped down, diving at White Beard. I snatched my kitten, put him into my satchel, and ran to the side gate, passed the Studebaker, and toward the boxcars pulling out of town.

CHAPTER TWENTY EIGHT

THE RETURN OF THE CHICKEN HAWK

CHUG. CHUG. CHUG. CHUG. THE boxcars rumbled passed the bushes. I counted thirteen cars. I peeked into the bag at White Beard, and he meowed. His paws reached for me and his green eyes begged for a rescue.

"Hold on, White Beard. We're catching a train. You're riding the magic carpet ride today." I clutched the top of the satchel with my right hand, jogging beside the train. I ran alongside the clickety clack of steel, reached with my left hand, and swung my foot upward to the ladder. "Geronimo."

I tumbled into the boxcar and saw a blur of something behind me. The train rolled passed the bushes, and I looked out the boxcar door. Nothing. It must have been a bird.

The train moved away from the station, and I held White Beard in my lap as I sat in the door of the boxcar swinging my feet. "Look, White Beard." I propped his head up, his pointy ears twitching in the wind. "The tracks run beside the highway, and this road takes us home. We'll get off here on the way back."

White Beard curled up in my lap, purring a kitty song. His purr kept time with the click-clack, bump and roar of the train. The rickety ride and scenes of the countryside caused me to lose track of how far the train had gone.

When the boxcars slowed to a pace I could outrun, I put White Beard at one end of the empty boxcar and held onto the door with one arm. I leaned out to see why the train was inching along and a blur ducked inside the boxcar behind me. Was there a hobo on the train with me?

The crunch, crunch steps of a neighing horse made me look ahead. I nearly fell from the boxcar when I saw JJ Ross in his big white hat riding his horse beside the train. He was searching inside every boxcar, probably hunting for suspects.

"White Beard." I ran to him and tossed him inside my bag. "We've got to jump. And we've got to go now."

I tumbled down the slope and ripped my overalls on my right knee. A stick jabbed me in the elbow and a sting shot through my arm. I clutched the satchel with a fist trying to keep from smashing White Beard. We bounced together like potatoes falling from a wagon, plunging into a thicket of weeds and bushes.

I stopped sliding and rolling just as JJ Ross rode by on his horse. White Beard's meows echoed my silent screams of fear, those trapped in my throat. He made enough noise for ten kittens. The meowing caused the horse to kick his hind legs, but when JJ Ross pulled on the reins, the horse settled down, giving one last snort at the bush. The Lone Ranger kicked his horse and rode on. I was out of breath and I rubbed my arm. I'd have another scar for show and tell at school.

The train creaked along, picking up speed. Guess the conductor got the all-clear sign. The train headed north and I scaled to the top of the tracks. I skidded down the slope on the other side as the last boxcar passed by. This way, as cars drove by on the highway, no one could see me. I'm short enough to move in the open and tall enough to look ahead.

I replayed Skip's words in my mind, remembering what he told me. If this is the farm, I'll find the secret. If this is the farm, I'll find the treasure.

198

Untied Shoelace

What's the crunching sound in the gravel behind me? Who is following me?

I darted behind the big oak by the pond, a kind of snaky spot with rotten wood. My PF Flyers sunk into the muddy, swampy ground, and a turtle popped his head up. He dove under the water when he saw me.

I had to hide from the crunchy steps. They were coming faster and getting louder. I rubbed White Beard's head and he purred. Meowing at the wrong time might cause me to fall backwards into the swamp or cause the stalker to grab me.

The crunch-crunch sound stopped, started, and then faded. I circled the oak, waiting for the person to get along, to get away from me.

"*Meow... Meow...*"

"White Beard," I whispered. "Not now."

The scuttle sound of gravel moving under shoes started again. "Are you there? Where are you?" A woman's voice called to me.

I peeked around the tree. "Mahlee? What are you doing? Are you following me?"

"I was on the side porch when you ran from the manor. I've got to watch out for you. I promised your daddy."

I tapped my fingers on her tin can and pointed at the pillowcase hanging on her shoulder. "Are those your belongings in the pillowcase?"

"Might be. I've got to figure this *staying* part out. I need to make sure you're okay first. I might take a ride to nowhere and see where I land." Mahlee stomped her boots in the mud, trying to get unglued in the sinking ground.

I marched in a full circle around her. "You haven't worn those old boots in a long time. You have three skirts on. Your hair's not pinned back, either. You're running away, aren't you?"

Mahlee shook her head. "Not quite. I'm thinking on it, though."

"I might go with you. If I find Daddy's treasure, we could go back to our old ways."

"Treasure? Where?"

"It might be at the Stamps farm."

Mahlee mumbled and started walking in her own circle, this time around me. "Need to get away, to think. I've been in love before. When things get hard, they may forget you. Sometimes they leave. Or sometimes they fall into the Mississippi River."

Mahlee marched the other way and came right back to me, shaking her head.

I grabbed her shoulders. "Stop talking in circles. And stop going in circles. Do you think Ernie is gonna stop loving you?" I gave Mahlee a romance talk, hoping I didn't have to say much. I needed to get back to finding the treasure.

"I'm a hobo with a past and Ernie's dignified. He's a reporter with his own car. I'm nobody. Just a clunky woman with a big mouth."

I reached for her hand, as Mahlee mumbled. "Why is it always so dark?"

"Mahlee, stop mumbling. It's sunny. Come with me. Help me find what my daddy left behind. Ernie loves you. He does."

Mahlee squinted and scowled at me.

I rambled on. "Ernie thinks you're the kindest person in the house. Priscilla is bossy. Grandma is . . . Grandma. Taddy is too smart for his own good. I break promises. Ernie sees the potential in you." I used Harmon's words to help Mahlee.

"But, I'm afraid . . . I might break him."

"Then don't squeeze him so hard. He isn't the toughest man we've ever met." I tried to make her laugh or at least, yell at me.

"Girl, you've got a lot to learn when it comes to love." Mahlee tripped me with her boot, which gave her the chance to bellow a Mahlee-belly-holler. Her laughter rose like hope over the tracks. White Beard sat on my shoulder, clawing at my skin. He had stopped meowing, but his ears went back when Mahlee's squeal hit the high notes.

She got back to *why* she was following me. "So where is this farm? And where is this treasure?"

"It's up there somewhere."

Mahlee shook her head. "How do you know where to go?"

"Skip told me the treasure was where Daddy used to work. I've got to see if this is the place." I marched a few steps ahead. "That's it. We're here."

Sirens blared and we ducked behind the bushes in front of a dirt road. *Bweep bip - bip bweep.* The siren on the car whined like a broken horn as it headed toward Texarkana.

"So what do you think you're after?" Mahlee was unable to leave me alone. "Tell me. Where are we going?"

I petted White Beard. "I'm looking for a big rock at the end of the fourth row of the corn fields behind the house."

"What's under the rock? Tell me what we're after."

"There's got to be a money box buried in the ground."

"Your pa never had much money."

"He might have won it in a poker game. He might have saved his winnings for me."

Mahlee yanked on my arm. "Is that the house? I see buzzards flying over it."

"It's got to be. There's a cop car parked on the road in front."

We snuck to the back of the house to hide from a napping cop whose hat sat on his face.

I stood at the back porch looking at the door and I held my cat close. "Do you want to look inside? We could look at the bloody handprints. We might find clues to help with the case."

Mahlee sat on the step by the back porch. "I've seen enough blood. I don't need to see more."

I passed my fur ball to Mahlee's big hands. "I'm going in. Hold White Beard."

Inside the kitchen, I saw muddy footprints leading to a bloody spot on the floor. The red trail made my heart sting and I shivered. My heart sped up and the hair on my neck felt like spiders crawling on me.

A bloody handprint was smeared on the wall by the door. I stepped over the splotches of blood on the floor and saw more blood on the chair. I saw a broken window in the living room and more red spots on the wall leading down the hall. This was way too much blood, even for me.

"Mahlee, Mahlee. Get me out of here." I ran through the house, to the back porch, and jumped to the ground in one giant leap.

"Girl, I told you. There's no need to see all that blood. Now, you're gonna have them bad dreams at night. You'll see."

My tummy twisted in knots and I felt sick. My throat went thick and air got stuck in my ears. I went to the side of the house and threw up. I got dizzy, sweat ran down my face and I had to sit down. Then I took big breaths trying to get enough air.

Mahlee walked up and touched my shoulder. "Are you better now?" She sat White Beard on the ground. "Come on. Let's find your treasure."

I wiped the sweat from my head and pointed toward the corn field. "Let's go over there. Fourth row."

"How do you know which end to start with? It could be the other fourth row."

"Well, I hope I'm right. We'll find out." At the end of the stalks, the grass grew as high as my waist and after searching long enough for the sun to move over in the sky, Mahlee stumped her boot on an object. I ran to her side. "Did you kick a rock?"

"Could be. Get to digging."

I grabbed a stick and dug. A few inches into the dirt, I hit something, larger than what Mahlee had kicked. I moved away the dirt. It was a boulder. I kept digging. Blisters formed on my hands. Finally, my stick hit something. A Mason jar? I pulled the glass from the ground.

Mahlee leaned in, trying to see through the dirt stains. "What's inside?"

I twisted the rusted lid, but the jar must have been buried a long time. It didn't budge.

I handed the jar to Mahlee and even with her five-finger turn, the lid wouldn't move. She held the jar above her head. "Let's throw the jar on the ground."

I grabbed the jar from her. "Here she blows . . ." The glass splattered and the sparkles of broken glass flickered on the ground. I picked up a silver key and a piece of paper. The note read: Box 406, Stateline Fountain Bank. "What's this key for? I don't see any money."

"No money? But we have a key? Let me see that paper." Mahlee acted like she knew all the words, but she can only read small words.

I took the note from her. "So where is Stateline Fountain Bank?"

Mahlee rubbed her face. "Your grandma banks there. It's downtown by the hotel."

I put the key and the note in my overalls pocket, wondering what the key might open.

Mahlee twirled around. "Where's White Beard?"

I searched for my cat, raced between corn stalks, and cut through the field. "Here kitty kitty."

Mahlee inched along the rows. "I saw him a second ago. He was headed toward the farm house."

White Beard's meows echoed with the waving of the corn stalks in the breeze. "White Beard. Here kitty kitty. We need to get back to the manor."

Mahlee bellowed with a deep voice. "White Beard. Come to me. Right now."

"White Beard's gonna run from your gruff voice. Talk nicer to him and he might come to you."

She mocked me. "He's gonna run off … talk nicer …"

I froze next to a straw scarecrow at the sight of what looked like dried blood on the ground. A footprint in the blood from a shoe made me feel like straw, like I'd crumble, like I couldn't breathe.

Mahlee bumped into me. "Ms. Stamps must have run this way. She must have gone to the house on the hill."

The chug-chug of a train clanked a roar across the highway. We both stopped and stared at the boxcars rolling by. Birds flew above us along with a chicken hawk looking for lunch in the fields.

I pointed to the tracks. "We have to watch for a train heading toward town. One will be here soon." I hoped Mahlee would ride with me. If not, I might catch the next train out of town instead.

We took giant steps between the corn and I called White Beard, again. I was ready to get out of the field. We moved closer to the Stamps house, following the meows. "There's White Beard. He's on the porch steps."

A screeching sound from the sky caused me to spin around. I ran toward White Beard, who meowed nonstop.

Kee-eeeee-arr. Chwirk. Kee-eeeee-arr. Chwirk. The chicken hawk circled, swooped, screeched, and moved closer with each circle toward my kitty.

"No, no. Leave my kitty alone. He's mine. Shoo." I flapped my arms like a live scarecrow.

I stood between White Beard and the diving chicken hawk. The chicken hawk kept diving in for the kill, his claws ready to snatch my kitten. I swung my satchel in the air and waved it around like a crazy hobo girl. "Get away. Go. Get."

The chicken hawk lunged at me, his claws slicing my forearm in one big swoop. *Kee-eeeee-arr. Chwirk.*

I stumbled, toppled to the ground, and huddled over my kitty. "Mahlee, my guts are hanging out." The blood from my arm poured onto White Beard and I held onto him with my left hand. I faded like a slow train and got swallowed up by the fog of death.

CHAPTER TWENTY NINE

BOBO HEALS THE BOO-BOO

"WHERE AM I? AND WHO are you?" I inspected my right arm wrapped in gauze and a hard shell. The man with black hair buzzed around the room. His ears held giant cotton swabs. His white jacket hung around him and he flapped his arms. He held his hands to his chest and waved them at me. Did he think he was a fly? Or a bumble bee? "Where am I?"

The man buzzed and leaned toward me. "Buzz … buzz … Well, look who came back to us. We were worried. I'm Doctor Doogo Fly. I buzz around your room hoping my noises stir you."

He twirled around, flitted to the window, and bumped against the window pane with his body. "Buzz … buzz … Hello, world. Annie Grace Kree is alive."

"Where's my grandma? Where's Mahlee?" I pushed the sheet with my left arm. My right arm felt heavy. It ached and throbbed with its own heartbeat. "What's wrong my arm?"

"It's broken. That chicken hawk tore into you. They aren't usually after people. You saved your kitten during the attack though. I'll call your grandmother and let her know you're awake."

"Do you buzz around in everyone's hospital room?"

"I buzz in rooms where little girls need to smile." He buzzed one more time. "I'm new in Texarkana. I always wanted to be in the movies, but my father told me a doctor makes more money. I attended college for eight years and made my way to Michael Meagher Hospital from Missouri. I've stitched your arm and set the bone. That cast will stay on your arm for six weeks."

Dr. Fly felt of my head. "No fever. It's down." He lifted my chin. "Color looks good, too. I've checked on you every few hours since you came in."

"What day is it?"

"Monday afternoon. You've been asleep for two days talking to your kitten in your dreams and telling someone to get away from your buried treasure." Dr. Fly removed the cotton swabs from his ears.

I rubbed my hand over the cast. "I remember the bone sticking out of my skin. Do you know where my kitten is?"

"He's at your grandma's house. Your friend Mahlee tried to bleach him. Your grandma asked me if a little bleach on his head would kill him." Dr. Fly glanced at my chart.

"Bleach? Did he get sick?"

"Your kitten's fine. Your grandma made sure."

Dr. Fly made his buzzing noises and slipped out to the hall, but he stuck his head in for one last buzz. "I'll check on you before I go home tonight. I'll tell the nurse to call your grandma. Buzz … buzz … buzz … Good to see you alert."

"Wait. Are you supposed to be a fly or a bumble bee?"

"What's my name?"

"Dr. Doogo Fly. So you're a fly."

"Nope. I'm a bumble bee. Been a 'Fly' all my life. Bees make little kids laugh at the hospital, too." Dr. Fly flew down the hall, buzzing.

I watched the door for Grandma, and my mind was on last Saturday at the Stamps farm. I've lost a couple of days. I swung my legs to the side. "Whoa. My legs are wobbly." I sat on the mattress, moved to the chair, and inched along the wall babying my right arm. I stuck my head into the hallway, but my legs gave out, and I sunk to the floor, like a weak chicken hawk losing flight.

My right arm slammed into the wall. "Ouch. Help me."

A white blur rushed to me. "What in the world are you doing out of your room? This is a hospital. We have sick people here. I hope you didn't rip out any of those forty stitches."

"Forty stitches? I'm going to have a big scar." I cried, not wanting the nurse to help me, but she had stronger legs than me right now.

The drill sergeant wearing starched white clothes and white hose helped me stand and guided me to the bed. She folded the blanket around me. "Stay in this bed, young lady. If you need anything, I'll get it for you."

I tapped my fingers on the rail with my left hand. *Grandma, where are you?*

Giggles and chatter came from the hall and Grandma's laughter told me she was leading the way to my room.

She ran to my side and hugged me. "My baby girl. I've got your room ready for you. The Fallbrooks left on the train today. They're afraid to stay in Texarkana and will visit an aunt in Little Rock for the rest of the summer. They'll return to their apartment by fall. They hope."

Her embrace reminded me of cinnamon rolls right from the oven, gooey, sweet and warm. Grandma smelled like home.

Mahlee and Taddy shuffled around the bed on the other side waiting for me to get unfolded from Grandma.

I pointed at Taddy. "What do you have in your arms? What are you carrying?"

Taddy dropped the balloons to the floor and raced to the side where Grandma stood. He lowered the rail and kissed my cast. "Your scar will show the Blanton brothers how tough you are. Gilbert made fun of you today at recess. He said you were afraid of a chicken hawk. So my fist tightened, and I socked him."

"No way. You hit Gilbert?" I smiled at his bravery.

"I did. One punch took him out. I bloodied his nose. Ms. Reece escorted me to the hallway and told me if I'm gonna hit one Blanton brother, I better take out the other one, too." Taddy rushed to gather the balloons from the floor.

Mahlee hugged my head. "Girl, you gave me such a scare. White Beard has a few red spots left, and he's searched for you everywhere in the manor. He's been sleeping with me, but White Beard wants you."

My heart clapped at having Mahlee. At having Grandma Elsie. At having a best friend named Taddy. I'm the luckiest hobo girl in Texarkana.

Taddy showed me his balloon animals. "Bobo the Magician came to school today for our fourth-grade party before summer break. Bobo performed lots of tricks. He blew up balloons, tied them, and twisted them into animals, too. He made this blue cat for you and this green bird. And this pink dog. And this crown."

Taddy placed the orange crown around my head. He rambled on. "Bobo did a card trick and had me pick a card. He guessed the ace of hearts. It was my card. He let me keep it." Taddy pulled it from his slacks pocket.

I took the card from Taddy and handed it right back. "If I'd been in class today, I would have asked Bobo to make the Blanton brothers disappear, just like my daddy's ace of heart card."

Taddy laughed and chatted on. "You can't get rid of them but Mahlee can. After school, Lester and Gilbert waited on the playground by the tree challenging me to another fight. Mahlee met me after school and she clomped over to them, whispered in their ears, and they ran away." Taddy turned to Mahlee and smiled.

Mahlee smiled, too. "I told those boys what my pa told Dexter Dug, who used to pick on me. I figure the Blanton brothers will leave you both alone from now on. Tied by their toes in a pig pen isn't something they want to know more about."

I laughed and tugged on my crown. "I'm the queen of Michael Meagher Hospital and Beech Street Manor."

Taddy laughed, slapping a balloon animal at me.

I pulled on Mahlee's arm with my left hand. "So how did you get me here?"

CHAPTER THIRTY

THE LONE RANGER TO THE RESCUE

MAHLEE REACHED FOR THE BLUE balloon cat. "You're one lucky hobo kid. JJ Ross rode up when the chicken hawk dove for you a second time. He carried you to Old Post Road. I ran behind his horse carrying White Beard, but I went back for your satchel and lost sight of you."

She shuffled her feet. "Officer Teacup drove up with you in the car after JJ Ross took you to the investigation spot. It was down the highway from the Stamps farm. They were watching trains headed out of town."

Mahlee batted one of the balloons and kept talking. "I figured you were dead. I sat on the side of the road ready to leave when Officer Teacup got out of the car, grabbed my shoulders, and told me to get into his car. He turned on his sirens and you bled on his seats. But he got you here."

I wiped tears from my eyes. "Officer Teacup saved me? The cop who calls me a delinquent? Where's my satchel?"

"It's hanging on your bed post with your cap." Mahlee glanced at Taddy and Grandma. She leaned in to me and whispered in my ear. "I took the note and key from your pocket. They're in my tin can. They're safe."

Taddy hit a balloon toward Mahlee to distract her. "No secrets. No telling secrets."

I grinned at Taddy. "Mahlee told me she brought my satchel home and my hat. I'll need to make sure my red rock is inside the pocket when I get home. Will you look for me?"

"Sure. If I find the rock, do you want me to bring it to you?"

"No. I'm going home soon. Dr. Fly said so."

Grandma moved to the door. "Speaking of Dr. Fly, let me go to the nurse's station and find out when you can go home." Grandma left with Mahlee following her out of my room.

Taddy shuffled to my bed and sat on the edge of the mattress. "Pastor Cody came both days. We were here Sunday until the nurse ran us off. You had a blood transfusion. You lost a lot of blood. The doctor kept saying for every hour you make it, is another hour you'll live."

Taddy kicked his foot. "Pastor Cody let me sit in his lap in the chair by the window. I cried because I should have stopped you from going."

I grabbed the pink dog balloon with my left arm making it bark at Taddy. *Ruff. Ruff. Ruff.* "It's not your fault. I would have gone even if you had tried to stop me."

He grabbed the balloon. "Stop barking at me. Did you know Pastor Cody prayed for you? He kept saying in my ear, perfect love casts out fear. Lord, bring this little girl back to her family. She's made to last."

"He sure prays a lot."

"He is a pastor. Remember?"

"Smarty pants." I hit Taddy with the balloon.

Taddy touched my cast. "I've never had a real friend until you came to us. I'm getting used to having you here."

I scratched the top of my cast wishing I could touch my arm. "I'm getting used to you, too, even if you sneeze too much."

Taddy changed the subject. "I have 'vestigator news for you. Ernie said Kacey Stamps is still at this hospital."

"She is? Let's find her." I sat up.

Taddy rolled his eyes. "I shouldn't have told you. You're going to get us in trouble, aren't you?" Taddy pushed my shoulders back to the bed. "You've got to keep your cast dry, rest, and listen to the doctor before we can become the Lone Ranger and Tonto again."

"Stop talking. You're not a doctor-in-training. Think like me, it's more fun." I put my crown on Taddy's head. "I just want to ask her a few questions."

Taddy removed the crown. "I've hit a Blanton Street boy for you today. I'm not letting you get me in any more trouble. Mama gave me a list of chores for my punishment for the fight. Washing the walls on the carriage house will take four days to complete. They'll get dusty again. I'm not so sure it's worth doing."

I sat back up and swung my legs over, knocking Taddy out of the way as the balloon animals drifted to the tile floor. "I'll go by myself. You can wait here." I shuffled to the door and nearly fell over. "Get over here. I need someone to lean on."

"You're gonna fall." Taddy held my hand as we slipped to the elevator. My bare feet collected grit off the tile and my green pajamas made me a bright target to see.

"I'm staying behind. I am." Taddy kept saying this even when the elevator door opened. Even as I leaned on him. Even as he stepped inside.

Taddy folded his arms. "I'm not going with you. I'm not."

"Too late. You're already in the elevator. Let's go to each floor and see if a cop is posted outside her room." I pressed the number three button.

Taddy whined and held my arm. "Do you really think they'll have a cop guarding her room?"

"JJ Ross will want to keep her alive. If the bad man reads the paper, then he knows she's alive. He might come after her."

On the third floor, I held Taddy's arm, and we stuck our heads out. No cops on this floor, but two people stepped into the elevator making blubbering sounds. The lady in the dotted blue dress wiped a river of tears from her face. The man sobbed, too. He pushed the number one button, and we moved to the first floor. They stumbled out and held each other. If one let go the other would fall.

The elevator stopped on the fourth floor next, followed by the fifth floor. I held the elevator door open and we peeked out together. "Taddy, there's Officer Teacup. He's at the end of the hall."

Taddy backed up. "Officer Teacup knows us. He'll know we're up to more *delinquent* stuff if he sees us."

I grabbed Taddy's arm with my left, shoving him into the hospital room across from the elevator. The snoring man with his mouth open, snorted, and slept through our visit. We waited for the right time to slip to Ms. Stamps' room.

Officer Teacup danced to the nurse's station where a nurse wrote stuff on paper. He smiled at her, she grinned back. He leaned on the counter and asked her if she had time for coffee. She must have said yes, because she stood and they danced around the corner to the left. We watched from the doorway making sure Officer Teacup left.

I held onto the wall with my left arm, and we hurried to what I hoped was the right room. I opened the swinging door and we slipped inside. I flipped on the light. The sun had gone down and the shadows of the night were loose in the hospital—Taddy and Shoelace.

Untied Shoelace

We stood by the side of Kacey Stamps' bed. I leaned in and whispered. "Hi. I'm Shoelace. Can I ask you a question?"

Taddy pulled me back. "We should leave her alone. She's asleep. Her face is wrapped in gauze. She can't talk. She doesn't need us bothering her."

"But this is our chance. One question. Let's ask her one."

A buzzing sound rattled behind the door and came into the room.

We darted behind the big leather chair and peeked around the sides.

"I'm Dr. Doogo Fly, here to check on you, Ms. Stamps. To see if your bandages need changing."

I held my breath and hoped to escape as soon as he finished checking on Ms. Stamps. A swoosh came through the door. A person in a hood. A person wearing black boots.

Taddy whined. "We're gonna die."

The hooded person turned off the light and my hand went to my mouth. I held my breath trying not to cough or choke. Or move.

Cla-plunk. Cla-plunk. The huff-puff breathing sounds reminded me of the attack after Taddy's birthday party. *Cla-plunk.*

Dr. Fly yelled between *cla-plunks*. "Let go of me. Stop. No. Don't ..."

I tried to see around the arm of the chair and saw the shadow of arms waving. Another *swoosh.* More *cla-plunks.*

Dr. Fly cried, "Help me. Someone."

The crashing and snapping stopped. The room went silent, the calm before a tornado rushes in. I trembled and rocked. Taddy pushed closer to me.

The door flew open. "Officer Teacup, are you in here?" The uniform stood in the door and a beam of light from the hallway parted the darkness. Dr. Fly lay across the bottom of the bed. He didn't move.

I screamed from behind the chair. "Help us. Help. Save us."

The uniform called for assistance. "Nurse, I need backup. I need help now." He then rushed into the room and, as the door shut, the shadows returned, followed by three more *cla-plunks*. A breathing blob landed beside the chair. Is it huff-puff man? Or the uniform man?

Taddy whimpered. I could feel my heart beating in my ears. Taddy shook next to me, holding my hand.

The huff-puff man snorted, his words sounded like a person pretending to use an old man's voice. "You're next pretty lady. I should have finished you the other night. This iron pipe will."

I bolted from behind the chair, my words screaming at the shadow. "No. Stop. You have to stop." I called into the darkness.

Taddy screamed. "Don't kill Ms. Stamps."

A scuffle. A thud. Taddy crying. Another clunk. A clanking on the floor. By my foot. I reach for it. It's a pipe.

I swung the pipe at huff-puff man, but I tripped on Taddy who yelled. "Don't kill me. Don't..."

I dropped the pipe, rolled to the floor, and hit my broken arm on the tile. The door flew open again and Officer Teacup bolted into the room, switched the light on, and pointed his gun at huff-puff man. "Don't move. Put your hands up."

Huff-puff man reached for the pipe on the floor.

"I warned you. Stop. Give yourself up." Officer Teacup moved closer.

Taddy screamed and Officer Teacup flinched, giving huff-puff man just enough time to slam a fist into Officer Teacup's face. They toppled to the floor and huff-puff-man punched Officer Teacup, whacking him in the head with the pipe.

Officer Teacup wobbled to his feet, holding his head. Huff-puff man grabbed Taddy and chunked him in the air. Taddy became a soaring boy-rocket and landed on Officer Teacup, and they both fell to the floor.

Huff-puff man ran from the room as Officer Teacup bled on the floor. The other uniform by the chair moaned and Dr. Fly woke up.

I ran to Taddy.

"It's broken." Taddy held his right arm.

"Broken? But Officer Teacup caught you."

"No. He didn't break my arm. You did. You landed on my arm when you ran at the bad man." Taddy cuddled beside me like White Beard does when he's afraid. I put my arm around his shoulder. We waited.

Dr. Fly rubbed his head. "What happened? Who hit me?"

Whistles blew and the halls of the hospital became screams, stomps, and a bustle of noise. Three cops moved into Ms. Stamps' room, but they disappeared to search for the bad man.

JJ Ross came into the room. "The Phantom got away. Did anyone see him?"

We shook our heads *no*, but I wanted to say *yes*.

Dr. Fly moved to Ms. Stamps. "He must have hit me in the head. Ms. Stamps seems fine."

Taddy and me rocked. Taddy cradled his arm.

The Lone Ranger shook his head and put his hands on the butt of his pearl-handled guns as if he planned to get to the bottom of this.

Dr. Fly gathered Taddy into his arms, and I held onto the doctor's white coat.

As we walked to the elevator, JJ Ross called to us. "I will need to talk to both of you about why you were in Ms. Stamps' room. Expect to hear from me." He tipped his hat and gave me that awful wink.

CHAPTER THIRTY ONE

THE VESTIGATORS

"TELL ME WHY I SEE the names Annie Grace Kree and Thaddeus William Day, Jr. on this file?" Sheriff Haskell Surratt waved the folder and showed us the tab with our names printed on it.

"It's says Annie Grace Kree. I'm not sure why." I swung my foot in the big wooden chair as I sat across the desk from the sheriff. I glanced out the window.

The sheriff tapped the desk. "Excuse me. Daydreaming are we?"

I smiled, giving him my grin, the one with no real answers. "No. I'm looking around. Nice office."

Grandma tapped my shoulder. "Shoelace, the sheriff needs to ask you and Taddy a few questions. This is a murder investigation and you have put yourself in the middle of it."

"Yes ma'am."

Taddy kicked his feet. "We're going to jail. I'll never go to fifth grade. I've become a delinquent."

The sheriff continued his quizzing. "Mahlee, I'll have a few questions for you, too. You were at the Stamps farm with Annie Grace and I need answers. I need to figure out how you folks are connected to the Phantom Killer." He placed a red rock on the desk and pointed at me. "Is this yours?"

I grabbed the rock and kissed it. "Where did you get my rock? I carry it in my daddy's satchel."

"We found the rock at the Stamps house on the back porch. You must have dropped it." Sheriff Surratt grinned.

Officer Teacup came into the room greeting Grandma, Priscilla, and Mahlee. He squinted at Taddy and me. I'm not telling him anything, either.

I pointed to Officer Teacup's head with my good arm. "Your head looks better. How many stitches did you get? I got forty stitches. It's been nearly a week, my arm's better. Did you see Taddy's cast? He broke his arm too."

Grandma's arm on my shoulder told me to hush, but the ruckus in the hallway made us turn our heads. Officer Teacup closed the door, but the muffled sounds leaked through the key hole.

I pointed to the door. "What's going on in the hall? Did someone escape?"

The sheriff snapped his finger. "Never mind. Leave the police business to me. I need information from you, right now."

Sheriff Surratt opened the file. "So tell me, Annie Grace. Why were you at the Stockmen Restaurant on Sunday, March 24?"

"I was eating breakfast with my grandma. Did you know two people were found dead in a car?"

He grumbled and went on through his list. "So tell me why Pastor Cody Westside would take you to a church where a hobo was barricaded inside?"

"Pastor Cody's my friend. He prayed for me when I broke my arm." I plopped my right arm onto the desk. "Skip was my friend. Did you know Officer Teacup shot him through the side window of the church? He killed my spelling bee friend. Skip and me always had spelling bees on the rail. Have you ever won a spelling bee, Mr. Sheriff? I have."

He shut the folder. "I'm not Mr. Sheriff. I'm Sheriff Surratt to you. So tell me why you put soap in the town fountain?"

"It was Taddy's birthday. I wanted to make his birthday fun."

"See, we are going to jail," Taddy whined.

Priscilla patted his shoulder.

"So did you give your grandma's scarf to a man whose head got cracked open by the Phantom Killer?"

"Who told you about the scarf?"

"Your grandma."

Sheriff Surratt continued his drilling with more questions. "Did you follow a lady on Blanton Street?"

"Who told you I followed her?"

"Your classmates, Gilbert and Lester. And why were you trespassing at the Stamps farm? Your footprints are all through the house."

"How do you know they're mine? Could be yours. You got PF Flyers? If you do, you might have left prints on the floor."

"Little lady. You need to tell me why you went to the farm."

Taddy became a talking statue in his chair. "I'll tell. I'll tell. Don't throw us in jail."

Sheriff Surratt sent everybody to a side office. "Let me talk to Taddy and his mama." The door shut, but not before I saw the sheriff pulling out a note pad.

The uproar in the hallway grew to such a pitch that Officer Teacup left. Grandma and Mahlee followed him like puppies following a master. And just as I started to go behind them, the sheriff rushed into our little room. "The Phantom Killer has been arrested. He's being brought into custody now. The press is already in the building. How they found out is beyond me."

I peered out the second floor window. People were gathering and in the middle of the cameras, I saw the white hat. It was JJ Ross. He talked with his hands and gave them his glory-be-mine smile.

I opened the door to the sheriff's office and crashed into Priscilla, who was coming out the door herself. "Where is your grandma?"

I pointed to the hall. "She and Mahlee went to see what was going on."

Priscilla looked back at us. "I'll be right back. You two stay put."

We nodded.

I sat in a chair next to Taddy. "Did the sheriff ask you anything? Did he have time to make you talk?"

Taddy sat back in his chair. "No. Nothing."

"What were you going to tell him?"

Taddy raised his eyebrows. "I wanted to tell him how your daddy had died. How you wander off and how your grandma shakes her head at you. And how you're a good fighter."

"Taddy, I'm not sure I need your kind of help." I wandered to Officer Surratt's chair, mocking the sheriff. "Now tell me. What do you know about the murders?"

A file with the name *Presley Samson* lay on the desk. I opened it.

"Close the folder. That file belongs to the sheriff."

"I'm looking to see what the sheriff knows." I scooted to the floor, clutched the file, and slid under the sheriff's desk. "Watch the door. Whistle if you hear anyone coming."

"I can't whistle."

"What can you do?"

"I can sneeze."

"Good. That's your part." I opened the folder. "This woman, Presley Samson, told Officer Teacup things from the murders at the park. Listen to this. They think her husband, York, murdered Peyton Mars and Bay Jo Baxter in April. She gave them lots of clues. If she reads Ernie's stories, she's learned this stuff from the paper."

Taddy leaned over the top of the desk, his nose hanging in front of my folder. "You better put the file down. Stop reading. You're breaking the law. Those are private cop notes. This is their 'vestigation."

"Remember these names. York and Presley Samson. Could be important. I'm after the reward money. This is now a part of our 'vestigating, too."

I pinched Taddy's nose. "Get off the top of the desk. Listen to this. She told Officer Teacup that York put the saxophone in their trunk. Did you hear me? In their trunk."

Taddy slid from the top of the desk, crossed his legs Indian style, and pushed next to me taking the folder away. He pointed at the paper. "Look. They tossed it from the car by a fence at the park. But where at the park?"

I grabbed the pages from Taddy and read on. "Yea. But in this part, Presley Samson says another person gave them the saxophone the day after the murders. That's how the horn got inside the trunk of their car. This Presley woman has different stories. Her version of what happened keeps changing."

Taddy put his finger to his cheek, tapping. "So she keeps changing her story. Maybe she's trying to cover for another crime."

The thunderous cheering outside the windows behind the sheriff's chair caused us to bolt to our feet. Snowflakes of papers scattered to the floor.

I pressed my nose to the glass. "JJ Ross is talking to those people. The whole town is here."

Taddy scooted across the room to the other windows. "The cops have a man in custody. Let's go see."

"What? Now you want to be a 'vestigator?"

"Sure, this is news. I bet Ernie will be there to get the story."

We scooted out of the sheriff's office, found the stairs, and jumped on the steps two at a time. The first floor was filled with uniforms and men with cameras.

Taddy cupped his hands to his mouth. "Ernie. Ernie. Hey, Ernie."

Ernie kept taking notes on his pad.

Taddy ducked beneath the elbows and arm pits and inched over to him.

The room reeked of damp dirt, reminding me of Spring Lake Park at night. A hand touched my shoulder. "Shoelace, where's Taddy?" Priscilla pushed close to me.

"He's over there with Ernie." I bumped my head on her elbow. "Where's Mahlee and Grandma?"

"I lost them outside when we followed the news reporters. I'm sure they're somewhere in this crowd."

I tried to see around the wide people who were also taller than me.

Priscilla bent down to my ear. "I see a man in handcuffs. He's wearing a white shirt with tiny black stripes and a tie. He's kind of thin to be a murderer." She described him like Taddy would.

The flash of the cameras and the 'get-back-stay-clear' orders from the cops smashed the people against the wall. I crawled on my knees, protecting my broken arm from legs and bodies, and snuck to the front to see.

Untied Shoelace

The man in handcuffs shuffled by and I saw his loafers. Small ones. The boots in Ms. Stamps' hospital room the other night were huge compared to this man.

The handcuffed man's voice cut through the mob. "Will they put me in prison for life for stealing cars?"

The man standing above me answered. "They'll put you in prison for life for murder."

Other men and women chanted. "Murderer. Murderer."

The man beside me joined in. "Murderer. You'll pay for this."

The two cops holding onto the handcuffed man rushed him into a secure room across the hallway by Ernie. The door clanked shut. People in skirts and heels, in overalls and slacks pushed and trampled each other. They raced out the glass doors to the streets leaving me shoved in a corner.

The cheers sent me outside. I watched hats fly from heads. One man blasted his shotgun into the air. Birds flew from the oak trees. The voices chanted, "York Samson is the Phantom Killer. We're safe, now. We're safe, now. We're safe, now."

A lone man leaning on the concrete wall softly spoke. "But what if he's not the killer?"

CHAPTER THIRTY TWO

A TASTE OF BLOOD

IT'S BEEN FIVE WEEKS SINCE the Stamps murder. No one else has been murdered since the beginning of May. The cast on my right arm stinks. I may need to soak it in bleach. The arrest of York Samson stinks, too. Things don't add up. York steals cars, and his wife has lied in her police file.

"Taddy, take a whiff. Does my cast stink to you?"

"It stinks because you don't wash it." Taddy stuck his spoon in his oatmeal bowl and came to my side. He sniffed. "Your cast smells like school paste. Mama keeps washing mine with a rag. You might want to try some soap and water."

I put my cast to my nose again. "Yep, mine smells sour." I lost a bite of oatmeal from my mouth, and it splat onto my cast. Licking the oatmeal from the plaster, I made sure Taddy and me were alone. "I've been thinking. Your mama's baked the biscuits for church this morning and, since we're handing out songbooks for Pastor Cody, we could have a 'vestigators' talk by the creek."

Ernie popped into the kitchen holding a magazine under his arm, talking to himself. He glanced into the sauce pan on the stove. "Who made this? This is thick." Ernie spooned out three big scoops into a bowl.

Taddy pressed a glass of milk to his face with his head tilted back, leaving a white mustache on his lips. "Mama poured the oats in the pan while she baked the biscuits. I think she forgot to measure the water. It's a little gooey. Put butter and sugar in it. You'll like it, then."

Ernie placed his bowl on the table. "Where's Ms. Elsie?"

I gave myself a milk mustache, too. "Grandma went to the grocery store with Mahlee. She wanted to go before it got too hot. Did you know the sun has burned up the good air? The Coffeyville bricks in the alley could cook eggs, it's so hot."

Taddy corrected me. "You get your facts mixed up. This is a hot summer. Hottest in years. We still have good air, it's just hot air."

Ernie shuffled to the end of the kitchen. "I need to give your grandma my boarding room rent. I'm sure she could use the money." He pulled out a wad of bills and held the top from the brown ceramic jar with the yellow word *cookies* painted on it. "Her jar is empty. Times must be tight. I'll drop some extra money into the cookie jar."

I hope Ernie wasn't reminding me of how much the front room window had cost. I glued my eyes to his hands, watching him count and add, recount and consider. Ernie tossed the whole wad into the jar in one swoop. "You two keep quiet. Tell your grandma an angel came through the kitchen."

Taddy sat with his back toward Ernie. He agreed without knowing what he nodded to. I smiled. Seeing this side of Ernie was nice. He's become a rich reporter writing those murder stories.

Ernie put pats of butter and four spoons of sugar in his oatmeal. "Not bad. This tastes much better than it looks."

He placed the shiny magazine on the table and Taddy raised his head to get a glance. "That's *Life* magazine. Hey, Donna Reed is on the cover." Taddy moved where he could stand beside Ernie.

I swallowed a bite of oatmeal and shoved in another, talking with food in my mouth. "How do you know who the lady is?"

Taddy pointed to the image. "See, right there. It says Donna Reed."

"Smarty pants. Tonto should talk nicer to the Lone Ranger. Who is Donna Reed?"

Ernie smiled and opened the magazine. "She's a famous movie star."

White Beard jumped from a chair to the table and landed with his face in my bowl of oatmeal.

Achoo. Achoo. Taddy sneezed with a wheeze. "Get your cat off this table."

"Sorry. He wanted a bite." I picked up my speckled red-stained kitten and placed him on the floor. Living outside with the rest of his kitty-cat family might be next, since he keeps getting into food, the trash, and leaving little puddles on the floor. Grandma's grown tired of him. But I love him, messy or not. No matter where I go, White Beard will be with me.

Taddy frowned at me and wiped his nose with his hand. He turned to Ernie. "Did you write a story about the murders for the magazine?"

"I wish I had. A city reporter did. That's why I bought a copy. Texarkana is big news now. The paper in Dallas has run a story, too. I'm gonna need a copy of that, too." Ernie flipped the pages to the article. "The caption says, *Texarkana Terror*."

"Let me see." I slid my bowl across the table to get closer, grabbed my spoon, and remembered that my kitty ate out of the bowl. I pushed the bowl back.

Ernie recited the story out loud. "The Phantom killed in three-week intervals, and he attacked and murdered couples but left no clues. The local police, the FBI, and the Texas Rangers continue to search cooling trails."

I pulled the magazine right in front of me, near my chest. "The pictures show booby traps in houses and a picture of people in the Grim. There's Clara's family, with her ma and her pa. Even their dog, Spot, is in the picture. It says Bay Jo Baxter gave Clara a dog." I rubbed my hand over the photo, hard. "Wipe that smile off your face, little Ms. Clara fancy dress."

Ernie interrupted me. "They got one part right. The Phantom Killer is at large."

In unison, Taddy and me poured out questions. "What? It's not York Samson? Did he escape?"

Ernie's voice quivered. "He didn't escape. But York fell asleep when they gave him the truth serum and his finger prints are nowhere at the farm. And none of the other crime scenes have prints." He sucked in the rest of the hot morning air, and a hush swooped into the kitchen, wiping out the smell of freshly baked biscuits.

Taddy pulled up a chair, I fell back in mine, and we three sat in silence until Ernie broke the thickness. Ernie rubbed his face. "Catch me up. Where did you say everyone is?"

Taddy pointed toward his building. "Mama's at our apartment dusting off the furniture. She says we're moving home since the Phantom Killer is locked up. He is locked up, right?" Taddy looked at Ernie who didn't answer. "Maybe we should stay at the manor a little longer."

Taddy moved to the screen door, looking through the mesh. "She should be on her way back. It's time to leave for the creek."

I went to the door hoping to see Priscilla and turned back to Ernie, to answer his 'catch me up' question. "Mahlee and

Grandma went to the store, remember? Grandma's teaching her to bake a cobbler this afternoon."

Ernie read silently to himself, gave a delayed nod, and ate his oatmeal, and then spoke. "Cobbler. Now that does sound good."

Taddy paced around the kitchen. "It's been five weeks. All the killings happened in three-week periods. It's past time for a killing or attack. Maybe the Phantom Killer has left town."

White Beard hopped on the table, and I tossed him out to the yard. It was time for hobo church. Where is Priscilla?

Ring-a-ling. Ring-a-ling. Ring-a-ling.

Ernie hurried to the phone. "Calm down. There's blood coming under the closet door? I'm coming. Call the police." He slammed the phone down, raced to the kitchen counter drawer, grabbed his gun, and stormed out the door.

We raced out after Ernie, jumping the picket fence, even though we now had a gate. We went up the stairs to the second floor and followed Ernie to Taddy's apartment.

Priscilla stood in the hallway, crying and shaking her head. "No. Not another killing. Why would a murderer put a body in our apartment?" Priscilla ran across the hall and grabbed Taddy, holding him at her side at the top of the stairs.

The other three apartment doors stayed shut, but the scuffling behind the doors told me people were home. Taddy's entire apartment would fit inside the front room of the manor. Ernie has to be finished searching.

"Ernie? Did you find anything?" I peeked in.

"Stay back. There's blood on the floor by the closet next to the bathroom."

My PF Flyers inched through the doorway. Priscilla pulled my blonde pony-tail. "Annie Grace, get back here."

"I want to help Ernie. Let me go."

Priscilla's red-rimmed eyes, her face wrenched with fear, made me want to go inside even more.

Taddy yanked on my overalls. "Let Ernie check this out."

I slapped his hand off my shoulder, pulled away, and raced into the apartment.

Ernie waved for me to stop about two feet away from where he stood. "Wait there. Watch the blood." He bent over, turned the door knob on the closet, and opened the door. Suitcases tumbled from the top shelf, along with blankets and winter coats. They landed on Ernie and me. Ernie toppled backwards and bumped into me.

I slipped in the blood and tumbled to the floor.

Ernie's words were muffled. He tossed a pile of coats to the side. "Where's the body?" He dug through the rest of the clothes hanging in the closet, tossing totes, and throws on top of me.

"Hey. I'm under here."

My face hit the hardwood floor. My right ear and cheek stuck to the blood. I rolled over. The cast on my right arm slid off in pieces. The fall must have cracked the plaster. My arm felt great, until I saw the blood coming from a box. "Wait, what's this?"

Officer Teacup tore into the apartment, skidding on the floor in his shiny black shoes. "Ernie, what are you looking for in that closet?"

"The body. It's gone." Ernie shook his head. "Look for yourself."

I stood and Officer Teacup gave me his get-out-of-the-way stare. "Let me look."

I held the box in front of me, hoping they would look at it. "But Ernie. Officer Teacup. There's no dead body. A giant box of melted peppermints died in this closet. It's so hot in here. No wonder they melted." I pointed at the floor. "This is red peppermint candy on the floor … not blood." I swooshed my fingers in the red syrup, licking them as Taddy and Priscilla came into the room.

Taddy screamed. "What are you doing, Shoelace?"

Priscilla pushed me away from the sticky spot and Officer Teacup wasted no time checking out the goo on the floor. "Yep. Candy. Melted. Not blood. I have wasted my time coming to this side of town, once again."

Taddy reached for a box of the soaked gooey candy and showed his mama. "This is one of those boxes of candy canes the church ladies gave you last Christmas. We were storing them in here. Remember?"

Officer Teacup hurried down the stairs because his radio on the patrol car blasted words of an emergency. I opened the front window and eavesdropped.

The radio voice repeated. "We have an *11-79*. A car accident in front of Piggly Wiggly. Also an *11-44*. Two people deceased. Coroner needed."

CHAPTER THIRTY THREE

SWAY BACK RIDES

THREE POLICE CARS SAT IN the middle of the road blocking traffic.

"There's an ambulance." Taddy pushed my face against the glass in the back seat of Ernie's Studebaker.

Priscilla pointed from the seat in front of me as Ernie steered the car into Piggly Wiggly's parking lot. He stopped the car at the far end of the store.

I climbed from the car and caught my shoelace on the edge of the door. Untwisting myself, Taddy pushed me. "You're in the way. Move." Taddy monkey-climbed over me.

I fell forward and both my knees hit the hard clay. I dusted off and started looking for my grandma. I searched the faces in the crowd who gathered on the side of the road. I called Grandma more than a million times. I bounced like a pogo stick and went to where lopsided bales of hay sat sideways on the bed of a pickup truck. "Grandma. Grandma."

Taddy tapped me on the shoulder. "Why is there hay scattered on the highway?"

"I don't know." I saw Officer Teacup and ran to him. "Where's my Grandma? Where's Mahlee? Are they dead?"

"Your grandma? Your grandma's fine. Mahlee is, too. Two hobos got hurt riding with Pastor Cody. They fell from the bed of his pickup when another man lost his hay."

"They're alive? Where are they?"

"In the store. Let's go find them."

Pastor Cody walked up with Slow Tom and Fast Tim. Everyone talked at the same time to Officer Teacup, but he finally turned to me. "Just one second. I'll help you find your grandma and Mahlee."

I waited with my arms folded and Slow Tom rubbed the bandage on his forehead. "I got knocked from the truck. Hit my head. Cut it, too."

Fast Tim showed me his wounds. "I … I … sc … scraped … scraped … mmmmy … arm and my legs, ttt …ttore holes in my jeans. Well, more holes. The nnnnice … la la …lady in the ambulance wrapped gauze a … a …around my arm."

The two brothers compared injuries as if they were trying to outdo each other. The whole time, I crossed my arms, uncrossed them, and crossed them back, waiting on Officer Teacup.

I tugged on Officer Teacup's arm and knocked his pad to the ground. "If Grandma and Mahlee are alive, then why did the lady on your radio say there were dead people at the accident? Where is my grandma? Where is Mahlee? Your radio-lady scared me."

Officer Teacup knelt in front of me, grabbing both my hands as if he saw me for the first time. "Our dispatcher's new at the office. She's filling in. The measles have been going through our office. Ms. Hazel is sick. I'm sorry the call scared you."

I sobbed and Officer Teacup gathered me in his arms. "Look, there's your grandma and Mahlee coming out of the store now."

"Shoelace. Shoelace." Grandma's voice sang a bellowing noise of joy. Mahlee mumbled words under her breath and smiled.

Untied Shoelace

I rushed to Grandma's round body and squished myself as close as I could, grabbing Mahlee in the family embrace. "The dispatcher lady made me think you were in a car wreck. The voice on the radio said people died."

Grandma patted my head. "I'm not asking how you overheard the radio on a police car. Right now, let's check on Slow Tom and Fast Tim. I've got them a soda water to drink. This heat wave's going nowhere soon."

"They're doing good." I pointed them out in the crowd.

Ernie ran and snatched Mahlee into his arms. "Mahlee, are you all right?" He kissed her more times than I've ever kissed anyone.

"Yes. I'm fine. Ms. Elsie and me were shopping and digging through coupons when the crash caused everybody to jump and run to the front glass."

Ernie hugged Mahlee, and they cuddled right there in the parking lot.

Grandma dished out orders to Slow Tom and Fast Tim. "I'll make up the bed in the room by mine. No one's slept in there since Otto died. Both of you are coming to the manor. You can rest for a couple of days. Fried chicken might help you heal faster, too. And no chores. I promise."

Saying no to Grandma is hard, even for me. Hard for anyone.

Pastor Cody tried to change her mind. "I've got plenty of food at my house. Lots of hobos are still scared to return to Hobo Jungle. I've got a house full."

"In that case, you could use two less mouths to feed. It's settled. They're coming to the manor for a few days. They replaced the window in the front room, fixed the fence, and put in a new gate for me. I owe them. So bring them on over."

Pastor Cody scratched his head. I wanted to tell him to let it go. Grandma always wins.

On the way to the manor, Taddy and me leaned against the front seat listening to Priscilla's conversation with Grandma. The death of the peppermints at the apartment made Grandma laugh. Priscilla folded her arms, the same way I do when I'm in trouble or when Officer Teacup makes me wait. "Stop laughing at me. This isn't funny."

"But you saw melted red candy and assumed it was a dead body in your closet. That is funny. Priscilla, these murders have you rattled."

Priscilla's voice squealed. "Now don't laugh. I didn't know it was candy on the floor. Someone could have been murdered in the apartment. Stop laughing. It's not funny."

"It's very funny. Dead candy is not a dead body." Grandma's shoulders shook.

Priscilla smiled. "I guess it's a little funny."

Grandma and Priscilla laughed, and their giggles reminded me of kids playing in the park.

Touching Grandma's shoulder, I blurted out. "Ernie thinks the Phantom Killer is still loose. He thinks York Samson is just a car thief. I do, too. Besides, the gun at the Stamps farm was a .22 and the other gun was a .32. The fingerprints don't match and the farm isn't on lover's lane." I rattled on with my clues while Grandma and Priscilla talked louder than me. The most important words I've ever said were lost in the car.

Taddy pulled my sleeve. "Stop talking so much. They aren't listening."

I leaned back against the seat, crossing my arms.

Taddy punched me. "You are acting like White Beard when he gets kicked off the table. And just because the evidence doesn't add up doesn't mean it's not the same person. The killer could be trying to throw the cops off track."

"Really, off track? I hadn't thought about that. I wish they would listen to me. I have a lot to say. If I could talk as loud as Officer Teacup's car radio, they might listen to me."

Taddy shook his head. "Whiner."

"I am not a whiner." I stuck out my tongue at Taddy.

Grandma chatted away. "Priscilla, you and Taddy stay as long as you need to. We want you safe. We have enough pots and pans, and string, and locks to keep us protected. I've got my shotgun. I'm not sure if I shoot any better than Shoelace, but I'll use it if an intruder comes inside the manor." Grandma squeezed Priscilla's hand.

"Grandma, I'm talking. *Meow . . . meow.*"

Taddy whispered. "I'm calling you White Beard."

I slugged his arm and pushed him to the floor board. Taddy stuck his tongue out at me and climbed back into the seat.

I pulled on Grandma's sleeve five times. "Grandma. Grandma."

"What do you want?"

"Why did you ask Slow Tom and Fast Tim to stay with us?"

She turned the car down Beech Street. "They've been good to me."

I squirmed in my seat. "But we need paying boarders. Ernie put his rent money in the cookie jar this morning and a wad of bills to go with it. He said the jar was empty, needed replenishing."

Taddy scooted closer to me. "You were supposed to say an angel put the extra money in the jar."

"Ernie's no angel."

"He was this morning."

Grandma guided the car with her hands. Her knuckles are bigger than most folks. It must be from stirring cake batter.

"We've got plenty of food. We have beds, running water, and clothes. We have each other. We're rich. My pa taught me a lesson on being kind, whether your cookie jar is full or not."

Taddy and me sat shoulder to shoulder. We leaned on the front seat again.

"Remember your friend, Skip? He was also my friend. I've known him since we were little kids."

"No way, you've been friends that long?"

"Yes. Skip used to live in Hobo Jungle with his uncle. He used to pet our horse on Saturdays when we rode Sway Back into town. I always sat behind my pa. He sat lower than me in the swayed part."

"Was that the horse you grew up with?" My ears listened like this was a clue to an investigation.

"Yes, Sway Back was my pa's brown horse. No one rode him because he shuffled lopsided down the road." Grandma wiped her eye and sniffled. "Pa had to ride him out of that corral. He didn't like to leave. But on each trip, I'd get a piece of stick candy before we'd leave town, and Pa had a hard time getting Sway Back to go home. Once he was out, he stopped and licked the hand of every kid he saw."

Taddy tapped Grandma. "How old was Skip then?"

"About ten. Same as you two." Grandma steered the car around another corner, drove to Broad Street, and parked.

I peered out the window. "What are we doing here?"

"This is Hart's Drug. This corner used to have a general store before the fire." She pointed to the sidewalk. "I ate root beer stick candy right there. After the store burned, the owner built a drug store in its place. I can see a jar of candy on the counter, even now."

Grandma pointed to the spot by the pole and backed up the car. "Back then, you tied your horse out front and left him

238

while you shopped. One day, Skip whispered to Sway Back as I chomped on my candy. Pa asked him what he said to our horse. He told us he wished he could enter a spelling bee, because if he won, maybe the prize would be a stick of candy."

Taddy licked his lips. "I love root beer candy."

I licked my lips. "Me, too. I sure miss Skip. He was my friend."

Grandma nodded. "I miss him, too. My pa tossed Skip two copper pennies one day, and after that, Pa gave Skip pennies every time we rode to town. Pa also started buying stick candy for Skip, too."

I rubbed my eyes. "He should be alive. He got mixed up in something that went bad."

Grandma pulled the car into the alley and stopped by the carriage house. She turned to me. "We all get mixed up, sometimes. God helps me figure things out when my cookie jar runs low and fixing fried chicken for a couple of friends is what my pa would do. A soft quilt for Slow Tom and Fast Tim may feel like copper pennies to them. And that refills my cookie jar."

I had to tell Grandma the truth. "Grandma. your quilts can be a little scratchy. The one on my bed right now is soft. But Taddy said the one on his bed is itchy."

"Leave me out of this." He pinched my arm.

"Stop pinching me."

"Both of you. Stop it. It's been a long day. I'll make sure Slow Tom and Fast Tim have soft quilts. I can fix the laundry. But what am I going to do with you two?"

I whispered in Grandma's ear. "You could buy us root beer stick candy at the store next time."

Taddy shouted. "I love root beer candy."

At the house, Slow Tom and Fast Tim met us in the alley. Slow Tom grabbed a sack of groceries and bragged on Mahlee's jewelry. "I saw Mahlee's getting-married ring. But the blue ring on her other hand is the prettiest thing this side of the train tracks. I love that ring."

Priscilla scowled, and her head turned to Slow Tom with a jerk. "It's just a ring. Nothing special, unless it belongs to …" Her words trailed off and Priscilla dropped her grocery sack.

She ran into the house talking louder than she should. "I have to find out. I have to see. I bet the ring's stolen."

CHAPTER THIRTY FOUR

STAIRCASE VOICES

ERNIE MET US AT THE back door. "Ms. Elsie, Pastor Cody went to Hobo Jungle to let everyone know why he missed church. He thanked you for taking care of his buddies."

"I'm glad to have the company." Grandma bent down and picked up Priscilla's sack from the ground. "I'm glad this package of flour didn't pop."

I walked next to Grandma. "What's wrong with Priscilla? She's acting happy one day and sad the next. She's starting to act like Mahlee."

Grandma handed me the flour. "Women get cranky sometimes. She'll be fine."

Ernie rushed to the car and helped carry the rest of the grocery sacks inside. He hugged Mahlee and smooched with her on his last trip from the car. "I'll be back after supper. I've got to write a story on the accident for tomorrow's paper."

Mahlee headed upstairs, and I dug through the brown sacks looking for anything as good as root beer stick candy. I found a can of cocoa and remembered drinking my first cup at the house of a witch in Boone, Missouri. Nicest witch I've ever met.

Taddy dripped water on the floor from a glass and plopped down in a chair. Grandma escorted Slow Tom and Fast Tim up the stairs, showing them to their room. Her orders for them to rest came with *yes ma'am.*

Humming, she came down the stairs carrying a bunch of quilts in her arms. "I'm washing these. I'll make sure they come out of the washer soft. I'll watch the rinse cycle, get them hung on the clothesline, and then, I'll get the chicken frying."

As soon as the screen door to the kitchen slammed, Priscilla rushed to the bottom of the stairs. I followed her and she tapped her shoe on the first step. Her hand squeezed the rail like she was waiting for a signal to rush up the stairs.

Mahlee rounded the top of the stairs and bounced on each step, but she stopped half way down. "Priscilla. What are you doing? What's wrong?"

Priscilla marched toward Mahlee. "I see you're wearing the blue ring. When I first saw it on your hand at the Grim Hotel, I never expected to see you or the ring again. I'm seeing the ring whenever I bump into you. I have to know. My pa had a jeweler etch Margo's initials on the gold band. If that ring is hers, you'll see the letters MW for Margo Wall on the band."

Mahlee swung around holding her right hand outstretched, teasing. "It's on my finger. You can't read it unless I take it off."

Priscilla moved up another step. "Then take the ring off and let me see."

"A friend gave this to me. It's mine, it's not yours."

Priscilla tried to yank the ring from Mahlee's finger. My PF Flyers ran to the bottom of the stairs. "So, who is going to help me cut up the chicken for supper? Grandma doesn't like me to use knives."

Priscilla let go of Mahlee's hand and moved to the side of the rail. Mahlee gave her the evil squinty-eyed look.

I pranced to the kitchen hoping one of them would follow me.

"This is my ring."

"Let me look. If the band has initials, we'll know the truth."

Their arguing brought Taddy and me back to the front room. Mahlee pulled the ring from her hand and threw it at Priscilla's face. The gold clanked on the hardwood floor and rolled near Taddy's foot.

Priscilla got closer to Mahlee, closer than Ernie does when he's kissing her. "Don't throw things at me. Every time I see the ring, I wonder where my twin sister might be. Margo's been missing way too long …"

Mahlee pursed her lips. "But you're calling me a thief."

The arguing, spitting, and near pushing brought Slow Tom and Fast Tim from their room. They watched from the second floor rail, staying out of the fight. Taddy grabbed the ring from the floor the first chance he could and tucked it inside his pants pocket.

I moved to his side. "What are you doing?"

"Be quiet. Mama doesn't know where the ring went."

Mahlee raced to her room, shouting. "Why is it always so dark? Even at the manor." She returned and pulled on the old grocery cart loaded with her tin can, clothes, and the pillow Grandma had given her. "I'm leaving. Not staying here. I'm not a thief."

Thud-thud-thud.

I stood guard at the bottom of the stairs. "You have to stay. I need you."

"Move out of the way. I'm no thief. Priscilla wants the ring. She can have it. I'm going back to the rail."

I blocked her way. "No. You told Daddy you'd take care of me."

Mahlee shook her head. "You have your grandma. Besides, Priscilla has cast me out. Nobody calls me a thief. She thinks I'm no good. I'm probably not good enough for Ernie, either."

Taddy got between Mahlee and his mama. "Mama, stop fighting." He put his hand in his pocket and slapped the blue oval ring into his mama's hand. He turned to Mahlee. "Stay, please. Don't go."

Priscilla unfolded her palm, glanced at the band, and crumpled to the floor. She whispered, "MW. This is Margo's ring." Priscilla clutched the ring to her chest whispering Margo's name.

Mahlee rolled the cart across the front room, out the oval door, and across the porch. The cart clunked through the gate with me running behind her.

"Mahlee. Stay. Please stay." I called to her, but the clunking of her cart drowned out most of my words.

Mahlee pointed her finger at me. "You stay with your grandma. This is your home now." She pulled the engagement ring from her finger and threw it at me. "Give this to Ernie. I won't need it."

My last cries went unheard as she rounded the corner and headed toward the tracks. I slipped the ring into my pocket and ran back to my oak tree. I hugged the tree and sobbed. Writing a poem today will be easy. It's the day Priscilla ripped Mahlee and me apart.

I ran into the house to slug Priscilla, but I stopped in the doorway when Priscilla's voice shook the pictures on the wall.

"I didn't mean to yell at her. Or call her a thief. I pushed her too hard. I miss my sister. The stress gets to me."

244

Grandma rushed into the room. "What's going on in here? I can hear you screaming from the carriage house."

I stepped up to Grandma. "It's a fight. Priscilla did it. She ran Mahlee off over the ring."

Grandma hugged Priscilla. "We'll work this out. You'll see."

"Don't hug her. She's the reason for all the screaming." I put my hands in my pockets and inched toward Taddy, who sat on the bottom step of the stairs with his head tucked in his hands.

Slow Tom and Fast Tim must have ducked into their room.

Priscilla gazed at the ring. "My pa gave this ring to Margo after the kidnapping at the Grim. He hoped the ring would let her know her family loved her. The next week, a train jumped the tracks, and Pa's Model T got slammed by a boxcar. After Pa died, Margo lost reality. She heard voices and talked to them."

Taddy stood and moved next to his mama hanging on her skirt, taking in every word.

"Margo would go to Rose Hill Cemetery every day and talk to our pa at his marker. She also talked to other members of our family who were buried there." Priscilla gave Taddy a glance like she might have wished she'd kept those words inside her mouth.

Grandma's eyes widened and she shook her head. "Was she a happy little girl? Did she hear voices then?"

"She had happy times, but the voices in her head caused confusion. As she got older, the voices spoke to her and made her hide from people. Then one day she ran off and never came back." Tears rolled down Priscilla's cheeks. "All these murders and being afraid, I'm feeling trapped inside the house. And now, I've run Mahlee off. I love Mahlee. I have to go after her."

I went to the front door and turned the knob for her and Priscilla ran down the street, disappearing downtown. I wiped the tears from my face.

Taddy reached for my hand. He slipped his pudgy fingers around mine. "I'm sorry. Mahlee will come back."

Grandma scooted to the other side of me. She wrapped her arm around my shoulder. "My pa used to tell me families figure things out, and families stick together. Mahlee will figure this out. You'll see."

I held onto Taddy's hand wishing for a horse to take me far, far away. To a place where no one dies. To a place where no one cries. Where no one leaves. Where life comes without sway back moments and lost rings.

CHAPTER THIRTY FIVE

A STOLEN TREASURE

PRISCILLA WASTED NO TIME PACKING her belongings and insisting on Taddy doing the same. "Ms. Elsie, we appreciate the hospitality. This is Mahlee's home, and I've caused her undue harm. We'll go home. If we leave, she'll come back. Sorry to be such a bother. We stayed too long as it is."

Grandma kissed Taddy on the head. "You come over anytime. You're welcome here. We will always be family. Priscilla, do come for coffee soon." Grandma followed them out the back door, using her apron to wipe tears from her eyes.

I ran upstairs to my dresser. I wasn't saying goodbye to Priscilla. I'll tell Taddy bye later in the tree. I grabbed my treasure-key and the note that Mahlee had returned to me and tucked them in my pocket. I raced by Grandma at the kitchen door and jumped down the steps.

Grandma called to me through the screen. "Supper will be ready soon."

"I'm not hungry anymore. I'm never eating again. I'm watering my peanuts."

"But you love fried chicken. I'll have it ready in no time."

"I'm not hungry." I hurried to the yard and turned on the faucet, spraying water on White Beard's fur. He darted to the alley. The Three Stooges lapped water from the puddles, until

I sprayed them. I watered my plants, hoping for peanuts this fall, if I don't leave before then.

I watered the side wall of the carriage house and hosed the quilts hanging on the clothesline. The heat dried them before I could soak the next one, the sun hot like pain and sorrow.

Grandma yelled through the screen. "Shoelace, those quilts are for Slow Tom and Fast Tim. Enough watering."

"Yes ma'am." I drifted to the side of the house so she couldn't see me. I washed the dust off the picket fence, but as soon as Ernie parks his car the dirt will settle on the slats again. I need to figure out what my key goes to and if I have a hidden treasure. If Mahlee leaves, we could use some money for the trip.

I tossed the hose to the ground, hitting Rainbow in the head as she waddled to the shade by the back of the house. She's looking a little fat again. I hope she's eating too much and not making kittens.

Ernie skidded sideways in his Studebaker and splashed mud on me as he parked the car. He jumped from the driver's seat and ran into the backyard. I ran to him and pulled on his shirt. "I need your help."

He pushed my hand away. "It will have to wait. Ms. Elsie called the paper. Mahlee's not gone, is she?" He didn't wait for my answer and ran inside the house.

I turned the water off and followed him to the kitchen. Slow Tom and Fast Tim were sitting at the table watching Grandma flour the pieces of chicken. They were drinking tea, and their eyes were glued to the frying pan.

Grandma wiped her hands on her apron and tried to make Ernie slow down. "Ernie, calm down. Mahlee will come home." She held his shoulders, but he pulled away from her.

He sprinted up to the second floor, and I waited at the bottom to see what Ernie might do next.

I didn't wait long. Ernie raced down the stairs, and he knelt low enough to look me in the eyes. The sweat on his forehead poured into his eyes. "Shoelace, you know where Mahlee would hide. Take me there."

"Okay. Quit pulling on me."

I hurried out the door and hopped into Ernie's car. Ernie was right behind me, but he stormed back to the house. In minutes, he came running to the driver's side of the car. He opened the door and started to get in. "I forgot something."

Priscilla waved at him.

"What? I'm in hurry."

She handed Ernie a piece of paper. "Give this to Mahlee."

I glanced out the back window of the car as we drove away. Taddy came to his mama's side and gave me a small wave.

I turned around in the seat, pulled myself to the dash, and pointed for Ernie to turn right. "Go to Front Street. Park by Union Station. We can take the trail beside the creek. Mahlee hides under bridges when she's scared."

"Hold on." Ernie skidded into a parking place and jumped from the car. "Let's hurry." He dashed down the first trail we came to.

"Come back. That trail's called Axe Handle Trail for a reason."

Ernie stopped, his eyes bigger than an owl watching for mice at night. "Which way?"

"Follow me. I know these trails. We have to go through the thick brush. We'll probably get chiggers." My feet took off like I was being chased by railroad cops. I stopped when I heard a hissing sound and froze.

"Are we close?" Ernie asked, running into me.

"Be quiet. There's a copperhead. It's by that bush."

Ernie reached behind his back and yanked out a gun. He pointed the barrel at the snake. The whistle on a train sent birds fluttering from the brush. Ernie fired his gun at the snake and the blast rattled my bones as the snake's head exploded into pieces.

I screamed and jumped like a rabbit. "Why did you bring a gun?"

Ernie sighed. "There could be a killer hiding in these woods. I have to save Mahlee. She's the first woman I've ever loved. I can't live without her." Ernie tucked the gun back in his waist.

"I'm glad you brought it. You're a better shot than Grandma and me." I tugged on his arm, and we walked around the bend. "The bridge is up there. I see her cart by the hill. She's curled up with her pillow."

Standing by the rushing creek, the dark green pool of water under the tracks slapped foam waves on the bank. Ernie wiped his eyes, his sobs deep like rushing water. "What if she says no? I have to take her home with me."

"You go talk to her. I'll stay right here with her cart." I pulled the engagement ring from my pocket. "You'll need this."

Ernie climbed the embankment, taking steps forward and several back, determined to get there, even on all fours.

I saw Mahlee's tin can in the cart. It called to me and my fingers were tempted to take a peek. Watching Ernie try to convince Mahlee to come with us made me want to go up the hill. I tapped my fingers on the can again.

Trains chugged out of the station over the bridge, humming toward Rose Hill Cemetery. The engines pulled the boxcars along the tracks to a clackety-clackety hammering sound like a dozen metal doors slamming at the same time.

Ernie sat down by Mahlee's pillow stroking her hair. She swung and socked Ernie in the jaw. He fell a few feet down the hill and then crawled back to her.

Mahlee turned to Ernie, her eyes focusing. Ernie put his hand to his face to block the next blow, and she grabbed his face, kissing his already swollen jaw. She wrapped both arms around him.

He scooted closer to her, and his gun slipped from his belt, tumbling to my feet.

I picked it up and tried to hear what they were saying. Another train roared into the station, and the steam poured above us.

Ernie nodded, grabbed Mahlee's chin, and kissed her. She returned the kiss. They cuddled under the bridge, and I turned to watch the creek. I glanced to see if the kissing had stopped just as Ernie pulled the engagement ring from his pocket. He slipped the ring onto her left hand.

I jumped and shouted. "Mahlee's coming home. Mahlee's coming home." When I landed on the fourth jump, the gun slipped from my hand, and I dove for it. I saved the gun from falling into the water.

Ernie handed Mahlee the note from Priscilla. She wadded the paper up without reading the words and tossed the note to the ground. The paper rolled lopsided down the slope to the creek. I reached for the paper as a wave splashed at my feet, missed it, and the note rolled into the water, gone forever.

I lost my balance trying not to fall into the creek, landed sideways, and squeezed the handle of the gun when I tumbled to the ground. The blast underneath me went *p-taff* in my hand like a giant firework, shooting a bullet into the woods.

Mahlee waved her pillow above her head and ran to me with Ernie, who stumbled down the hill behind her. He searched for wounds. "Are you shot? Are you hurt? How did you get my gun?"

"It fell when you were kissing Mahlee."

Mahlee grabbed the gun from my hand and hit me with her pillow. "Leave guns alone. You need to learn how to use one. Until then, leave them be."

"Sorry. It was accident. I nearly fell in the water." I gave Mahlee my famous grin hoping she'd feel sorry for me.

Ernie snatched the gun from Mahlee, and she put her pillow in the cart. "I'll roll my cart into these bushes for now, but I'm taking my tin can with me."

I reached for the can. "I'll get it for you."

"No. Get away." Mahlee bumped me aside, and she knocked the can from the cart. It rolled to the ground and the lid popped off. Mahlee scrambled for her trinkets, scouring the bushes for her items. "It's gone. My gun is gone. Someone has stolen it."

I looked into the can. "Maybe you lost it."

"I never take the gun out. Someone took my gun."

Ernie patted her shoulder. "Honey, you probably lost your gun back when you were staying at Hobo Jungle. It's probably long gone. When did you last look inside your can?"

She shook her head like she was trying to remember. "Weeks. It's been weeks." She swatted Ernie's hand from her arm, stomped her boots, and pursed her lips. "I found that gun in '43 and now it's lost. I've never even used it. I never even got bullets for it."

Ernie held her hand. "You can use my gun anytime you want." He whispered in her ear, she smiled, and she clutched her tin can.

252

Untied Shoelace

I held Mahlee's waist as we sauntered to the car. I whispered toward her other ear, even though the words landed on her shoulder. "I'm glad you're coming back. I need you to watch out for me. So why didn't you read Priscilla's note?"

Mahlee shrugged her shoulders and sighed. "I don't care what she has to say."

Ernie gave me a glance like Grandma does when she wants me to be quiet.

In the car, I asked Ernie what I wanted to earlier, before he took me searching for Mahlee. "I need your help. My daddy left me a key and a note. What does Box 406, Stateline Fountain Bank mean?" I held the key out for Ernie to see.

He turned his head. "It's a safety deposit box key. People store important papers or even money inside boxes at the bank." Ernie steered the car to Stateline Avenue. "I have an idea. My friend, Mr. Shiloh, is the bank president. Let's see if he'll meet us. He owes me a couple of favors."

We waited outside the bank for thirty minutes until Mr. Shiloh got there. Too long for me to wait. Too long to watch Ernie and Mahlee kiss in the front seat of the car.

In the room with lots of key holes, Mahlee waited with me as I put my key into the small metal door. The container was bigger than a Corn Flakes box. Ernie stayed by the front doors with Mr. Shiloh, talking wrecks and murders.

"I hope this has the treasure." I opened the lid and saw a flour sack folded in thirds. I unfolded the canvas and peeked inside, seeing small pieces of paper. "What's this?"

Mahlee stuck her hand into the sack. "Receipts? They have your grandpa's name on them. Otto Kree."

Her puzzled gaze matched mine.

"So this is my grandpa's stuff? Why would my daddy have his pa's things?" I pushed my hand into the sack. "What's this? It's money. Lots of it. Look at this money."

Mahlee peered into the sack. "Bundles and bundles. Where did it come from?"

I threw the money down. "Grandpa got robbed on the same day he died. My daddy was the last to see him alive."

Mahlee wiped her lips, paced, and mumbled. She got lost in her own pain. "Your daddy had a few bad times. But he treated me good. I've had a few bad times myself. I should have never taken that blasted ring. On the night when darkness swallowed me up, a lady in the other hospital bed gave it to me. When she told them doctors she heard voices in her head, they carried her away screaming."

I clutched the money to my chest. "Was it Margo?"

"Yes. She looked like Priscilla, only with hard eyes."

"We have to tell Priscilla."

"No. Margo wanted to disappear." Mahlee cried sobs like those of a person whose past held more secrets, even more than Daddy buried with him falling from the train.

Tears streamed down my face. I never wanted to think Daddy might be a bad man. But if I 'vestigated Daddy, I'd say he was a thief.

I put the money back in the flour sack. "I've got to make this right." I turned to Mahlee and looked her in the eyes. "And we have to tell Priscilla about Margo."

Mahlee whispered, "I'm not telling Priscilla anything. I'm not talking to her."

CHAPTER THIRTY SIX

GIGGLES FOR SHOELACE

"WHITE BEARD. STOP CHEWING ON those five dollar bills." I yanked the money from kitty's mouth although his claw ripped the end of one bill. "White Beard, you're tearing the money in pieces and making me lose count."

He meowed, pounced into the stacks on the mattress, and scattered the money. I put the bills back into stacks and recounted the Lincolns, the Hamiltons, and the Jacksons. Every afternoon after chores, I sit on my bed and count the treasure. The first four days after I carried the flour sack to my room, I counted nearly the same amount but different.

"This is a lot of money." I tickled White Beard's tummy, his claws latching onto my wrist. He hung above the treasure and slipped from my arm, smashing into the bills with a poof, and he attacked the money.

I started giving Mahlee a bundle of bills. At first, she argued with me, but then I reminded her how this would help Grandma with the rent. Mahlee's been dropping money into the cookie jar every few days.

I shoved White Beard to the other side of the mattress and he pounced back. He attacked the money again, diving at the bills and making a mess of my stacks. "White Beard. I'm going to toss you into the yard if you don't stop."

"Meow…Meow…" White Beard rubbed his head on my arm saying he was sorry with each meow.

Creak-a-tink. Tink-a-creak.

The loose wood on the stairs told me Ernie, Mahlee, or Grandma might be coming to my room. Slow Tom and Fast Tim left two days ago. They stayed longer than planned, but right now, only four of us live at the manor.

Grandma called through the door. "Shoelace. I've got the best news for you. You're going to be excited." She tapped on the door and the twisting of the knob sent me into a mad dash. I shoved the money into the sack and into the closet.

A muffled meow came from inside the sack. "Oh no." I unfolded White Beard from the bundle of ones, leaned against the dresser on my elbow, and cradled my kitty.

The bedroom door opened and Grandma danced into the room, grinning. "I've arranged a summer visit with relatives for you in New Boston. This will be a good time for you to meet your cousins. Sally O'Malley is a second cousin to a first cousin to the third cousin on my mother's side. Or maybe the fifth cousin to my third. No matter. They're relatives."

"Do I have to go?"

"This will be fun for you. You'll have someone to play with. Most of the people in town are feeling better since the Phantom Killer is sitting in jail. Time to resume our lives."

"I want to stay here. I don't want to go. Taddy and me visit at night in our trees. Let me stay here."

She fluffed one of my pillows. "The O'Malley's will be here in fifteen minutes. They live near Highway 1840 and they plan to take you swimming at Crystal Spring's pond in Maud tomorrow."

"I can't swim. I'll have to wade." I fell across the bed on my stomach, kicked my feet, and hung my arms to the floor.

"Get your satchel and grab your clothes. I'll watch the cats while you're gone. You will have fun. I'll come for you

Saturday morning around nine before I go to the grocery store."

"How far away did you say?" I moved from the bed and stuffed a clean pair of overalls and a shirt into my bag. I put my engineer cap on my head, hiding my nappy-uncombed hair. I tied my shoelaces as White Beard jumped from the bed, and a five dollar bill floated to the floor in front of me.

"White Beard. Silly cat." I hugged my kitten, laughed, and rolled on the floor. I put the five into my pocket before Grandma saw it.

Grandma popped my hind side. "Get yourself to the front porch. The O'Malley's will be here soon."

I hurried to the front room and went to the porch. A brown rusty pickup parked by the fence. Three people bounced from the cab, and Grandma introduced Mr. O'Malley and Mrs. O'Malley and Sally, whose freckles were bigger than her ears. She had brown spots on her arms, too. She was taller than me and wore overalls like mine.

I pointed at Sally's face. "Has anyone ever told you how you got those freckles?"

Sally touched her nose. "No. Ma has a few. I figure she gave them to me." Sally rubbed the freckles on her arm.

I shook my head. "My daddy told me people who have lots of freckles followed too close to a cow's tail and cow poop splattered on them."

Sally slugged my arm. "Good one. That's the best joke. I never knew following a cow caused freckles." She laughed hard, grabbed her tummy, and tooted.

I giggled and thought about slugging her back, but my fists laughed instead. Sally's pa and ma broke out in laughter, too. Mrs. O'Malley tapped me on the arm. "Sally toots at church, in the store, at the doctor, and in her sleep. Shoelace, you better watch out. Sally may toot under the cover tonight."

"Too hot for covers." I laughed at how the O'Malley's laughed at themselves. Their laughter filled the truck and leaked out the opened windows for the entire thirty minute drive to their farm house in the country.

"So this is where you live?" I pointed to a run-down white frame house sitting beside a barn and a coral. The house sat off the highway on a dirt trail barely wide enough for the pickup.

"Yep. Old home place," Sally's pa said. "We have the biggest climbing tree in the county. I made a tree house for Sally, and she sleeps in the tree most of the time, but since you're company, Ma washed the sheets, and you and Sally get the bed."

"I can sleep in the tree house. Outside would be great." I was happy to be with a barefoot Sally who spit like a boy when her pa mentioned the tree house.

"You two go climb the tree or skip rocks in the pond by the ducks. Watch for water moccasins. Ma cooked a mess of stew and cornbread. We'll eat in an hour."

We strutted passed the screened-in porch.

Sally picked up a stick and let it click-click along the side of the house.

I hurried to keep up with Sally's strut, running into a pile of wood, knocking a couple of pieces of timber to the ground. "Sorry. These PF Flyers run fast, but they can trip me up."

"Leave it. We'll stack the wood later. Come on. You'll like my tree house."

I craned my neck back and looked up. "Did your pa nail those pieces of wood on the trunk to make a ladder and build those walls for you?" I stepped onto the first rung.

"Yep. Pa loves wood. He loves to use his axe, and he loves hammering nails, too."

Untied Shoelace

"I love your tree house. Can we go up?"

Sally tugged on my sleeve. "Sure. But you have to take an oath."

"A what?" I jumped to the ground.

She spit on her both of her hands, rubbed them together, and held them out. "Stick your hands out, palms open."

Obeying Sally, I held them out as she chanted and rubbed spit onto my skin. "Now say this. Two cows. Two cows. One horse."

I repeated. "Two cows. Two cows. One horse."

"Good. Say this. One horse. One horse. Two cows."

"Can't we just climb the tree?"

Sally giggled and jumped on the first rung. "Come on. I'm messing with ya. We can see the whole world from up here."

Sally yelled at me. "Watch out for monsters and flying fanged ducks. They might come for us."

I heard a car's engine roar like someone kept the gas pedal pressed down too long. "Do people race down your road?"

"Naw. No one bothers us out here."

A cloud of dust rose above the trees at the end of the road, and the sound of the engine faded.

CHAPTER THIRTY SEVEN

MONSTER AT DARK

FOR THE NEXT TWO HOURS Sally and me conquered the seas, sailing around the world in her tree house. We used sticks and drummed on the walls. "Whala-whala-go-back to the seas. Whala-whala-go-back to the seas." Sally told me the chant would ward off evil sea monsters and keep the flying fanged ducks from attacking us.

I peeked through one of the tree house windows. "The ducks are flapping in the pond, their fangs are hanging from under their bills, and their wings are growing." I fell to the floor only to rise to my feet. I saw a car parked at the end of the road and I started to say something, but Sally handed me a weapon-stick to defend the fort.

"Take this. Hold it with both hands. In three seconds, the stick will turn into a sword." Sally screamed and knelt, hiding behind a box in the tree house. "Watch out. Those ducks are strong and will pull you from the tree. They eat my ma's stew and her cornbread when no one is watching."

A voice on the ground called to us, echoing in the night air. "Sally. Shoelace. Time for supper. Stew's ready. Ma has the bowls on the table."

"Is it safe to come down? Are the fanged ducks gone?" Sally asked.

Pa played along with her. "I've put them to sleep with my magic tree wand. You'll be safe for hours."

260

Untied Shoelace

We climbed down the tree, hurried to the kitchen, and ate the yummiest stew made with corn, carrots, beef, and onions. The cornbread crumbled in my mouth and melted like cake.

After supper, Sally's pa scared us with ghost stories of four-legged monsters in the pond. He said they come after little blonde girls.

I removed my cap. "I have blonde hair."

Sally giggled. "I have brown hair. I'm safe."

Her pa said, "Nope. You will be gobbled up because on Wednesday nights the monsters like brown haired girls and blonde."

We screamed, rolled on the floor, and laughed like sisters. The sun hung behind the trees. Our laughter rose as the night set in and an owl hooted. The contest to see which frog had the loudest croak rang out like someone playing drums.

The past few hours had been fun. I was glad Grandma made plans for me to spend time with Sally. This has turned out great. Taddy would like Sally, too.

Sally's ma came into the living room wiping her hands on a kitchen towel. "You two can listen to the radio if you want. I've got the dial set on Orson Welles. Tonight's show is *War of the Worlds*. It first played in 1938 on Halloween. A show about alien invasions from Mars."

Sally ran to change clothes. I stood and headed to the pickup to get my satchel.

Mrs. O'Malley called to me. "Your bag is on the bed. I brought the satchel in for you when you and Sally ran to the tree house."

"Thank you. I usually remember my satchel."

A few minutes later, Sally and I pulled the quilt over our feet, but the air hung like a damp rag, and I kicked off the covers and leaned on the pillow. Sally copied me.

Mrs. O'Malley adjusted the pull-down shade to let the air in.

"I'm leaving the shade up a little and the window cracked. We need the breeze coming through the house. It's muggy tonight." Sally's ma and pa sat at the bottom of the bed, ready to listen to Orson Welles with us.

Scuttle-thud. Scuttle-thud.

Pa shuffled to the window and moved the shade. "Those darn fanged ducks come to the house like pets. Sally feeds them scraps. Noisy little guys tonight."

He came to the bed as a *thud-thump-thud* rippled through the opened window.

"Get your gun, Pa. Those aren't ducks."

Before he left the bedroom, the front door knob jiggled on the porch. Sally's pa called to the darkness outside. "Who's there? What do you want?"

Rat-a-tat. Rat-a-tat. Ting-Thump. Thump. Thump. Rat-a-tat.

Mr. O'Malley turned out the living room light and went to the window beside the front door. He peeked out the window.

Mrs. O'Malley scooted across the floor. "A neighbor would knock on the door."

The lone light left on in the house came from the bulb above the bed. Mrs. O'Malley yanked on the string turning the house to darkness and shadows.

Sally scooted close to me. "Ma, what's wrong?"

The *thup-thup-thup* ran alongside the wood on the outside of the house going all the way to the rear.

Mrs. O'Malley lifted the quilt hanging from the mattress. "Under the bed. Both of you. Hurry. Not sure who's here. But no one should be."

Untied Shoelace

The three of us crawled under the bed, the dust sticking to my night shirt like glue on paper. "Should we call the cops?" I was itching to look out the window.

Mrs. O'Malley put her hand to her face.

Rat-a-tat. Rat-a-tat. Rat-a-tat. Thump-thud.

Sally's words dropped from her lips as she shook. "That's the kitchen door."

I slid across the floor on my knees peeking passed the doorway to the kitchen. "I see a beam of light. The person has a flashlight."

In the front room, Mr. O'Malley whispered. "Maybe it's a drunk. We do live by the highway and strays wander in. Fred borrowed my shotgun just today. He needed it to run off the coyotes bothering his chickens."

The rumble of a car's motor idled by the back of the house, and I rambled to the kitchen window to see.

Sally called to me. "Shoelace, stay in the bedroom."

My feet stuck to the floor and the light from the flashlight shown under the door again. "Someone's on the back porch." I pulled the curtain to the side and peeked out. I saw a shadow.

A car's headlights lit the backyard and the person on the porch jumped, and the heavy steps pounded the ground. The shadow-person had a mask.

Huff-puff, huff-puff.

I ran to the front bedroom, peeking under the slit in the open window. A crashing sound like wood falling told me the person tripped on the wood beside the house. And the car's headlights shone in the front yard now.

Sally grabbed my night shirt and yanked me to the floor. "What are you doing?"

I pulled loose from her. "It's got to be the Phantom Killer. I heard the breathing. I saw the mask."

Mr. O'Malley called to us from the front room. "The car's leaving and stirring up dust on the road. We've got to call and report this."

Mrs. O'Malley turned the light on above the bed. "Pa, I need to talk to you. Today in Texarkana, a man stumbled into me in the store. He knocked a rack of clothes over, his face turned white, and he stared at me."

Mr. O'Malley frowned. "You think he followed you home?"

Mrs. O'Malley shrugged her shoulders.

I moved next to her. "What did the man look like?"

Mrs. O'Malley said, "Only thing I remember is he had dark hair. It might have spooked him when the lady behind the counter called me Ms. Stamps, too."

I jumped in with my 'vestigator voice. "Ernie, the reporter who lives with us doesn't think the Phantom Killer has been caught." I moved closer to Mrs. O'Malley, her hot breath felt like fear.

Mr. O'Malley rubbed his chin. "But everyone says the Phantom Killer is in jail."

"Someone is in jail, but I don't think he's the murderer. All the pieces don't add up. Ernie has lots of clues. I have some, too. No one believes him or me."

Mrs. O'Malley paced around the room. "Maybe the man was the Phantom Killer and maybe he came for me. Pa, even you said I could be Kacey's twin."

Mr. O'Malley ordered us all to get dressed. "We're going to Texarkana to spend the night at the manor. But first, we need to get this reported."

Officer Teacup arrived in his patrol car along with two other police cars. He asked the O'Malley's questions, and he saw me peeking at him from the bedroom. He wrinkled his nose like he wanted to ask how I was involved, but he moved on.

The other officers took the front door and the kitchen door from their hinges and loaded them into Mr. O'Malley's pickup. Officer Teacup asked Mr. O'Malley to take them to the police station. "Drop them at the back of the station. We're checking them for finger prints."

On the ride to Grandma's house, we sat squashed together sweating from the humid air. Mr. O'Malley tapped on the steering wheel. "Why would the police need our doors? Why not simply take the knobs? Why would they want or need the whole door? I don't understand."

I bounced in the seat with each pothole in the dirt road. I planned to talk to Ernie. He's covered every attack and murder. He has to write the O'Malley story because the man in jail can't be the Phantom Killer. I have to tell him that I saw the mask.

Grandma's gonna have to get those pots and pans out again. Those who have doors need to lock them. And those who need doors better get them.

CHAPTER THIRTY EIGHT

A PEANUT FOR YOUR THOUGHTS

ERNIE STOOD AT THE BOTTOM of the stairs in the front room talking on the phone. "What? You're not running the piece?" His finger's tapped on the wall, making a woodpecker tapping sound.

"This is the fifth time you've changed your mind. The attack happened weeks ago. The people in Texarkana have a right to know. This story could make me famous, and there's a good chance York Sampson is simply a car thief. A better chance he's not the Phantom Killer." Ernie slammed the receiver down.

He stormed up the stairs. "What? Spying on me? Don't look at me like that. I tried to get the word out. The paper won't run my story. I can only do so much."

I went to my room and counted my treasure money. I wish I could be a writer. Maybe, I should start my own paper. I rubbed White Beard's ears and watched Rainbow wander in from the balcony through the open door. "Rainbow. Stop moping. Larry, Moe and Curly will be happy at Sally's house. She loved all three of them. She couldn't pick just one. She'll protect them from the fanged ducks. Don't worry."

For the rest of the summer, Ernie covered other stories at the paper. His editor ran the one on the opening of the new shoe store, the end of the heat wave, and other pieces. But the newspaper never did run the O'Malley's story. That got tucked away like it never happened.

However, the last murder was back in May. Ernie talks about the loose ends and missing pieces, like no matching fingerprints and the missing saxophone.

The last story in the paper announced the capture of the Phantom Killer, and people believe the murderer has been caught. I hope they are right. But I think they are wrong.

Grandma is shopping without worry. So are the neighbors. Mr. Darnell has returned for the fair to have his hot roasted peanut booth. Kids are playing out after dark. Kites are flying in the fall breeze. Trains come and go, and a new school year started two months ago. I have Ms. Reece as my teacher again. She moved to the fifth grade with our class.

I bunny-hopped down the stairs. Grandma stacked toast on the table for breakfast. Mr. Darnell said, "I sure missed the cooking from this house, Ms. Elsie. You're the best cook. You even make toast taste great."

"Thank you. I love the kitchen. It's my favorite room." Grandma smiled and stacked more toast in front of Mr. Darnell.

I grabbed a slice of toast, ran out the door, and went to check on my peanuts. "Nothing. I have a garden of green plants but no peanuts."

Taddy hung on the gate, waving at me. "Hey. Mama said you can go with us to Church by the Creek."

I nodded. "I'll be right back." I hurried to my room, grabbed my satchel, and tossed in a part of the treasure. I raced to join Priscilla and Taddy for the five block walk to Swampoodle Creek.

Grandma stuck her head out.

"Be careful. Listen to Priscilla."

"Yes ma'am."

I caught Taddy and slapped him on the shoulder. He dropped the sack of biscuits to the ground. "Be careful."

"Sorry. I'm excited. This is the first time we've been together besides in the tree or at school. We get to hand out songbooks, too."

Taddy picked up the sack. "You nearly made me splatter biscuits in the dirt."

"I said I was sorry."

Priscilla took the sack from Taddy. She smiled at me. "How's Mahlee?"

I grinned back. "Grandma is keeping her busy. Mahlee's learned to make preserves and to starch clothes. She's even baked a cake, but she baked it too long. It was kind of dry. She'll have to work on that." Having Taddy by my side made me skip and twirl, made me talkative.

At the creek, Pastor Cody set out wooden chairs from his pickup. Billy Joe, Taddy, and me grabbed songbooks from the front seat. "I have a secret. Can I trust you two?" I glanced at them. "Can I?"

They said yes in unison.

Billy Joe pointed to the sky. "Hey, a kite. It's stuck in the tree. I'm getting it after church."

A *clop-clop-clop* came up behind me. Texas Ranger JJ Ross stopped his horse beside us. "Secret? Tell me about your secret."

I made up a story. "I've found a kite. It's stuck in the tree. Can you climb trees? You could get it for us."

"I don't climb trees. I've got an investigation to finish."

"To finish? You've caught the Phantom Killer. Your work should be done." I hurried up the trunk, wishing I would learn to keep my mouth shut. I pulled the kite loose from the branch

268

and my foot slipped. The kite swooped from my hand, sailing above JJ Ross, circling his horse like a bumble bee.

JJ Ross pulled on the reins. "You've spooked my horse." The horse raised his front legs and galloped along Broad Street with JJ Ross hanging on for his life.

I jumped to the ground and Taddy patted me on the back. "Way to get rid of the Lone Ranger."

I gazed down the street. "Why is the Lone Ranger still in town?" I stared at the run-away horse. "The case must still be open. Or JJ Ross would leave."

Pastor Cody carried his Bible to the front near the chairs. "Church starts in ten minutes. Everyone gather around."

I got back to my plan to help out my hobo friends. Billy Joe and Taddy agreed to five punches from me if they told on me. I showed them the money in my satchel.

"Where did you get all this money?" Billy Joe let it run through his fingers.

"Never mind. Just help me do this."

Taddy knew Skip's story, the part with the jar and the note, and the money at the bank. On late night talks in our oak trees, I told Taddy how my daddy might have been a bad man, too.

I handed Billy Joe and Taddy a wad of ones. "I want to put a dollar in each songbook, one for each hobo. Take this money and put it inside Pastor's Cody's Bible, too. I'm fixing my daddy's wrongs."

Billy Joe grabbed my ear. "But where did you get the money?"

"It's my daddy's treasure. I'll tell you all about it someday."

After Priscilla passed out biscuits, Pastor Cody told his church folks to turn to the song *I'll Fly Away* in their books.

Slow Tom grabbed a songbook and something fell to the ground. "God sent money from heaven. I found a dollar."

Fast Tim opened his songbook. "God sent me … me … money, too." He waved the dollar above his head.

"You both found money?" Pastor Cody held his Bible sideways as a ten dollar bill slipped from the pages of his teaching book. He bent down and picked the bill up. "I have money, too."

Pastor Cody had the biggest grin I've ever seen on his tan face as he watched the money fly from the pages of the songbooks. "We have an angel in our midst. We must thank God for providing for our needs, today."

I stood near the tall weeds by the creek watching from behind the chairs. Billy Joe and Taddy turned to me, smiling.

Priscilla danced and opened a songbook. "What's this?" She glanced around like she was trying to figure out why everyone had money.

Taddy tugged on my sleeve. "Did you see Slow Tom's face? His wrinkles even smiled. The lady with the baby in her lap cried. We put money in a dozen books. Everyone's surprised and laughing. They're saying God is good."

After the preaching, Pastor Cody walked over to Slow Tom and Fast Tim. "Your ma's sick in Baton Rouge. Take this ten and catch the train to see her before she passes. Use part of it for a bath and both of you buy a new shirt before you leave." He stepped away, but turned to the brothers. "You know, God is good even when our pockets are empty. His goodness never changes."

Slow Tom and Fast Tim grinned and nodded.

I strutted up to Pastor Cody, tugging on his shirt. "Why did you give your money away?"

Pastor Cody smiled. "I can't out give God. An angel would know that." He smiled, tapped me on the head, and folded chairs.

Taddy mocked me from behind. "An angel would know that. Don't get any ideas. You aren't an angel."

"I might be. You never know." I clutched my satchel and grabbed another ten dollar bill. I ran and put the money on the driver's seat of Pastor Cody's truck.

Priscilla waved for us to come along, and Taddy and me hurried. We skipped down Broad Street toward home.

Priscilla reached for Taddy's hand, and he reached for mine.

Taddy eyed me. "The fair starts next Thursday on Halloween. Can you come with us?"

I swung Taddy's arm high and low like a swing on the playground. "I'm going with Grandma. She's entered her jelly and hot sauce in the contest. Mahlee's entered her canning, too. Ernie told Mahlee he would meet her at the fair since he's writing a story on the hot roasted peanuts coming to the county. But I can meet you by Mr. Darnell's peanut stand."

For the next four nights, Taddy and me practiced our spelling words in the oak trees between our houses. I held the list of words. The next word was engineer. I pretended to spell the word for Skip, "E-N-G-I-N-E-E-R." I could nearly see Skip's grin.

Taddy sat in his tree across from me, giggling at my goofy lost gaze.

"Stop laughing at me. I'll push you from this tree."

"You did push me once. When we first met here in the tree last January."

"I didn't push you. I watched you fall."

"You were worried you'd get blamed for my death."

"I was not. I knew you were faking. You didn't scare me."

271

Taddy challenged me to spell the next word. "Spell memorable."

"That's easy. It's spelled T-A-D-D-Y."

CHAPTER THIRTY NINE

LIFE'S NOT FAIR

"MAHLEE. HURRY. THE JUDGING AT the fair is tonight. They always give out the prizes for the best canning on the first night. You might win a ribbon. Hurry. I have to stop at the filling station for gas." Grandma stepped to the cookie jar, reached inside, and pulled out the bills. "This cookie jar has extra money these days. I've told Ernie to stop putting his hard earned money in the jar."

I leaned on the counter beside her. "Maybe, Ernie's an angel." I smiled like a cat whose tongue was too long.

Mahlee came stomping into the room. "Ready. I'm ready. I had to put bobby pins in my hair, and I had trouble buttoning my skirt, too."

"It might be the cake you've been eating since Grandma taught you to bake." I jogged out the door to the car.

Grandma parked the car in one of the grassy fields at Spring Lake Park. The Ferris Wheel lit up the whole park with a spotlight of color, like a sideways sun with seats. The music played on the Merry Go Round, and the horses rose and fell with each tune coming from the center of the ride. Kids were dressed in costumes for the contest. Not me.

Six months ago, Peyton Mars and Bay Jo Baxter were murdered at this park, but tonight the fair felt like a party to celebrate life.

Last Halloween, I went trick or treating as a hobo. This Halloween, I'm at a fair. Two little girls ran by me with fluffy pink stuff on sticks. "Grandma, what are they eating?"

"Cotton candy. Sweet pink sugar." She licked her lips. "Here's enough money for sweets and for the rides, too."

Before I could say thank you, Grandma and Mahlee hurried to the other side of the fair grounds.

I ran to the man selling pink clouds. "Cotton candy, please."

The man with sticky fingers handed me the candy. I bit into the crunchy sugar and the goo filled my cheeks with sweet grit. Then, the sugar melted, and a pink cloud of tasty candy made me want another pink cloud. "Yum. This is good."

I ran to Mr. Darnell's hot roasted peanut booth. "Hey, Mr. Darnell. Are you selling lots of peanuts?" I handed him a coin.

He placed a sack of peanuts in my hand. "Yes. Sales are great. By the end of the week, everyone in Texarkana will remember the peanuts from Georgia."

A group of girls wearing dresses and shiny shoes ran to Mr. Darnell. "Peanuts. We want peanuts."

An arm on my shoulder caused me to spin around and my left hand made a fist.

"It's me. Taddy."

"You know how I am when people sneak up behind me." I unfolded my fingers. "No costume?"

"No. I thought of dressing like a Tonto, but you would have made fun of me." Taddy ran his fingers through his hair. "My mama went to see if Grandma Elsie won a ribbon." He sniffed the peanuts.

I held the bag under Taddy's nose. "Want one? They're good."

"Naw. They probably taste like roasted pinto beans." Taddy backed up and wrinkled his nose.

I turned toward the tents. "Did you say your mama went to talk to Grandma?"

"Yep."

"We better warn her."

"Why?"

"Cause Mahlee's with her."

Taddy twisted me toward the Ferris Wheel. "Mahlee's on the Ferris Wheel with Ernie. I saw them getting on a second ago."

We watched the sideways wonder wheel.

He pointed. "See, there they are."

Mahlee and Ernie snuggled on the up and over, and down we-go ride. At the fair, there are plenty of rides to make you dizzy, rides to take your breath, and rides to send you from the earth in twists and circles.

I pointed to the ride beside the Merry Go Round. "Let's ride those fire trucks going in a circle."

"That's for little kids."

"I'm a little kid. Come watch me ride." I took off running and hoped Taddy would come with me. His short and fast breaths told me he was behind me.

"Hold my peanuts. I'm riding this." I bought a ticket and climbed into the mini-size fire engine, holding the steering wheel thinking I had to guide the truck around the tracks. "You're gonna wish you rode with me."

"I'll wait here. We can ride the Ferris Wheel next."

I guided the fire engine around the track, intent on keeping it from falling. I got close to the guard rail, turning the wheel the other way. A fair ride should be easier to steer.

Clara paraded over to the side of the ride and licked her double-scooped vanilla ice cream cone. "Little hobo girl, the track holds the fire engine and all the other cars in place. You don't have to drive. Kiddie rides go by themselves. You're just a hobo girl and you don't belong here."

I jumped from the fire engine, crawled under the fence, and pushed Clara's ice cream into her nose. I ran passed Taddy and hid behind Mr. Darnell's peanut stand. I leaned on the fence hoping to stay out of trouble until Clara forgot about me.

The fountain sprayed water into the park's pond and the wind blew, causing the leaves to rustle and float to the ground. "I'm going home. This fair isn't so fun after all. I just don't fit in. Clara will make fun of me if I go back."

Climbing the wobbly fence sent me to the ground, and I dropped my cap. The moon shone on the water, and the light of the Ferris Wheel made the water look as if the sideways wheel had fallen into the pond. I watched the reflection at the same spot where Pastor Cody carried us fishing and wading in the spring.

The big oak tree towered above me like Clara does. Its branches made fun of me, too. The wind somehow made this tree talk to me, and the brushing of the leaves in the night air mocked me. Then I remembered splashing in the water that day and how playing with Taddy and Billy Joe replaced my fears with laughter.

I wrapped my hands around my knees and rocked, crying, feeling alone and lonely. I stared at the ripples in the water. The lake was low because of the heat wave that lasted all summer.

Ernie wrote a story about how swimming holes and creeks ran dry and dusty in our county. My tears could fill the creeks and all the lakes.

Untied Shoelace

A ripple in the water reflected something in the mud. I unfolded myself and reached into the pond. I yanked. I pulled. I held something rusty. I struggled to pull the metal from the mud. It finally came loose. I wiped it off and ran my hand over the curves. I had just pulled a horn from the lake. Could this be Bay Jo Baxter's missing saxophone?

I lugged the horn to the edge of the fairgrounds and placed it behind a bush near Mr. Darnell's peanut stand. My heart raced, my breaths were short, and my hands muddy. I wiped them on my overalls and stepped into the light in front of the booth.

I had to find Taddy.

A shriek, like I made the day I learned Chops was a girl cat pierced the night air. A woman screamed for help. "This little boy's having trouble breathing. His face is turning blue."

I pushed up to the people who circled around someone. "Taddy?" I fell to the ground beside him. He lay on his back gasping for air. His eyes begged me to help. He clutched a sack of peanuts.

Taddy mouthed one word. "Peanut."

Someone pushed me away, and arms reached for Taddy. They were long, strong arms belonging to Mahlee. She snatched Taddy from the ground and charged to the parking lot with Ernie on her heels. As they disappeared, people applauded and cheered them on.

At the hospital, Grandma stopped by the front driveway to let Priscilla out of the car. I climbed from the car, too, and ran behind her. I skidded to a stop. Mahlee sat in the grass, holding her arms around her own shoulders, mumbling.

"Is Taddy…?"

Her mumbling grew louder than my questions.

I shook her. "Mahlee. Stop. Tell me if Taddy is alive."

"Why is it always so dark?" She rocked and hit her head against the side of the building. She mumbled.

I moved closer to her. "You brought Taddy here. Is he alive?"

Ernie came out the front door passing Grandma who went inside. He glanced at Mahlee, shook his head, and pulled me to his side. "When I carried Taddy inside, Mahlee refused to come into the hospital. She sat by the wall and has been mumbling since we got here."

He moved near her, but Mahlee slapped his arm away.

Pastor Cody arrived and went inside, petting my head as he hurried by.

"Does anybody know if Taddy is alive?" I screamed at the highest Kree pitch, the one ready to break eardrums if no one answered me.

The door to the hospital opened and Priscilla raced out. I froze. Ernie, too. And Mahlee stopped rocking. Priscilla's arms swung as if she might hit Mahlee, but they draped like leaves falling from a tree around her neck. "You saved my boy's life. You saved my Taddy. He's going to make it. The doctor said he's allergic to peanuts."

Priscilla's wails matched Mahlee's cry and Ernie's sobs matched my howls.

Ernie hugged Mahlee. Mahlee hugged me. I hugged Priscilla. And Priscilla hugged Ernie.

Our tears became shouts of joy. Our joy became filled with hope. My hope became filled with life. Taddy was alive.

Priscilla put her hand to Mahlee's face, turning her chin. "I'm sorry for accusing you of taking the ring. I had no right to treat you that way."

Mahlee smiled, stood, and guided Priscilla to the door. Mahlee stopped and backed up a couple of steps. "I'm waiting

here. Hospitals are scary places for me on Halloween."
Mahlee tapped Priscilla on the shoulder. "But we are friends,
again."

They hugged, and Priscilla hurried inside the hospital.

Ernie met up with Pastor Cody and they talked for a
second on the sidewalk. As Ernie waved goodbye to Pastor, he
looked at me. "I'm going to check on Taddy."

I inched up to Mahlee. "Why won't you go into the
hospital? You always come to see me when I get hurt."

Mahlee sat on the ground by the wall and covered her
eyes. "Bad things happen on Halloween. Little girls
disappear."

"What do you mean?" I sat beside her.

She rocked and her words got mixed up. "Taddy. Hurt at
fair. Lizzy Beth hurt me there. Wrong day. Bad night. Took
the little girl from my sight."

"Who is Lizzy Beth?"

Mahlee made a screeching sound like a kitten caught with
its tail in the door. She swung at me and shoved me
backwards, sending me tumbling. I crouched on the ground
waiting for her fists. She rolled her eyes and blinked fast. She
collapsed on the ground like a rag doll. "No more pain. No
more."

"Taddy's gonna be fine. He's just allergic to peanuts."

I touched her arm. She slapped it away.

I moved closer to look her in the eye. "Why did you push
me? I don't understand." I wanted to hit her. My fists clinched
as Mahlee rushed at me.

"Sorry. Sorry. Sorry. Lizzy Beth. I am sorry." Mahlee
pulled me to her chest.

"I'm Shoelace. Remember me?" I felt like a page in her
past had been torn from the book and the page bled onto me.

She focused on my face, ran her fingers across my nose, and I cringed. She then ran her fingers across my forehead. "My little girl. My Annie Grace Kree."

"That's me. But … who is Lizzy Beth?" I hoped the shoving had ended.

Mahlee sighed, breathed in, held her breath, exhaled, and clomped in a circle. "My … my little girl. I gave her to the doctor one Halloween in Memphis. I never saw her again." Her hands held each other. She stopped, turned, and stomped. "The rail would be too hard for a baby. Too hard to hold. Too hard to protect. Too hard to explain to the daddy."

I remembered the night in the carriage house when the PF Flyers found my feet. The same night Mahlee dropped her tin can and a picture of a small baby fell out. I wiped the tear under Mahlee's eye. "The picture you keep. Is that a picture of Lizzy Beth?"

More heavy breathing. "Yes. Lizzy Beth was born on Halloween. That's all I have of her. She's three today. Halloween is dark and bad, a trick day. No treats."

Tears leaked out like a rushing river and together we crumpled to the ground. We sat. We rocked. And we cried. Then, we sat and leaned on each other.

Mr. Darnell showed up and looked at us sitting on the ground. "Is he …?"

I rose to my feet, wiping myself off. "Taddy's gonna live. He's allergic to peanuts."

"But I never sold him any peanuts."

I rubbed my head. "Oh no! I gave my peanuts to Taddy when I rode the fire engine. No. No. He ate … my peanuts."

I ran from the hospital down the road to the manor, the longest three blocks ever. In the backyard, I yanked up the green plants. "White Beard, get out from under my feet." I pulled and ripped them from the ground. I grabbed the shovel and dug the rest of the plants up. "I don't want to see another peanut as long as I live."

Crunch. Crunch. Crunch.

I stepped on a pile of plants and cracking noises popped under my shoes. I picked up a shell … a shell of a peanut. I grabbed a handful of shells from the dirt. More peanuts. So many. It looked like a giant bowl of peanuts got spilled in the garden. *No one told me peanuts grow underground.*

I crunched a handful of peanuts in my fist and propped the shovel on the side of the carriage house. I ran to my tree, climbed the branches, and leaned back on the trunk.

I pulled my poetry can from the hole and read some of my poems. I reached for another poem and saw the sticker that might match the one on Bay Jo's music case. I touched it and tossed the sticker aside and picked up a piece of paper with exact corners. *Taddy folds paper this way at school.*

I pulled the paper from the Hills Bros. can and straddled the limb. I cried as I read:

> *A friend never gets in your way*
> *Unless you happen to be*
> *Climbing an oak tree.*
> *Then, she'll race you*
> *Until you are blue.*
> *I dream of climbing trees*
> *With Annie Grace Kree.*
> *Up in the air where we are free.*
> *Please, God. Don't let her die.*
> *By Thaddeus William Day, Jr. May 4, 1946.*

I wiped my eyes and folded the note in a less perfect, more crinkled way. I stuck my new-most-favorite poem into the can.

White Beard pounced onto my lap and purred as Grandma and Ernie drove up.

Everyone unfolded themselves from the cars. Mahlee and Mr. Darnell shuffled to the kitchen door. Priscilla strolled to the side gate with a small brown-headed boy, her arm on his shoulders. "Thank you, Ms. Elsie. Night everyone."

I tumbled from the tree and ran to Taddy. "You didn't have to spend the night at the hospital? I'm tree-climbing happy to see you." I hugged him. "You could have died."

Taddy sighed and sounded tired. "I got better fast. Dr. Fly made sure. Did you know Dr. Fly thinks he's a bumble bee?"

"Did he buzz by your bed?" I shoved him, not letting him answer because my hands reacted without my permission.

Taddy stumbled back a step, and I pulled him toward me. I gave him the biggest Annie Grace Kree hug. "I found your poem in the tree tonight after I dug up my peanut plants. You might become a pretty good poet if you keep it up."

Taddy laughed. "I like reading your poems better."

I tapped him on the arm. "Did you know that peanuts grow in the ground?"

Achoo. Achoo. "Your cat is following me. And yes, everyone knows where peanuts grow." Taddy wiped his nose on his sleeve. *Achoo. Achoo.*

We both laughed and Priscilla told Taddy to hurry, that it was getting late.

White Beard rubbed his head against my leg and Rainbow padded along the top of Ernie's car, plopping her fat body on the hood.

Ernie turned from the door. "I'm gonna get me a cat."

Rainbow jumped from the Studebaker and darted up the tree.

Untied Shoelace

I walked Taddy home to his apartment. For those few steps, we pretended to be bumble bees. *Buzz. Buzz. Buzz.*

"Get off my car. Shoelace, get your cat." Ernie screamed at White Beard who now sat licking a paw on top of his car.

Taddy and me laughed. We ignored Ernie and buzzed like bumble bees, again.

I looked back at the manor. My thoughts were also on Mahlee. Someday, I hope she finds Lizzy Beth. Until then, I could pretend to be her little girl.

Buzz. Buzz. Buzz.

CHAPTER FORTY

THE COLOR OF CHRISTMAS

THE NEXT TWO MONTHS RAIN poured like Morton's salt streaming from a salt shaker. The cold winds and the storms filled the creeks and the ponds. Many roads flooded. Pastor Cody held church for the hobos at his house because Swampoodle Creek ran over at the banks. Slow Tom and Fast Tim came back after their mama died, and their mama left a wad of money for them. They bought Pastor Cody new chairs for creek church and moved into a house.

After the fair, a man picking up trash discovered Bay Jo's horn by the fence where I left it the night Taddy ate my peanuts. Ernie became the famous reporter Taddy knew he would. Texas Ranger JJ Ross and his men left town. And York Samson is off at a prison for stealing cars. The murder case against him never stuck.

Not long after the fair, a Negro man was found on the tracks by the park. No one linked his death to the murders or figured out if there was a connection. Whoever stabbed him knows the answer.

School's better. I've spent one day in the office. I brought a bunch of empty whiskey bottles for show and tell. One of the hobos at the creek is living for God now. Buddy Bill stopped drinking months ago and gave me his empty bottles. Ms. Reece told us to create the perfect town, and I glued whiskey bottles together. The perfect town would be made of glass with no secrets, no attacks, and no killings.

In the office, I sat at the principal's desk. "Mr. Meldrum, why am I here? I don't understand."

He folded his hands on the desk, smiled, and nodded. "We're having a competition. A student from each school around the four-states area is sending a fifth grader to tell what the best town might be. A town without secrets could win. What do you think? Would you like to represent Central School?"

"Me? I would love to." I ran around the desk, hugged Mr. Meldrum and felt his arms reach around my back. I melted in his embrace and it felt like my daddy's hug from long ago.

I miss Daddy's hugs and his smile. He's not a bad man. He just did a few bad things. I've made a few of his wrongs right. The money he stole from Grandpa has helped people in town. He would be proud. But I guess, for now, I'll keep that a secret. Only Mahlee knows. And Taddy. Billy Joe knows, too. Oh, and God knows, too. Oh yea, and Pastor Cody. I told him, too. He would have found out from God anyway.

Thanksgiving dinner has come and gone. I had more than oranges and apples this year. Grandma roasted a turkey and Mahlee made the dressing. "Mahlee, that's the best dressing I've ever had." I had told her how good it tasted, but the heavy spices made me burp for hours. She was thrilled to help Grandma in the kitchen.

Priscilla baked homemade biscuits, and Taddy and me licked the bowl when Grandma made a chocolate cake. Ernie ate the last piece of cake, again.

Now it's Christmas Eve, and we're having a party. Grandma baked batches of gingerbread cookies, enough for everyone at hobo church. Enough for us. She let Taddy and me bite off the legs of the first hot ones out of the oven. She also mixed eggs, cream, nutmeg, milk, and sugar in a bowl and called the drink eggnog.

Grandma sipped on a cup and sat in the big chair next to the Christmas tree with her green scarf around her neck. "I love the snowflakes you and Taddy made. The popcorn strung around the tree is reflecting the colors from the lights, too."

I touched a candy cane and saw my reflection in the front window pane. "The candy canes are my favorite."

I've gotten taller, my hair is longer, and Grandma braids my hair now. I admired my PF Flyers. My big toe has worn out the spot on the side. The shoes felt tighter than they should, but they are still the best shoes ever. If I'm growing, my feet must be, too.

Taddy danced and waved his hand in front of my frozen stare. "Here's a few more icicles. Let's finish putting them on the tree."

I tossed the icicles onto a branch, and we hung the paper chain around the branches, too.

Mahlee and Ernie came in from the kitchen. Mahlee picked a few stray icicles from the floor. "When will the others be here?"

Grandma put her drink down. "Priscilla should be here any second. She ran to the apartment for something. Pastor Cody, Slow Tom, and Fast Tim will be here in ten minutes." Grandma sipped on her eggnog like White Beard slurping milk. "The O'Malley's were coming, but the highway's flooded. We'll see them after Christmas."

I wandered to the display by the fireplace on the mantle, stood on my tiptoes, and picked up the ceramic cow by the manger. "Grandma. I guess Jesus had cows. Wonder if they ever got loose from his boxcars?"

Grandma giggled. "He didn't have boxcars. But, I'm sure his cows strayed at times."

White Beard came out from under Grandma's chair and scooted to the bottom of the tree next to the presents. Grandma swooshed him away with her foot. "We'll open gifts when everyone gets here."

I picked up the box with my name. "What's this? Is it breakable?" I shook the box hard, no noises or rattles inside.

"It's not breakable, but you'll like it. It's from Priscilla and Taddy."

I put the box down and smiled.

Grandma stood and tilted her head toward the window. "Pastor Cody is here and Priscilla's right behind him. They better hurry. The rain's coming in sheets, and the temperature's dropping. We might get some ice tonight."

Once we settled in around the fire with each other, Grandma handed out her gifts to her friends. Ernie received a fountain pen. Mahlee got new hair combs. Priscilla got a new aluminum biscuit cutter, and Taddy got a sack of root beer stick candy.

"You're not allergic to root beer, are you?" I grabbed his sack, which he stole right back.

"Naw. Just cats and peanuts. And you."

Grandma gave Pastor Cody a bookmark for his Bible. She gave Slow Tom and Fast Tim two of her homemade quilts.

Slow Tom rubbed his hands on the quilt. "Mine's soft."

Fast Tim grinned. "Mine's a ... a ... lit ... lit ... tle itchy."

Everyone laughed.

Priscilla sat on the couch beside Mahlee making Ernie move over. "I have a present for you."

Mahlee put her hand to her chest. "For me?"

"Yes. A special present for you." Priscilla handed a box to Mahlee.

Mahlee pulled on the curly blue ribbon and lifted the lid. She pulled out a ring with a blue stone. Was that Margo's ring?

Mahlee dropped the blue ribbon on the floor, her hand waving in the air. "I can't take this. I can't take your sister's ring."

"This is your ring. It's not Margo's ring. It's new, just for you. I bought you a matching one. I even had the jeweler engrave your initials."

Mahlee pulled the band closer. "The initials are MD. I've never told anyone my last name. Always been just Mahlee."

"The M is for Mahlee. The D is for Day. I want you to have my last name. I can always use another sister." Priscilla and Mahlee stuck to each other like icicles on a Christmas tree, like ice on a road. Like sisters at Christmas.

"Thank you. You are my sister. Always," Mahlee said.

Grandma got up from her chair. "I have a very special present for you." She handed me a tiny box.

"What is this?" I shook the box and tore into the paper. "A harmonica? My mama played one." My smile was so big my molars were showing.

"I know. I figured it was time to add a little music to your life." Grandma kissed the top of my head as I made squeaky noises with the harmonica.

Taddy grabbed it from me. "Awful. Just awful. You need lessons."

I took the harmonica from his grasp. "I will learn to play this. You'll see." I turned to Grandma. "Thank you. This is the best."

I carried a present to Grandma. "This is for you. It's from me."

Grandma put her eggnog on the side table and unwrapped the brown paper sack with the red ribbon.

"Hurry, open it." Taddy piped in, moving next to her.

I stood on the other side of her chair.

"What in the world?" She unfolded the flour sack and opened the bag, pulling out handfuls of money. "What? I don't understand."

"Let's say Grandpa left this for you." I reached inside and pulled out another wad of money, piling the bills onto her lap. "This will help you keep the manor fixed up and fix the things I break. The cookie jar will never be empty again."

Pastor Cody strolled up to Grandma. "It looks like an angel is watching out for you, Ms. Elsie. And I've heard from a good source, this money isn't stolen. It's a gift."

Taddy came to my side of the chair and whispered in my ear. "Don't get any ideas. You're not an angel."

I slugged him and he sneezed.

White Beard scaled the Christmas tree and I thought I heard footsteps on the porch. I listened. Nope. It must be the wind.

CHAPTER FORTY ONE

ANGEL AT SWAMPOODLE

"WHITE BEARD, GET DOWN FROM that Christmas tree. You're gonna ruin Grandma's angel." He clawed at the wings, dangled from a branch, and bounced on popcorn decorations.

I scooted a stool across Grandma's polished floor, my feet lagged behind, and I slipped, my red rock falling from my pocket. I picked the rock up and stuck it inside my overalls, making a Christmas wish. I hoped this would be the best Christmas ever. White Beard meowed, his paw caught on a ribbon. He must be making a kitty-Christmas wish. I tossed him to the floor and he scampered off.

I stuck the angel back in place on top of the tree. "Grandma, look, the angel is happy again."

Grandma grinned. "Good. All my angels are in place now."

I saw a black curtain swoop by the window. "Someone's on the porch. Maybe the O'Malley's made it down their road." I ran to the front door, turned the knob, and let the cold, dark night slip into the house. "Sally, is that you?"

A blur clunked across the street as the gate bounced in the wind. I moved to the front steps by the rail.

Pastor Cody pulled me by my overalls. "Go inside. Stay there. That's not Sally." He sprinted to the fence and watched the darkness. "Someone's running down the street. I'll be right back."

Grandma shuffled to the porch and stood next to me. "Pastor Cody, come back. We're having eggnog. It's Christmas Eve. Take your truck. It's raining."

Mahlee came up on the other side. "Where's he going?"

I pointed toward the tracks. "Someone was on the porch. He ran off."

Ernie stepped outside with a cup of eggnog. "I'll get my car. Wait here." He set the cup on the table by the rocker and went to the side street to get his car.

Mahlee looked at me.

I raised my eyebrows.

Together we galloped like horses into the night and out the gate.

Mahlee darted in front of me and I chased her to the creek, along the trail, and up to the tracks. We hunted for Pastor Cody who had disappeared in the rain.

Clunk. Clunk. Thud. I toppled over a blob like the night at Spring Lake Park. Only this blob pushed me off and handed out orders. "Get off me. Be careful. The trail's washed out."

I stepped in every muddy footprint Mahlee made. A clap of thunder and a flash of lightning lit the sky and sent me back to my knees. I stood, sloshed along, and trailed Mahlee beside a moving train. Mahlee jumped into an open boxcar that was headed toward the bridge.

I stopped, scared to move. The rushing sound of the waves in the creek caused fear to rush through me. If the porch-shadow lurked inside the boxcar, he might hurt Mahlee. I went after her.

I got a leg on the ladder and made a Geronimo swing. I tumbled into the boxcar. I fell against the wall and the crashing shadows were falling over crates. The screams mixed with the lightning and a thud landed at my feet. The cry, one I've heard before.

It felt like I was inside one of my nightmares.

"Mahlee? Is that you?"

The moan gave me the *yes* I needed.

A big hand squeezed my arm and I screamed. "No. No. Don't hurt me." My arm snapped. "Aeeeiou … I want my daddy."

The hand let go and the cloudy voice spoke. "I'm sorry. I am. Please forgive me. I've hurt you."

When does a shadow apologize? And why?

The lightning streaked through the boxcar and Mahlee knocked the shadow down. His head lay over the edge of the open door. He wore a mask. He kicked her and they rolled back inside the car, knocking me to the wall in the back, over by some crates. "Ouch. My arm."

Mahlee reached for the man's neck, lost her balance, and fell backwards like a paper note falling down a hill. She plummeted from the train with a cry. "Shoelace, jump. Get off the train. It's the Phantom Killer."

I propped myself on the wall, hoping to leap from the boxcar. I peeked out the door, holding my hurt arm, and the train inched across the bridge above Swampoodle Creek. The train bumped, and I toppled to my knees.

The masked shadow twisted my good arm. "You should have left me alone. You wouldn't understand." His voice was sad and vaguely familiar.

On the next lightning strike, I lunged for his face, ripping the mask from his head. The sky went black and a squeal of the train picking up speed sent me to the floor. I coughed and tears ran from my eyes. But I had the mask.

Untied Shoelace

Then the light flashed in the sky again and I saw his . . . hands over his face. He turned away. But I saw … the black boots.

I tripped on a crate, flipped in the air, and tumbled to the creek. I held onto the mask and hit the icy water like a rocket. My head bumped against something hard on the bottom. My right arm twisted behind my back. I was trapped by the undercurrent.

My head popped above the water, and my fingers held a death grip on the mask. I gasped for air. "Help me. I can't swim." I swallowed more water, choked, and went back under.

I felt numb, my legs cold, and, in a place deep inside me, I prayed to God, *save me*. My body went limp. *God, find me in this water. I have Annie Grace Kree potential. Please let me live.*

A hand on my arm. A push to the top. I gasped for air. The grasp felt like a strong hand from my past. The hand shoved me to the bank, and my face stuck to the mud. I crawled to a spot by a tree, hugged the mask, and waited. I shivered and my sobs broke free. "Daddy. Daddy. Why did you have to leave me?"

I rocked and cried. Time stopped. I held my breath. Sobbed. I felt my breaths jerking with short gasps. I curled into a ball in the wet mud and shook, hugging the mask like it was a pillow.

Then steps came my way. Thudding. Purposed. Another hand touched my shoulder. "I've searched everywhere for you. Ernie told me you and Mahlee didn't stay put. So I came back for you." Pastor Cody wrapped his arms around me. The hug felt like God was holding me. Warm. Safe. Rescued.

"My arm. The bone's cracked again."

"I'll be careful. What's that in your other hand?"

I unfolded my fingers. "It's a mask. The man on the train was wearing it."

Pastor Cody stuffed the mask into his pocket. "Did you see who it was?"

I squinted, trying to remember. Nothing. It was like a nightmare. There one second. Gone the next. "No. It was too dark."

"It doesn't matter right now. I need to get you home."

Pastor Cody cradled me in his arms and ran the entire way to the manor. Grandma was waiting for me on the porch and she took her green scarf and made a sling for my dangling arm.

Slow Tom wrapped his quilt around me after Pastor Cody sat me in a rocker.

My hobo friends were soaked. "Slow Tom, you're wet. Fast Tim, you're wet, too."

"We was out looking for you," Slow Tom said. "We couldn't find you in this storm."

I recognized the faces of friends and family. Grandma. Pastor Cody and Priscilla. And Taddy. Slow Tom and Fast Tim. Ernie and …

I sat up and looked around. "Where is Mahlee? She's not here."

Pastor Cody pointed to the gate. "There she is."

Ernie ran to her and Mahlee rushed by him. She came to the porch, arms out, and hugged me. She bumped my right arm.

"Ouch. It's broken."

Mahlee gazed at me. "I've been searching along the creek. I saw you fall from the train into the water. I never could find you."

I touched Mahlee's face. "Your head is bleeding. You have cuts all over you."

She ran her fingers across her brow. "I'll heal, so long as you are alive."

"I nearly drowned. Someone saved me. Was it you?"

"No. I never found you. I was afraid I'd lost you in the creek."

Grandma peeked at my arm. "Pastor Cody saved you. He brought you home."

Pastor Cody stepped closer. "No. I found Shoelace curled up under a tree. Someone else must have pulled her from the creek."

Taddy inched in front of Pastor. "Maybe it was an angel."

I slapped Taddy's shoulder with my left hand. "So, you believe in angels now?"

"Maybe. You are here." He wiped a tear from his face.

Pastor Cody held out the mask. "We may have chased after the Phantom Killer tonight. He could have killed us."

Ernie drooled and grabbed the mask. "Did this come off the person who ran from the porch? Or did you happen upon the Phantom Killer? Either way, I knew it. I knew he was still loose." He hurried into the house to call the paper and he called Officer Teacup at home, telling him to meet us at the hospital.

Then everyone argued about whose car we would take. Ernie wanted to drive his Studebaker to the emergency room. Grandma wanted to take her car. And Pastor Cody jingled his keys to his truck. It looks like we're all taking a ride to the hospital on Christmas Eve.

Pastor Cody swooped me into his arms again, but this time my red rock clunked to the porch. He bent down and grabbed the rock. "I'm surprised you didn't lose this in the creek."

"It's my lucky rock." I put the rock into my pocket with my left hand.

Slow Tom and Fast Tim waved to us from the porch as we took two cars and a pickup truck to the hospital.

On the way, I talked nonstop to Taddy. "Who do you think saved me from the river? What do you think? Tell me. I have to know. You know, I could have solved the murders if I had seen the face of that man in the boxcar tonight. JJ Ross won't believe how close I got to solving the entire thing. Say something."

Taddy sighed. "You haven't taken a breath. You talk too much. Be quiet. We've got to get your arm fixed."

"Do you think someone is watching over me? I might have an angel." I teased Taddy. "I bet you don't have an angel. Oh wait. I could be your angel."

Taddy choked on spit. "No way. Angels don't break."

At the hospital, my arm got a new cast. Dr. Fly buzzed around Taddy and me singing Christmas songs. Mahlee and Ernie hugged together on a wall after she got stitches in her head.

Priscilla and Pastor Cody held hands and prayed for me at the bottom of the bed. Grandma invited Dr. Fly for Christmas dinner tomorrow along with the starchy nurse.

Officer Teacup appeared, took some notes, and talked to Pastor Cody. "We have boot prints leading down the hill away from the tracks to the creek. The same boot prints show up again by a tree. Then they lead back to the tracks and they stop there." Officer Teacup scratched his head. "Only thing we can figure is, he hopped a train."

Ernie walked up and handed Officer Teacup the mask. The mask didn't look so scary without a person behind it.

Untied Shoelace

Grandma interrupted their talking and put an arm around Officer Teacup. "You could probably use a home-cooked meal. Come join us for Christmas dinner tomorrow. I have enough for everyone."

He cut me a smile. "I would love to join you."

I nearly choked!

**

In bed, with the house all quiet, I wrote a poem.

> *Tonight, I'm afraid to sleep.*
> *When I close my eyes, I see a shadow*
> *Of a face in a boxcar.*
> *The skin melts and oozes like honey.*
> *And bumble bees fly right by.*
> *I run down the tracks.*
> *I fall from the bridge.*
> *And jerk awake on the floor.*

I folded the paper, sat in my bed, and cradled White Beard. I kissed his paw. I'll wait for the sun to come up before I go to sleep. Or maybe I will go across the hall and get in bed with my grandma. She's moved back to her room, and being alone in mine means I can't see her smile while she snores. It also means I can't put her arm over me if I'm scared.

EPILOGUE

MAHLEE SHUFFLED IN HER NEW loafers. "Stop playing tag in the post office."

Taddy tagged me one more time.

I gave him my *what for* look. "It doesn't count if you tag my cast."

"Does, too."

I placed my package on the counter. "How much postage do I need to mail this to St. Louis, Missouri?"

Mahlee dug in her purse, a Christmas present from Ernie. A small bag for hair combs and lipstick. Someone needs to show her how to keep the color inside her lips.

Mahlee paid the clerk and I tagged Taddy.

"Not fair. I was waiting until we got outside."

Mahlee placed herself between us. "Eddie Card will be happy to see you're returning the PF Flyers you borrowed from his carriage house."

I nodded. "Grandma bought a new pair for me to mail. If we ever go to Missouri again, we might find out who gets the shoes."

I looked down at the new red PF Flyers on my own feet. The ones Taddy and Priscilla gave me for Christmas.

Taddy announced. "She put a book inside the box, the one Pastor Cody gave her, *The Hero on Strange Hill* and a dollar in each shoe. Plus some socks."

I grabbed Taddy by the arm and twisted it behind his back. "You tell everything you know. Maybe you should get shipped off to Missouri."

Bent in half, he yelled. "Tell Mahlee why. Tell her. I'm not scared of you."

I pushed Taddy ahead of me, letting go of his wrist. "I borrowed a pair of socks from a hobo once. It's time to give them back. Maybe, the kid who gets the new shoes might want to read about a hero, too."

Mahlee squeezed my hand. "I know a little hero."

I spun around. "Geronimo."

Mahlee twirled around playing with me and wobbled to get her balance. We hurried outside, and I saw Ernie sitting in the passenger side of his car with the window down. "You three hurry up. I've got a train to catch for Memphis. We might have another lover's lane murder."

Mahlee called to us. "You two walking or riding? I've got to drive Ernie to the train station."

"I'm not riding with you. Taddy and me will walk back. You just got your driver's license, and I've seen how you drive. I'm not ready for that. Hey, Mahlee, what's your last name? You've got to have one for a license."

"Mahlee Beth Shaw-Day." She hurried to the car and hopped into the driver's seat. The wheels of the car bounced over the curb.

Taddy pranced in a big circle around me in front of the post office. "Let's race to the fountain. It's only a block."

"No, I'd rather skip."

A lady came out of the post office carrying two big boxes. One tumbled to the sidewalk at my feet. I picked the box up. "Here ya go, lady."

"Thank you. You're an angel."

I smiled.

Taddy frowned.

I skipped up to Taddy. "My birthday's in two weeks. January sixteenth. I'll be eleven. We could ride a boxcar for my birthday this year. My cast will be off by then."

Taddy sighed. "The magic carpet ride with Annie Grace Kree never ends."

I giggled. "Race you to the fountain."

"So long as you aren't making bubbles when we get there."

"No promises." I touched my pockets with both hands. One side had soap powder. The other pocket held part of a rainbow caught last year in church through a stained glass window.

At the fountain, I opened the rainbow pocket hoping for enough color to make my nightmares go away. Since Christmas, I dream about masks, of drowning, and of black boots. And I keep yelling and falling from my bed.

Grandma said it's time to get back to climbing my oak tree. To passing out songbooks. To writing my poems. To hugging White Beard and playing with Taddy.

Taddy ran his hand through the water at the fountain by the bank. "Shoelace, look at the rainbow. The sun's shining through the spray. You don't want to miss this."

Taddy was right. I've missed too many rainbows already.

**

Grandma zoomed up in her car. "Shoelace. Taddy. Get in the car. We've got to pack. We're headed to Wheelock Academy in Millerton, Oklahoma. Priscilla received a letter from Margo. She's working with Choctaw Indian girls. She's alive."

Untied Shoelace

I tucked the rest of the rainbow into my pocket and sprinkled white speckles of soap powder into the water with my other hand.

Taddy just shook his head. "Officer Teacup won't be happy."

We ran like steam engines to Grandma's car. Oklahoma here we come.

DISCUSSION GUIDE

1   Shoelace lost her daddy over a bridge. She was forced to leave him behind in the waters of the Mississippi River, and she found new life waiting for her at the manor. A hand on her shoulder will guide her steps. Have you lost someone and found yourself running back for them? Where does your help come from? How do you move on?

2   Tin Can Mahlee carried secrets from her past. Have your choices kept you from emptying the can of regret? Do you struggle to make good decisions? Have you ever asked the Lord to guide you as you open the lid and seek Him?

3   Grandma Elsie Kree wrapped an apron of love around her family. She served them and showed love beyond the cookie jar of life. How can you serve someone?

4   Reporter, Ernie Surratt had dreams to become famous. He put everything into writing stories for the paper until he met Tin Can Mahlee. Who has touched your life and changed your story? Was it for good? For God? Or was it selfish? Or was it to hide some dark secret?

5   Priscilla, a widow in town serves at Church by the
    Creek. She is often caught up in chores and routine.
    Her twin sister is missing and she feels the loss. What
    if you could pass out a peppermint of love, who would
    you give it to? Your sister? Your neighbor? Or a
    stranger?

6   Taddy makes friends with a little hobo girl even
    though he's allergic to her. Have you ever made
    friends with someone only to see the potential in them?
    How can you reach out with kindness? How can you
    help them find their potential?

7   Pastor Cody Westside loved with arms like his father,
    loving the outcast. He made a difference in the lives of
    the hobo. In the lives of those he met. Is there a way
    you can reach out with arms to love? If so, will you?

8   Texas Ranger JJ Ross loved his celebrity role in the
    pursuit of the Phantom Killer. Have you ever allowed
    yourself to get too puffed up? What can you do to
    humble yourself? How could this change your life?

9   The Phantom Killer attacked and murdered people. His
    mask hid him. The darkness kept him from the light,
    but he was never hidden from God. How do we hide
    from God? What would we change if we thought about
    being transparent and real in our walk with God?

*You have surrounded me on every side, behind me and before
me, and You have placed Your hand gently on my shoulder.*

Psalm 139:5 (Voice)

Pam Kumpe

BOOKS BY PAM KUMPE

See You in the Funny Papers – Humor Devotional

Scoop of Inspiration – Humor Devotional

In the Lick of Time – Children's Book

Things I Learned in Jail – Book of Hope

www.pamkumpe.com